Other Jericho Books, listed in chronological order, by T. F. Platt are:

If We Make it to Jericho
The Brown Mud of Jericho
I've Baked a Fresh Cobbler
I'll Always Take Care Of The Trees
It is Edith's Tree
She Wears It for Her Loved One, Oh So Far Away
The Three Door Dodge
You Did Okay
Pig Iron Trucker

Hermit Shack

A JERICHO BOOK

by

T. F. PLATT

authorHOUSE®

AuthorHouse™
1663 Liberty Drive
Bloomington, IN 47403
www.authorhouse.com
Phone: 1-800-839-8640

First published by AuthorHouse 06/23/2011

ISBN: 978-1-4567-3350-6 (e)
ISBN: 978-1-4567-3349-0 (sc)

Library of Congress Control Number: 2011901553

Printed in the United States of America

Dedication

For my family

Acknowledgements

The author wishes to thank family members and friends; notably Rena Baker, Michael Baker, Buck Platt, Helen Platt, Violet Robinson, Jim Robinson, Peggy Schneider, Kathleen Heimendinger, and Bessie Morehouse who have read one or more of the Jericho Books prior to publication. Their comments have been helpful and appreciated.

For the original idea of Hermit Shack and the book title of Hermit Shack, the author owes his son, Marvin, who wrote the original story for a writing competition while in junior high school

Introduction

As in all books of the Jericho series, Hermit Shack is fiction. The characters of the books are fiction written in honor of the author's grandfather, Clarence Groner, and the author's mother, Edith Marie Groner Platt, and their descendents. The geography used in the books is similar to that of the communities in Michigan where Clarence Groner and Edith Marie Groner Platt and T.F. Platt, and others of the Groner and Platt families, resided and toiled through much of their lives. The books aren't in any sense biographical, although the real Clarence and Edith for a time lived on a road called Jericho Road and Clarence did work briefly in a paper mill nearby.

Jericho Books written to include events from 1944 through 1971 cover a time frame wherein characters in the book could be based upon the author or upon persons of the author's actual acquaintance. In Hermit Shack some readers may see a bit of themselves in an otherwise fictional character. One such AKA character is T. F. Platt and what that character does in the story is somewhat in line with actual events of the author.

Hermit Shack opens in 1971. Nathan and Luisa Platt and their four children are visited by Aunt Edith, Uncle Harold, and Grandma Clydis. Uncle Harold decided to show Professor Nathan Platt a pair of human bones found in a gravel pit near Manitou Prairie, Michigan. A hunt ensued for a murderer. Family members and friends pitched in to help. Along the way they hear gruesome tales of an "abominable snowman" and wonder if it isn't really a wild human beast that would willfully dispatch a foe for food, for liquor, for fear, or for vengeance. Tracking the abominable becomes part of the hunt for the big hermit.

Along the way youthful romance buds, reminding adults of how suddenly a childhood may end.

Hermit Shack is the tenth of the Jericho Books by T. F. Platt. The Jericho stories are intended for adults and young adults. The stories do not include explicit interpersonal interactions and they omit profanity.

Chapter One

M IAH PLATT STUDIED THE RAILROAD station wall clock for the umpteenth time, deciding again that it wasn't running, that it had at last stopped. The Amtrak schedule chalked on a black board beneath the clock insisted that the westbound Amtrak diesel was due in at 6:05 a. m., and chalked next to the time, the statement, "on time" punctuated the promise. From his hard oaken bench he could see no more than could anyone else as the waiting room offered no view of the rails or the trains. His mother Luisa sat quietly reading a precious issue of the Saturday Evening Post. The Post was slated for demise, ceasing publication after a run of 145 years, and she was reading to miss not a single word. He'd not seen her eyes visit the wall clock or the chalked on schedule board even once during the endless hour and more he'd flustered. Seeing her with the Post prompted his mind's eye to again review scenes from his clandestine issue of Penthouse, a new magazine just beginning its run, that a friend'd passed to him at the recent 'School's Out' picnic. His thinking caused a silly grin to crease his cheeks.

"Is the train on time?"

His head jerked.

Someone had awakened the sleepy stationmaster to ask the very question that jumped around in Miah's mind in competition with his scenes of Penthouse. "Yes," the stationmaster'd replied, but Miah knew that reply only assured that one more Jackson, Michigan train station denizen now sat upon hard oak and fretted whether the wall clock was at all running. That sorry denizen likely would ponder with him whether a rail passenger service just starting that March of 1971 could be reliably on time. Then: Oh, wow, what's this? His mind'd popped like a firecracker!

The stationmaster'd just unlocked the double doors to the passenger apron!

Two big steps carried him to that now open portal to the action scene. In that doorway he collided with his mother who had the Post tucked under an arm and was rushing with her head twisted eastward with an ear cocked to catch that first decibel of Amtrak rumble. Jostled from behind by the newcomer, he clambered on past his Mom and then he too faced the huge eastern glow of the sun on its climb to best the horizon. Quickly, like his Mom, a hand came up to shade his eyes from old sol's awakening. They waited on tiptoe for a first glimpse of the burry-sounding monster.

Burrrrr! Burrrr! They could hear the Claxton's brassy Burrrr! from out around a bend in the rails. The thrilling beast blasted into view and then it tore past them, seeming way too fast to be stopping, but then miraculously, it stopped with the passenger coach doors abreast the apron. A black suited conductor carrying a yellow-colored step stool stepped down, turned, and placed the stool next to the doorway from the coach. Grandma Clydis Groner appeared in the doorway. Guided by the conductor and by Uncle Harold's strong hands, Grandma stood from the train. Uncle Harold reached bags that were pushed into view by Aunt Edith. He helped Aunt Edith negotiate the stool. Hugs and back pats came next.

"Jeremiah, how you've grown."

"Twelve now, or is it thirteen?"

"Twelve." He was proud to hear his voice'd pitched low for his reply. Carrying one of the bags, he walked along with Uncle Harold James. "We brought our '68 Pontiac station wagon, so there's room."

"Great, I'll ride with you in the rumble seat."

They put Grandma into the passenger seat up front. Half or better of the rear seat was taken up by the bags. Aunt Edith and Luisa smiled in at Uncle Harold and Miah. Each lap of the pair held a bag. "Watch your head." Luisa lowered the rear hatch. Instantly Harold and Miah were in a tiny world of their own, and able to view scenery the others just passed. The train station grew smaller as they pulled away.

"How were the sky scrapers?"

"You know, the most fun was to re-visit the Woolworth's Building. It opened in 1913 and your Aunt Edith actually became friends with a lady who had a daughter who worked there in Woolworth's. Then while I was in World War I, Edith and her grandparents visited the building with that friend of Edith's. My turn came in 1923 when Edith and I were there on honeymoon. It's only 792 feet tall, but it means a lot to us.

"The Empire State Building was spectacular from the outside, a very gracious and elegant structure, and inside we looked out from several observation sites. That thing's 1250 feet tall. We got off on the 78th floor and on the 79th. It's hard to imagine that on a Sunday morning in 1945 an American B-25 bomber crashed into the building at just about where we were standing. I shivered even though no sign of the accident was evident. The three in the bomber were killed and down below ten churchgoers were killed; hit by debris we were told. They're going to build an even taller building, we heard, that's to be called the World Trade Center. That'll be taller than the Empire State. In a restaurant we heard there's likely to be two of those trade center buildings. They'll be some sight to see one day."

Up front, eighty-four-year-old Grandma Clydis Groner nodded then scrunched in her seat to the tolerance of the seat belt. She fell sweetly asleep. From the rear seat sixty-six year old Aunt Edith James kept running commentary with Luisa at the wheel as well as with Uncle Harold James and Miah to her rear. "I'm so thankful for cotton-polyester blends. The next trip I won't even carry along my steam iron." To her rear, Miah shifted the bag to ease circulation back to his legs. Uncle Harold grinned at him, knowing the bag was Edith's. "How about at Montgomery Wards?" Aunt Edith continued. "Do they have the cotton-polyesters?"

"We stock them in all clothing departments, polyester linens, too. I'm glad I get a discount by working there. Very little ironing required."

"If you see a McDonald's ahead, stop. On me. Grandma loves their new apple pies and she needs the energy as you can see."

"One in the next town near the college. I'm afraid I can get hooked on the Big Mac. It's a wonderful new sandwich but I really do not need the calories. Bookkeeping work just doesn't exhaust the calories." Soon she was slowing for the turn into McDonald's. Edith reached forward and jostled her mother.

"Momma, McDonald's coming up."

Grandma jerked awake. "Praise the Lord," she said, "decent food after that train. You'd think they'd have a dining car on the morning's run. It's wonderful to have McDonald's. Did you hear that beef consumption in United States is at 113 pounds per person per year? I'd say that hamburgers are a very big seller, but I'm not up to one today. Order an apple pie treat for me. I'll wait in the car."

"No, come in. They have a restroom."

"Leave me in here," Uncle Harold said. At seventy-one he was beginning to admire leisure, that in contrast to aches and cramps should he move from his present roost. "Just bring a Big Mac and some cold water."

She heaved up the rear hatch and swung down the tail gate; on the bossy side as usual, "No, you get out. You'll be more crimped yet by the time you ride clear on to and a little beyond Manitou Prairie." She reached the bag from his lap.

"There's a rack atop." Miah hoped his comment might elicit a notion in his aunt. "We have some stay-down stretchy cords under this seat."

She heaved her bag containing the steam iron and several million other solid objects off his lap. Seeing the relief on his face, she said. "Will you see to it?"

"Sure." His voice, he could feel it, had dropped several octaves and he with obvious pride of manhood's blooming, alit beside his Aunt Edith.

"My, how you've grown," she said. "Is a Big Mac and fries what you had in mind? What to drink, malted or cola?" She felt his shoulder. "Harold, now don't strain yourself on the bags. Leave the tough stuff to our Miah."

"Strawberry malted."

"Ditto that," Uncle Harold began crawling from the cramped compartment. "But no fries, just a Big Mac and a strawberry malted."

"Okay. Dear, now you take it easy. If your heart pitters or patters or whatever it does improperly, s-t-o-p. We don't want another attack."

"Miah'll take good care of me."

Aunt Edith hurried to catch up with Luisa and Grandma. Miah and Harold looked on, both marveling at the preserved condition of Grandma Clydis. Clydis'd been the living image of Venus de Milo since her teens. Putting on a few pounds during twilight had only emphasized curvaceous grandeur. Aunt Edith was a bit slab-sided but consistently caused a pop-eyed condition in males and caused many a male to instantly squeeze off several inches of waist, to throw back at the shoulders, and to be glad he'd thought to use Dial, apply Bam roll-on, rub in a little dab of Brylcreem and to include a generous splash of Old Spice after-shave. At thirty-three Luisa still held her wholesome teen physique so convincingly that one expected to see bobby socks and saddle shoes gracing her agile gliding feet. Looking after them, Miah studied but a moment before his eye caught a notice posted in the window the ladies approached; '3.5 million burgers sold everyday.' Hunger pangs swept him. Reluctantly he pulled his eyes away; thinking, one Big Mac should do it for me, but a foot did move toward Aunt Edith and his deep voice almost called after her to double his order. He managed a turn in time to see that Uncle Harold was to duty rather than temptation or daydreaming. He was pulling the stretchy tie-down cords from under the seat.

Mom, Aunt, and Grandma soon returned, two of the three taking no notice of the rooftop handiwork creditable to Miah and Harold. Aunt Edith said, "My, that'll hold in a tornado." If they'd had more than the dozen stretchy cords, they'd have tried to install them. The roof looked like a love fest between two gigantic black tarantulas. The 'men' grinned at one another as Aunt Edith handed in the provender and closed the tailgate and hatch.

Oldest sister ten-year-old Omi was on the court setting up croquet as the big Pontiac swung into the yard. "Naomi, how you've grown!" That comment served to bring her on the run.

"Hi, Aunt Edith. I knew you liked croquet."

"You don't mean Red Ball Edith, do you? I've mellowed some but will meet your challenge right after you consume a Big Mac."

"Great."

"Call Cia and Nic before the ice all melts in the pop." Mom handed the McDonald's bag to her blond curly-haired oldest daughter.

"Nic's scout master called and is coming to pick him up to go on a rock hunt. He's putting on his new tennies. Cia's in the kitchen taking pictures of some birds outside. Grandma Clydis, here, let me carry your purse. The cobble stones aren't laid even along here; so watch your step."

"Smoothest over here." Luisa took grandma's arm. "Nathan left it smoother over here."

Six-year-old Nic charged up with his new tennies gripping like a tree frog's toes. He snap turned to fall in with Uncle Harold and Miah. "Uncle Harold, you can come to find stones."

Uncle Harold walked along with a hand on Nic's shoulder. "Nicodemus, you've grown into quite a boy scout."

"Cub Scout, he is. That's even way below Tenderfoot."

Big brother's do tend to weigh heavy," Uncle Harold said. "Why, rock gathering is one of my favorite activities; if your scoutmaster doesn't mind."

"Nic, get in here to eat McDonald's." Big sisters, Harold thought, can also at times weigh heavy.

Eight-year-old Cia turned from the window as the group entered the kitchen. "Phoenicia, are you having any luck? Take a break. We've McDonald's for you kids to eat before the ice all melts in the cola."

"I've taken up almost the whole roll of Kodachrome," Cia said. "My Blue Bird leader says if they're good enough, she can enlarge them for my album."

"That's a pretty project," Grandma Clydis said. "Your Grandpa Clarence always liked the birds. He fed them all those years. Oh, the time we had watching them. One of your Aunt Edith's first words was 'bird'. She said, 'bird, bird.' Oh, so cute."

"How about Delbert and Joe? Did Aunt Edith say?"

"I can't recall although I'm sure your Aunt Edith could. It's like you children, the mom always remembers the early words."

"My boys, both Delbert and Joe, began with dada," Aunt Edith said.

"Nic said dada before he said mama."

"A mother should always expect that and not be upset, and I'm sure your mama recognized that dada is easiest, we think, for a tiny tot to say," Grandma Clydis said. "And by the way, we saw Delbert and Pinky and your three cousins in New Jersey when we were visiting light houses. We visited the Sandy Hook light and the Twin Lights. Delbert's whole family was near Twin Lights swimming in the Atlantic. The five of them were tanned to coppery and your Cousin Pinky would still fit into the bikini she had on back just after the Korean War. That's when Mr. Rearch invented the bikini and hers was the first any of us had seen. That was sure a shocker. Their Ralph is as tall as his dad now and the girls you'd think were twins. On close look, though, Pam is two inches taller than Rebby."

"Grandma, Rebby's oldest."

"And shortest; we all grow to the size God intended, and she's beautiful as she knows."

"How about Uncle Ward and Aunt Doreena and Ron and Skip? Are they both still lifting weights? Is Brandy like a woman?"

"Oh sure, they want the physique of their dad. Your Uncle Ward, though, developed his way without any special effort. He held the envy of boys and girls alike. Doreena chuckles that her boys work so hard at training; but she's very proud of them, too. And their older sister Brandy is a grown up lady and has begun working at Wolverine Shoes. She will learn all about making them before she's trained in international sales."

"Gosh, Brandy'll go all over the world." Omi rolled her eyes. "And, gosh," she said, "she may even marry someone abroad. That would be too bad in a way because I know Emma planned on sitting her children."

"Her children? Now, hold on, dear, Brandy isn't even betrothed to anyone, yet. Even if Emma is the oldest daughter of Cousin Joe and Parrot, what's Emma thinking about?"

"Cousin Emma said that seeing as how she cared so much for baby Ardene while her mother worked payroll at the Wolverine shoe factory, she looked forward to baby sitting for pay and Hulda was the next oldest of the cousins but she wouldn't likely get married real soon and have babies because Aunt Edith told Momma that Hulda's going for a PhD."

"Why, that Hulda," Grandma Clydis turned to eye Aunt Edith. "Edith why didn't you say your youngest would stay in college?"

"I will, Momma, but I've just heard so little so far so I've waited."

"Oh, Omi, I see your point now about Emma's baby sitting. And, girls, did you know that Robert and Clarence are already dating girls? Your Uncle Joe and Aunt Parrot are feeling like old folks, they said when last I visited there. Little Edith is attending Bible School for her first time this year. And you should see their youngest, my namesake, little Clydis. Oh, such a pretty little tyke."

"Just like you, Grandma, at that age, huh?"

"Oh, I'm sure," Grandma joked. "I'm glad cameras weren't too common back in those days."

"Aunt Satin and Uncle Jim moved so far north. Do you see them often?"

"Thank goodness for the annual family reunion. I'm so glad to see all of you youngsters, even the youngsters that are now middle aged. Remind your folks always to come. But, wonderfully, besides reunion, Satin and Jim did visit us a time back and also they were at Grandpa's funeral. They had Daphne, Melody, and Ramey with them. I said who's minding the others and your Aunt Satin said, 'Nobody, gosh Grandma, our baby Samuel is eleven, didn't you know. Mag, May, and Janet are helping at their church day camp over along the Muskegon River. Samuel's on a hike with his scout group.'"

While Aunt Edith and Grandma Clydis continued their visit with the girls and Nic around the table, Luisa had gone to the bedroom to change into work clothes. She emerged with a neat dark blue skirt and a flowered cotton-polyester blouse.

"I must rush away," she said. "I've bean counting to do in the cash office at Montgomery Wards. Nathan should be home any minute. His summer classes only go until noon."

"Aunt Edith," Omi said, "it's time we tried the croquet court."

Grandma Clydis ignored Omi and Edith's choice of croquet. She turned to Cia: "Phoenicia, do you have some bird pictures for me to see? Through the years, your grandfather and I learned to name all of them that came to the feeders."

"Sure, I'm supposed to learn all of them for my project."

"Well, I'm off to help mow at Lakeview cemetery," Miah said.

"Uncle Harold, my scoutmaster just drove in."

* * *

Tiny heads bobbed and waving arms fluttered from the windows of Mr. Merit's Ford Bronco. A boy named Alvin Beach cuddled to the scoutmaster to make room for Uncle Harold. Nic sat on Uncle Harold's knee and had one leg pressed to his friend and an arm rested across the seat behind him. Leaning across Alvin, Nic's high voice pealed a decibel above his squeaky fellow Cub Scouts to say, "Mr. Merit, this is my Uncle Harold."

Blyth Merit nodded and returned Harold's grin and nod. Less than a mile farther south along Peach Road, the Bronco cleaved into the Digger

Marl's yard, and on through his yard to follow a dirt two-track another fifty yards to arrive onto the loading area of Digger's gravel pit.

"Boys, as you know, Manitou County Michigan is an ideal place to find a great many different types of stone. Who can tell me why that is true?"

Amid the giggles and squeaks a tiny voice levered forth the words, "The glacier."

"Correct, Lars. Lars, you may hand out these plastic bags." Lars hopped to the assignment. "In each bag, boys, is a card. Write your name on the card then leave the card in the bag. Mr. James has a pencil you may borrow if needed."

Harold's hand shot to his shirt pocket. "Sure enough," he said. Several of the larruping cubbies needed to borrow his Ever-Sharp mechanical pencil.

"Now, to the pit, men."

The reason the boys were wearing old clothes instead of the beautiful decorative yellow scarves and dark blue Cub Scout uniforms and the cute yellow cap was immediately obvious. The boys attacked the wall of the pit like thunder bolts bent upon perpetrating an avalanche. Their ambition was to scale the wall to their highest before tumbling back down amid dust, dirt, and a hail of stones of myriad size and description. On the floor of the pit, at a safe distance, Harold and Blyth began picking stones, placing them into little piles of similar types. Finally the exhausted sweaty cubbies came away from the wall, each with several stones, each of the stones with a dissimilar morphology. "Gather here, boys."

They formed a jagged line of constantly wiggling rag muffins. "Mr. James has a list of stone types for each of you. Identify your stones as to type, check each type off your list. Keep your stones and your list in your own plastic bag. Ask Mr. James or me if you need help."

It seemed a matter of seconds before the squirming cupids had finished their collections, except for tiny Alvin Beach. "Uncle Merit is this sedimentary?"

Mr. Merit turned the stone around and around in his hand. "Gosh, Alvin, I don't know." He passed the stone to Mr. James.

"My guess is that it's not stone, boys. Some kind of bone, I will say."

"An old bone, is that a fossil?"

"No, so it wouldn't be kept with your stone collection. Alvin, may I keep it? I'll trade a geode for it." He held the geode for all to see."

"Geode, sure! What is it?"

In the brief moment the boys were silently in wait of his answer, Mr. James said, "Sedimentary, a stone with mineral crystals formed inside."

Alvin stood proudly with his serendipity. The others tore back to the wall of the pit. Dust rolled. Harold began a frantic search for another boy stopping stone.

"Hey, I got one!" The voice echoed from the wall of the pit. A small hand rose above the tumult. "Here, I got one!"

"Gerald, come here with it!" Gerald brought with him a gaggle of sillies. They swooped in on Mr. James.

"Here."

Harold carefully examined the specimen. "Well," he rubbed his chin. "Not a stone, alright. How about I trade a fossil for it?"

"Yeah! What of?"

And the rest of the troop chorused in treble octaves, "What of?"

"Trilobite, okay?" He held out the small fractured rock. Clearly something different was sticking out of it.

"Gee, uh, sure." Gerald traded for the fossil.

"It is an extinct arthropod from the Paleozoic Era," Mr. Merit said. "They are found in ancient rocks of former oceans or inland seas worldwide. Wonderful find, Gerald." Mr. Merit jotted the information, along with an added fact, "more than 200 million years old," on the back of his business card and handed it to Gerald. "Put this card in with your stone collection."

At the head of their driveway, Uncle Harold and Nic hopped from the Bronco. Nic raced for the croquet court, arriving in time to hear Red Ball Edith's ball clack against the end pole. "Oh, Nic," Aunt Edith called. "We can start a new game."

Clack.

Omi had finished second to Red Ball Aunt Edith, but ahead of Cia. Cia didn't bother to finish the half dozen hoops to her finish. She carried her black ball over to Nic and the others. "I dare you to use this black ball, Nic. It's sure not lucky."

"Naw, I want green."

"It's blue this round for me. No more with that hoop dodger black."

"Papa likes that black one anyway," Nic advised.

"Aunt Edith," Omi said. "I'll trade the orange ball for the red."

"Not, on a rainbow," Aunt Edith joked. "You can see why I'm known as Red Ball Edith. Orange, you may see, is really your special color. Give it another try. You'll see"

* * *

Uncle Harold placed the ancient-appearing bone fragments onto the table in front of Professor Nathan Platt. Saying nothing about them, he began stirring creamer into his Kroger brand coffee. Nathan studied the specimens, turning them around and around in his hands. "Human, is my guess."

"What is?" Grandma Clydis had awakened at the sounds of Harold and Nathan in the kitchen.

"Bones, old ones." He pulled a chair out for Grandma, but swung the chair to face himself. "Good thing you're bare foot, Grandma. I need a foot such as yours."

She sat down and he reached for her foot. "Now, you aren't going to tickle me are you?"

"Who, me? Why, Grandma, I recall twas you who told me it takes two to tickle. One just can't tickle oneself. I never have actually tested that theory." He raised Grandma's foot to his lap. "But, sorry, Grandma, no tickling today. This one," he held the bone beside her foot, "is the heel bone. It's called the calcaneus. The other is a foot bone from about here." He held the bone next to her foot. "My guess it's the navicular, located at the top of the foot. Of course, these bones may be from a different primate, but I'd bet they're human."

"We'd hoped to visit the college," Grandma said.

"We have looked forward to such a visit, Professor."

"We could leave Red Ball Edith here with the kids."

Harold went out to inform Aunt Edith. "Dear, you can all come but we've only the pickup. Tomorrow we're all going in to see the campus. Nathan agrees that these bones we found may be important."

"We can't quit the game. Omi and Cia are past me and that sleeper Nic is close on my tail. I can't believe sixty-six years have slowed me so."

Harold chuckled. He couldn't believe anyone could actually beat his wife at croquet. At the light blue Chevrolet pickup, he assisted Grandma

Clydis from her step stool and into the cab. He stood with the step stool in his hand, prepared to set it into the pick-up's box for use later. In so doing he caught a glimpse of Red Ball Edith and saw a distinctive look of determination in her poise.

He knew that Red Ball Edith wasn't kidding. She was possessed of determination modeled to her hero of heroes, Golda Meir, Prime Minister of Israel, who declared, 'To be or not to be is not a question of compromise, either you be or you don't be.' Red Ball Edith would win or not win, but she'd be in the fight all the way; and so would Omi, Cia, and Nic. He was proud of the whole bunch as he heaved into the cab on the driver's side then slid to the middle position.

With the Chevy parked near the lower door of the science building, Nathan led the way through the door and pressed 'up' at the handy Otis elevator. In the hallway upstairs a student hailed his professor. "Prof, do you know yet?"

"Can't come to it yet, John. How are you doing?"

"I'll keep asking and mulling, but can't conclude anything yet."

"See you tomorrow then, John." The student rushed on down the hall.

"John's in my History of Biology class," he explained. "He and I are trying to agree on the meaning of soul."

"Soul, really," Grandma was surprised. "Why, I, uh, well, I guess I don't really know. Of the Bible, do you mean?"

"Yes, as applied to religion. We're after what soul meant in the beginning; that is, we want to know what soul meant when any being first had one. We conjecture that'd define the first humans. Today there're many meanings of soul, as you know, but the first meaning of soul is; logically, still the main one. Questions like that can keep one's mind occupied."

"What do you think it is?"

The door to his laboratory swung inwards. "I don't know. I hope we come up with it." He approached the human skeleton where it hung from a stand. "Fortunately there are some easier questions. Folks, compare these bones to the skeleton while I ferret out a box of foot bones."

The bones perfectly matched the human calcaneus and navicular bone of the right foot. "No doubt, do you agree? I see no point in comparing them to other primates. How about it?"

"Human all right."

"Real old?"

"Weathered a lot, but the actual age will be hard to determine. Impossible really, unless other evidence is forth coming. We'd better go now to visit Sheriff Puller's office. This is no joking matter, to my notion."

They arrived home just in time to begin supper preparation. Nathan and the children that summer were attempting to ease Luisa a bit by cooking supper on weekdays. Normally the meal would be an uncomplicated affair, like a double order of Cost Cutter brand Macaroni and Cheese or with a double dose of one of many varieties of Hamburger Helper. He began pulling pots and pans from a cupboard. "I'd thought macaroni goulash tonight. Any better ideas?"

"Simpler the better," Aunt Edith said. "I'm bushed. I'm liable to sack out with Grandma unless I'm desperately needed."

"Go to it, Aunt Edith. The kids and I usually come through well enough. Luisa is sometimes pretty bushed when she gets home so anything looks good to her, I think."

"Omi, it's your turn to set the table." Cia was stationed at a calendar with the days marked with names of the children."

"Nic, don't run off without helping Miah with the dishes."

* * *

With the stupendous aroma of macaroni goulash heading the air, Luisa entered the house with a smile. Uncle Harold contributed broken up lettuce leaves tossed in a bowl with cut grapes, pineapple, and tiny cubes of apple, the whole made desirable by a splash of sugared and watered-down salad dressing. Aunt Edith arose from her rest in time to place salad plates and to check out Omi's table setting. Nic arrived with tumblers, Miah with the gallon jug of homogenized whole milk. Grandma said a prayer, putting in a request for God's help for Luisa's hands.

"Luisa, have you had a diagnosis? I'm very concerned for you."

She held her leather-braced hands above her plate. "No, but the doctor thinks rheumatism or tendonitis. Right after work, I put on the braces and wear them as often as I can until time to go back to work.

The hands aren't too bad then until late in my shift. No one at work has seen the braces."

"Age thirty-three is just too young an age to be suffering so. How about a paraffin bath? Grandpa Delibar tried that for arthritis."

"No help, though I tried it as directed. Just resting my hands has worked the best." She dug the salad server into the salad bowl. "Children, how was your afternoon?"

"We mowed and trimmed at the cemetery. Mr. Istir thinks he knows a good way to put broken grave stones back together. We'll work on that in the morning."

"Well, Aunt Edith beat Omi and me at croquet."

"Just once. I'm afraid my prowess in that game revealed their route to my defeat. Nic even had me cornered in that last game. Say, kids, don't you have a baseball and bat?"

"Sure, after supper."

"Alvin and Gerald found some bones that were not stones like we were supposed to find."

Nathan quickly explained about the bones and that Sheriff Puller was meeting them at the gravel pit at one o'clock the next afternoon. "Most interesting," Aunt Edith said, "actual human bones. Real old, were they?"

"We can't determine the age without more to go on."

"A grave, you've found, do you think?"

"We'll know more tomorrow. Harold thought he saw little Gerald, one of the Cub Scouts, actually pluck his bone specimen from the wall of the gravel pit."

"If a grave is found, look for any item of clothing," Aunt Edith advised. "Shoes, too, are important. Apparel is dated, we know. For example finding cotton-polyester blend some day in the future would date the find as more recent than 1970."

Aunt Edith and Grandma Clydis looked to be on the edge of their chairs.

The other adults knew the implication.

Aunt Edith and Grandma Clydis were about to launch the whole family into yet another of their projects. Thoughts of that prospect set pitter-patter in the hearts of those around the table.

Chapter Two

TWO BOXES OF KELLOGG'S FROSTED Mini Wheat, a half a loaf of whole wheat toast topped with butter, oleomargarine, or strawberry jam, and washed down by two quarts of reconstituted orange juice along with plenty of coffee was breakfast. Nic rushed to the television to catch Sesame Street on PBS, the screen clearing in time to see Big Bird enter the scene. Following Big Bird and the other Sesame friends, Nic would dial in CBS for a session with Captain Kangaroo. For old time's sake, Omi and Cia often joined him for the Captain. Now in his fourteenth year, all of the children had grown up with Captain Kangaroo. Miah, too, would've preferred to stay and watch his friend the captain. Mr. Istir, though, would be waiting at the Lakeview cemetery.

Professor Nathan left to meet his summer classes, General Biology and The History of Biology. On his heels Miah pedaled for the cemetery. Talk at the table swiftly settled on Luisa's braced hands. "Does your insurance cover expenses like the braces?"

"The college covers us with Blue Cross and Blue Shield. These braces however aren't prescription. Mrs. Woods, she lives across the road," she nodded the direction, "in the gray house, recommended the braces. Her husband was a dentist. She's in Oak Ridge, Tennessee at present to visit family. Our girls are caring for her cats."

"I heard that Blue Cross now covers 68 million families, that's double the number from when they first began. Ask your doctor to prescribe the braces. That must surely be a good insurance company to be serving so broadly."

"I guess it wouldn't hurt me to ask." She checked the wall clock. "Say, we'd better be getting ready. Nathan has a short break around ten-thirty." She called into the living room: "Kids, turn that off right after Captain Kangaroo. We're going to the college and we'll be there for lunch."

"I'm wearing slacks and anklets," Grandma Clydis announced. "It'll save pulling on pantyhose."

"I'm wearing slacks and also pantyhose," Aunt Edith said. "I like the feel of them. The paper said that over six hundred million pairs have been sold. Why, one would expect," she caught Grandma's eye, "they've become standard apparel for all women every day."

"I'm sure glad men aren't wearing those," Harold said, winking at Grandma Clydis. "They look like over-tight long johns."

"Men have the wrong kind of legs, anyway; too hairy," Edith scoffed. "Why the time they'd take shaving their legs."

"I do need a few minutes to shave this handsome face." He downed the last drops of his cup of coffee then headed for the bathroom.

"I'm glad peace in on the way," Grandma Clydis said in changing the subject, "what with Miah and Hi and others of the cousins swiftly growing toward draft age; and many, please, God, protect them, are already that age."

"It's wonderful," Aunt Edith said to get Grandma Clydis onto an alternate topic, "that whenever we speak of either Miah or Hi the other cousin pops into mind. Those two are as close as brothers."

"They've always been close. But Edith, like you, I do so hate, hate war."

"At least they'll be illegible to vote. In June the 26th Amendment was ratified, you know, lowering the voting age to 18. Now if the young men could vote on whether war or not, we'd have something."

"I'm glad the boys haven't mentioned Audie Murphy. He died, you know?"

"The war hero, the most decorated soldier in our nation's history; what happened?

"Airplane crash. He was only forty-six. He's buried now at Arlington."

"I hate war. I can't see why even religious people seem to want war."

"The world needs a lot more women to be in charge, but no, it seems there's always to be a rabble-rouser guy, or a committee of them, in charge."

"When Ho Chi Minh died I hoped that'd end the trouble over there. No such luck. Government men seem to relish war. You're right; we need to elect far more women into government."

"Well those Paris Peace Talks and President Nixon's Vietnamization Policy, they're at least getting some of them home from that smelly jungle, swampy yuck paddies; and the horrible bloodshed. I want our young men to be home." Edith looked angry. Talk of war always reminded her of Harold going off to World War I. "I think it's awful of them to lock up Lt. Calley." Edith postured as though to paste somebody. "He was in a terrible war, for corn sakes. Mylai couldn't have been all that different than any other day of that war."

"I read in a column that they may reduce his sentence."

"I'd pardon him."

"Well, we'd better all get ready to go." She began clearing the table. "Girls, after the Captain, hurry over and care for the cats. We must soon get going."

The girls tore out the door. Mom's command of "Get the mail" and the slamming door sounded simultaneous. "Couldn't have heard," she said.

Having finished his shave, Uncle Harold said. "I'll go get it."

Clad in red slacks and a light blue blouse, Grandma emerged from her room in time to declare, "It's a wonder there's mail at all. Isn't it eight cents to mail a letter nowadays? Recall three cents back in 1932. That was enough through fifty-eight. Then it went wild; four cents in 1958, five in '63, then six, and now eight. Whole families'll be losing track of one another."

Edith stood with her face to the ceiling and she looked to have a finger in her eye. "What you'll do to avoid glasses," Grandma said. "Does that hurt?"

"Soft contact lenses, no they're a blessing, Momma. You should try some for reading glasses."

"Tiny little things that disappear when dropped. I've trouble enough just finding my regular reading glasses."

"Ready," Luisa said. "Nic, let's go now. Turn that off."

Nic rode up front between Uncle Harold and Grandma. Omi and Cia scrambled over the back seat and on into the rumble seat, leaving the back seat for Mom and Aunt Edith. Turning her head until her neck cricked didn't turn Grandma far enough to be one on one with Luisa. Her words shot right into Harold's ear when she asked, "Did they give you that diethylstilbestrol, that DES with your pregnancies?"

Harold brushed across his ear. "Huh?"

"Not you. Luisa, did they?"

"Yes, and I see now that it's warned against, but we're not having more."

"I see it's recommended, too," Aunt Edith said, "that one gain only twenty to twenty five pounds during a pregnancy. I gained in excess of that for our boys. They turned out wonderful but I had a time getting back into my clothes. You look great. How much did you gain?"

"Edith, I wasn't talking about that," Grandma complained. "That DES, I want to know. It's harmful now they tell us. Could that cause rheumatism, say in one's hands?"

"My doctor hasn't said so, but I'll ask."

Harold parked the station wagon next to the light blue Chevy pickup. Nic was a step behind his sisters racing for the elevator, pausing a moment he contemplated his mysterious sibs. They'd sardined themselves in the opening elevator door in concerted effort to be first to press the '2' button. Omi's hand gained position and was cuffed by Cia and the '2' lit up; they didn't know who pushed it. At the second floor the elevator door opened and they stood looking out at the Biology Department.

The professor was in sight. "Nathan, what is that smell by the elevator?"

"Formaldehyde used to preserve specimens. There's a Comparative Anatomy session today; mainly pre-medical students. I'm lucky my work is primarily with living specimens." He conducted them through his laboratory rooms and his lecture rooms and his office. "Carol," he said upon entering his office, "you know Luisa and Omi, Cia, and Nic. This is Grandma Clydis, Uncle Harold and Aunt Edith. Here are the keys to the Pontiac. Please tour them around the campus and land them at the cafeteria. Can you join us for lunch?"

"Sure. Come on, folks. I work in the arboretum and, just our luck, there's oodles in bloom and with the waterfall working, you'll be captivated. However, I want us to leave by way of the door on this floor instead of the elevator. There are things to see before we land in the Pontiac."

Out on the sidewalk, she said, "I came to college to be a political science student but I had to take Professor Platt's required course in Biology. This summer I am serving as his laboratory assistant in that course. I still study political science but I want to teach natural science in an elementary school.

"I missed a lab session in that required course of Professor Platt's. He said that to make it up he'd conduct a sidewalk tour followed by an oral quiz. There were three of us truants, all of us frightened. The class lasted from the door we just came out of to around the building on our right to arrive in the parking lot." She pointed, "See that green on the wall? That is Protococcus, a simple green algae that now I see about everywhere I look. On the nearby tree, see the bluegreen scaly growth. Those are lichens; a lichen is an organism with a fungus body that has algae growing inside it. Now look along the ground near the tree and some is also on the tree. What is that? Moss, you say. That is correct. Now which is the north side of the tree? Which, Nic, do you know?"

"Where the moss is?"

"No, in this case the moss is growing on the east side of the tree, not the north. Where the moss, the lichens, and the algae live is due to there being sufficient light and moisture for their growth. It's an environmental factor, nothing to do with the cardinal points of a compass. Edith, do you see any flowering plants around?"

"Dandelions. I see no other flowers."

"You've seen the moss, lichens, and algae. I wish we could see a fern right now, as well. But, now see the evergreen ahead on our left. Of the plant forms we can see from where we're standing, the algae, lichens, moss, the evergreen, and also the ferns; none of them are flowering plants; they produce no flowers. All of the other types of plants we can see from here are flowering plants." She paused, looked all around, the others in mimic.

"What flowers? I don't see . . ."

"Many types of flowers have no petals so people do not know they're viewing flowering plants. Come over by the post where the lawn folks missed trimming. I hope to show you the flowers and fruit on grass plants. Friends, Prof Platt went on and on. By the time we'd returned to the science building, every one of us truants had become budding biologists."

Carol drove them all around the campus pointing out historic buildings and dormitories, frat houses, the quad, the field house, and on and on. At the arboretum she let them scatter but cautioned that hearing the Pontiac horn toot was a vital prelude to lunch with the professor in the college cafeteria.

* * *

After savoring an amazing variety of foods at the college cafeteria, the family hurried home. Quickly then, several of the family gathered at Digger's gravel pit in wait of Sheriff Puller. At the gravel pit as the patrol car pulled in, Grandma Clydis flashed her deputy sheriff's badge for Sheriff Wayne Puller to see. "Deputy Clydis Groner," she introduced herself. "My husband, like me, was a deputy most of his life." She introduced deputies Harold and Edith. "All three of us are members of the Kent County Sheriff's Department. We want to assist in this investigation. My grandchildren will also assist. May we work cooperatively?"

"Gosh, yes, Mrs. Groner, I've heard of you folks. My cousin Bertram Benson is the town marshal at your hometown of Leadford. Cooperate, you bet. I'm inclined to have one of you leading the charge."

"Let Harold and Edith pull straws."

"No need, sheriff, Edith wins. I never could keep up with her."

"They're kidding, Wayne," Edith said. "You charge, we follow."

"Discussion and cooperation as we go along," Wayne countered. "We're tickled pink to have you." By then Sheriff Wayne Puller stood with Nic on his shoulders.

Working from his perch upon the sheriff's shoulders, Nic probed the pit wall. In minutes, he'd pried loose another bone. "Foot bone," Grandma Clydis said. She placed the bone in an evidence bag.

"That's it, Wayne," Edith called. "I see a larger bone now and it's about ready to fall out. I'll guess the tibia, the shin bone. We're into a grave."

Hand up my camera for Nic to use. He can get a snap of this. I'll also keep snapping as we dig. Shovel work from atop, and hand and finger tools from here." Nic snapped several photos of the bone they could see. "I'll call in a couple of bucket trucks from the electric Power Department. Harold, there's a couple of shovels in my trunk."

Sheriff Wayne Puller went to his squad car and popped the trunk latch. He then reached into the front seat for his radio. He called the Power Department.

After a few minutes, Harold and Omi arrived into position atop the grave. They laid out canvases and measured and marked a rectangle of sod to be lifted. "Dear," Uncle Harold called down. "My guess is that when buried the grave would've been back a-ways from the rim of the gravel pit. Removal of the gravel through the years has now exposed the body. I see Miah nearing with his bicycle. I want him to dig while I look for a fence line to identify the original pit brink. Maybe Digger has some photographs as well, or can think up an answer or two."

"Hey, Uncle Harold. Why don't you let me dig; save yourself."

"Miah, you've talked me into it. After the sod is removed you dig away only a few inches at a time. Place all of the dirt on a canvas. My guess is the grave's only about three foot deep. Any thing that looks like material evidence, measure and mark where found and place it and the info into its own plastic bag."

"Harold," Grandma Clydis called," I know Digger Marl is at work or we could ask him. So lets you and I look for a fence that may have been across the pit. I'd think the body would've been buried inside a fence rather than over it to another side of one."

"You're thinking like me, Momma, that the body was carried here from the woods behind me. I don't see a fence now, but to the east is a rundown fence, probably a property line fence. We maybe could find an intersection."

A pair of bucket trucks pulled in and backed into position by following hand and voice direction from Deputy Edith. Her deputy sheriff badge was pinned to her denim shirt. A second sheriff's department car drove into the scene. "Edith, remember me?"

"You look and sound familiar, but I won't guess."

"Babe Faygard Toberton is my mother. I'm Fanny Gillespie now. My husband is the fire chief."

"Isn't it a small wonderful world? Will you join me in a bucket?"

"Sure, I'll get my gloves. Also I'll lock my service belt into the trunk of my car."

In one bucket Fanny and Edith dug meticulously into the grave.

They removed bones and some rotted cloth. "Hey, I think we're exposing a belt."

"Hey, up above. You may stop digging now. Dirt and gravel are starting to rain into our excavation."

From the other bucket, Cia said. I can feel a big bone way in. Nic and I've dug little deep holes. Aunt Edith, I'm afraid it's a skull."

"Y – y- es," Nic said. "I think I f – f - feel a tooth."

"Wayne," Edith called, "I think these kids can come down now. I'd bet they are at the skull. A minute ago I saw they'd drawn out part of a hat brim or bill."

"Great," Sheriff Wayne Puller was jubilant. "Come on down kids; good job. Now I'll get in there; give you kids a rest."

Answering a radio call to her husband, the fire chief, the fire department rigged flood lights as dark came on. Grave excavators used handheld flashlights and dug with one hand, also holding a light for one another as required. Work was completed by nine that night. Edith rode with Deputy Fanny while Harold rode with Sheriff Wayne. The group accompanied the skeletal remains to Lansing, Michigan for autopsy. Every other speck of material evidence went with them to the State Police Crime Laboratory.

As suspected at the exhuming, the subject was male. He was determined to be around five foot eight and one hundred fifty to sixty-five pounds. His teeth were more than half missing, seemingly as though at a sign of any tooth trouble, that tooth had been extracted rather than repaired. That with the exception of the front incisors and canines which were all present and in fairly good, repaired, condition. Cause of death was determined quickly; skull fracture.

A blunt object was used. The object was more likely a club than a rock because of the shape of the fracture. The shape of the fracture also ruled out a hammer or axe or similar object as the weapon. The victim had been struck from above. The neck vertebrae were also slightly damaged due to the head moving sharply rearward and slightly to the victim's left.

Too tired to travel home that night, Edith and Harold checked into a hotel. Fanny Gillespie rode back to Manitou Prairie with Sheriff Puller, leaving her patrol car for the Jameses to use the following day. In their room, Edith dialed Nathan and Luisa. She delivered her message, hung the receiver, and plopped rearward. Her head came to rest on Harold's abdomen but he felt it there not at all as he'd already plunged into the Land of Nod.

* * *

On the Saturday following the exhumation of Mr. John Doe, a large white highly decorated Mack camper pulled into the James yard. Nathan had been puttering at lawn care to use up time as he'd been anxiously waiting the thrilling vehicle's arrival. Helio C. Outhe, Uncle Helio, an Athabascan Indian trucker from Alaska had telephoned Nathan at his office. "How's Grandma getting along? We didn't want her to plan on our arrival lest she go batty with preparation."

"She's fine; a little less agile, as you know."

"Sleeps a lot, does she?"

"Several naps a day and the same all night, but it seems to add to enough sleep. We all agree that without Grandpa Clarence, she gets along better when not at home."

"This new camper has two bedrooms, bath in each. I sure hope she'll travel some with us. Her bedroom converts to the living room for daytime. It has picture windows, a frig and a radio, record and tape player, and a television with video tape player. That room's about half the size of ours, but, of course the kitchen's in our room too. Good oven, we had TV dinners all the way back across. We'll be to your place a little before noon."

"Great. We'll see you then."

Now the gleaming custom-made camper sat in the Platt yard. Aunt Anna Mae and Uncle Helio grinned from their bucket seats. Upon the pearl white background paint, an artist had painted lush scenes of Alaska even to portrayals of wildlife with young and of fantastic salmon leaping from frothing water. The couple had made their dreams come true. They sold their brick house at Leadford and moved in with Momma Clydis to help her get by. If not for their moving in, Grandma may have had an even worse time of it. She wouldn't go into the bedroom where Grandpa Clarence had transitioned into heaven. Anna Mae and Helio had moved into that master bedroom and they set Momma up in a room where Clarence's folks had completed their twilight.

The train trip that Grandma Clydis Groner had taken with Harold and Edith James to New York and vicinity had been carefully planned. The visit with Nathan and family was also due to family planning. Not only had the visiting stretched Grandma's time away from her Leadford home, it had given Helio and Anna Mae time to fetch the gleaming new rig from a contractor in Bangor, Maine. All of the traveling and visiting had given needed diversion to Grandma Clydis. Adding to their delight, they now discovered that Grandma not only was enjoying the present diversion, she was embroiled in it. Of all things, she and the others were into a murder investigation. "Momma," Helio said, "You take the cake."

Grandma Clydis looked up from ruffling the fur of Old Sniffer. The venerable old guard dog had made the trip east with Helio and Anna Mae. "What's wrong with his neck? It's chaffed and the hair's gone." In dog's age Old Sniffer was the oldest member of the family.

"We'll get to that in a minute," Uncle Helio said.

"Grandma, Aunt Edith," Aunt Anna Mae wanted their attention for an important announcement, "we are to be blessed with another generation of Sniffer and Snifferettes."

"Oh, where is she?" Again Grandma bent to examine Old Sniffer, moving her hand over a chaffed area that was nude of hair. "She do this to him?" Grandma turned and pulled at a door of the camper.

"Grandma, she's not in there. Sniffer's mate is out east yet, where they built our new home on wheels. They promised at least a Little Sniffer and a sparkling new Snifferette, but wouldn't part with their beloved Trixy."

Helio placed an arm around his shapely fifty-two-year-old mate. "It'll mean a return trip out there for us, Momma, and we'll want you along."

"It does look like room enough in there for three people." She turned again to peer at Old Sniffer.

"Sure thing, plenty of room for three; come in and look it over."

"Momma, tell us all about the murder investigation while we look. I never cease being surprised at what you and Edith get into."

"Actually, bones were discovered by Nic's Cub Scout troop." Nic came on the run from the croquet court, dropping his mallet onto the grass at about the half way point. He slid up to Grandma. Grandma Clydis placed a hand on Nic's shoulder. "Nic, I'm surprised that old Sniffer dog isn't at your side. Where did he go off to?" Grandma stood at the camper door but scanned the yard; seemingly unaware of the gleaming camper.

"Nic, how you've grown," Aunt Anna Mae said as she fingered his hair. "Don't worry about old Sniffer. He'll be around at the other door where he likes the steps better. Too, he's yet a bit under the weather. Go and gather your sibs for a look around in this our rolling home on wheels."

His sisters had just finished the round of croquet and were hurrying into the scene. Old Sniffer emerged from behind the huge camper and slowly walked toward the girls with his tail slowly wagging. "Where'd we get the dog?" Cia began patting Old Sniffer. His tail swung lethargically.

"From the camper, silly." Omi reached for a pat at the old dog. "Why isn't he happy?"

"Aunt Anna Mae, can he come into your camper?"

"Oh, sure. He has a special bucket seat up front. He's a bit tired yet, is all. He's had a day and more at trying to regurgitate a pot holder. A little rest now and he'll be fine. I have some Jergens hand lotion you can rub on his neck."

Once inside, Old Sniffer pulled himself into a third bucket seat, the seat located between the two other up front buckets. He immediately placed his nose forward as if directing the vehicle along the way. Omi met him there with the Jergens. The remainder of the group toured right on past him and he whined and pranced his front feet.

Uncle Helio lifted him from the seat. "You aren't going to drive just now, boy. Come and help with the tour then there's kids to play with. That'll do you good." Omi reached anew to pat his fur.

"How'd he get hurt?"

"Your Aunt Anna Mae started to tell about it." Uncle Helio opened a refrigerator and pulled out a large gob of ground beef. With his tail wagging feebly, Old Sniffer wolfed it down. He lapped some water from a bowl set half under the driver's bucket then moved with Omi and Uncle Helio down through the camper to the living room where he wandered on into the celebration.

Aunt Edith had entered the camper by a rear door. She paused to pat Old Sniffer. She said to Uncle Helio, "Old Sniffer seems to be on his last legs. He didn't rush up to me to beg that I ruffle his fur. It's a good thing he found Trixy in time. How did he hurt his neck?"

"Oh, he's going to be okay now," Helio sounded casual, "he worked more than a day to regurgitate a pot holder."

"He what?" She reached a hand to Helio's shoulder and held there. "Regurgitated a - did you say a pot holder?"

"The dog vet thought it caught in his esophagus. Old Sniffer about wore all the hair and hide off his neck trying to get the pot holder back out. The vet said it'd likely need to work its way on into the stomach before he could hope to regurgitate it.

"We fed him our left over pancakes every morning so as not to waste them. Old Sniffer soon could catch a pancake in mid air and swallow it down with a single gulp.

"Couple of days ago Anna Mae was baking some rolls for us to eat on the road. Old Sniffer was yet hungry or likely curious as he often is. Well, Anna Mae was taking hot rolls out of the oven, using pot holders, you know. Old Sniffer reached under Anna Mae's arm to get a whiff of those rolls.

"She quick like undertook to shoo him away and a pot holder went flying. He nabbed it in mid air and swallowed that pot holder in a single gulp; like as if it were a pancake. He worked a lot of the time driving to here to get it out, but finally it went on down and it got slippery as the vet said it would. Then he regurgitated it back up."

Aunt Edith stood rubbing her head. She and Helio bent to examine again that amazing old dog. Aunt Edith and Omi sat down beside him where that valiant old mutt laid on the floor of the camper living room. He placed his head lovingly on Aunt Edith's friendly foot. He sighed tiredly, contentedly when Omi smoothed his fur.

Having exited the rear door of the camper, stocky fifty-six-year-old Uncle Helio fell in beside his nephew. "We have two friges in there. I hear you've a load of salmon. The experiments go okay?"

At thirty-seven Nathan had put on love handles and a slight pod in front, stature now resembling his stocky Alaskan Uncle. The two were fond of one another yet had little interests in common with the exception of salmon and of fond memories of Alaska. "These are cold water salmon from the Upper Peninsula. They were trapped in a stream off Lake Superior. We were able to remove their mercury all right while they were still living. This we know because fish from the same batches but not treated still contained mercury.

"All fish at the fourth hour following treatment or sham treatment, as in our controls, were allowed to die like they would if caught commercially or by a fisherman. Samples were taken from a shoulder and a dorsal fin of each fish for testing in our lab. No doubt, our treatment will remove mercury from living fish without apparent injury to the fish.

"The fish that had the mercury removed have been stored at minus eighty degrees ever since, but do you think I've been able to give them away?"

"People are funny."

"Yes, they say, 'from an experiment?' They think I'm nuts or something."

"A love I still miss from Alaska is the fish camp, that one you visited, on the Tanana River. Visitors would come by tour boat to watch the fish wheel and the ladies butchering the fish. In just seconds they could have a big beautiful fish all cleaned and hanging on the line. I worked there part of one summer, but didn't want any more. You probably heard idiocy while you milked those cows while visitors watched. One day I heard a spectator say, 'You mean it kills the fish?' and another said to me, 'you mean you catch them just to kill them?' I couldn't answer such questions."

"I was over at the main barn one day to sew up a teat a cow had stepped on. Several stitches were required and the poor cow jerked and raised a foot with each stitch. A woman came over there; the woman left her group, I mean, and came into an area where visitors aren't encouraged to go. 'It serves you right,' she said to me, 'for pasturing these cows.' Oh, I said; looking up at her. 'Snakes do this,' she said. 'You'd think you'd know better.' I was flabbergasted, and still can't think of what I should've said to her. That gal just walked on back to her friends. I guess all people are ignorant about at least something."

"Yeah, or most everything."

"That's sure a nice outfit you've fixed up," Nathan wanted a change of subject.

Helio gleefully returned to discussing his new camper. "The truck has our sleeper compartment and small kitchen ahead of the fifth wheel, I'm not sure you noticed, so the main camper is removed just like any other semi trailer. When one has removed the semi trailer part, a door closes at the rear of the cab and also one closes in the front wall of the camper. So with the camper removed, I just have a truck a little longer than most for my hauls. I figure to haul freight another ten years or so.

"Anna Mae often rides along on hauls. Old Sniffer thinks that extra bucket seat in the cab is his, but really we hoped Momma may decide to ride along on trucking trips as well as on camping excursions. There are steps we can pull down at the passenger door of the cab and at two of the camper doors to make it easier to get in."

"Uncle Helio that camper is a beautiful and well thought out project. I did take note of the two refrigerators in there. How about a trip into the college for a load of salmon? The kids would enjoy helping with that.

"By the time we're loaded, it'll be time to pick up Luisa at Wards. On Saturday her shift is until noon as the store closes at noon."

"By gum, let's do it."

"Nathan," Aunt Edith called. "I'm phoning in an order to Kentucky Fried Chicken, including a good extra bunch of their biscuits. Can you pick it up around noon? Momma and I'll prepare a salad to go with."

"Yes, be sure Omi knows what you ordered. I'll likely send Omi and Cia in to get it."

The kids had a grand time tossing fish into the parking lot from Prof Platt's second floor laboratory. The fish were wrapped in Saran Wrap with the treated fish tagged with a yellow tab. All treated fish had had their mercury removed while untreated fish still held their mercury, but could be eaten sparingly, that is by following the Michigan state rules for Great Lakes fish consumption. All of the fish were harder than rocks. Helio couldn't imagine cold as cold as minus eighty although he'd seen fifty and sixty below a few times in Alaska. A tossed fish struck his head making him a believer. The friges in the camper were packed except for a small space for lunch makings needed in their getting home to Leadford.

Luisa was surprised upon leaving Montgomery Ward just after noon to see that a huge white vehicle upon which artists had rendered elaborate scenery blocked the route to where she'd parked the station wagon. Especially she was anxious because her hand braces were under the car seat – and her hands were hurting. Frustrated she approached the behemoth with her eyes darting, seeking the shortest route around the blessed thing. Almost in her face a door swung open. "Luisa, my dear, come in here."

Luisa looked into the bright eyes of Grandma Clydis. "Why, hello."

Edith dropped down from the passenger door of the cab. "Luisa, your braces are in here."

"Fine." Entering the door being held open by Grandma Clydis, Luisa said, "Well, what is this?" She stood in the kitchen/bedroom with her eyes scanning in near disbelief. "My guess is Aunt Anna Mae and Uncle Helio?"

"Yes, it's their camper. When not traveling on the road, a door opens to make the truck and the camper a big open set of rooms. If no other way, communication with the cab is by intercom."

"Come forward," Anna Mae's voiced came out a speaker near Luisa's head. "We've an extra bucket seat here for you."

Luisa occupied the middle bucket seat and Aunt Anna Mae helped her into the braces. "Aah, that does feel better."

"Nathan and the kids helped to fill our friges with rock hard salmon. They've gone on now to Kentucky Fried Chicken to pick up a couple of buckets of lunch."

"All set?" Helio set the gleaming Mack camper into motion. 'Bridge Over Troubled Waters,' by Simon and Garfunkel began wafting into the cab. Helio cocked an ear. "Grandma picks good background music. We think she likes our new car."

"Car? This is bigger than a bus."

"We sold our other truck and we sold the house then we saved near twenty-four hundred by not buying a standard kind of new car."

"Oh, I see. Nice outfit."

A ways south of town on their way home they passed a cemetery. Anna Mae pointed. "Look." A Pontiac station wagon with a load of chicken, biscuits, and children was parked amidst the grave stones. Uncle Harold stood with Mr. Istir and Miah. Miah was pointing to something on the ground.

Chapter Three

CONVERSATION OPENED AT LUNCH WITH a comment from Miah. "Mr. Istir says there's a severe drought in Russia and China. He says he wouldn't wish a dust bowl on anyone like his folks suffered in Oklahoma; his family's from there."

Cia looked up from her cratered drumstick. "What were you showing Uncle Harold, a dust bowl?"

"What's that?" Nic spoke around a nice savor of biscuit.

"It's when you don't get rain for a long time so the ground gets dry, dry, dry, and very dusty," Omi said, and went directly to her next bite of crispy thigh.

"Around here? I must've been real little."

"For what, Nic?"

Nic chug-a-lugged half his tumbler of milk. "What Miah showed you, that dust bowl."

"No, Nic, I was showing a broken grave stone, but we talked about a dust bowl before you came to the cemetery."

"Oh, who broke it?"

"The grave stone, we don't know for sure. People drive into the cemetery sometimes just to vandalize it. They can hit the grave stones with their bumpers and push them over or break them off their bases. That's a bad thing to do."

"Strange that you can't find the rest of that one you showed us."

"A lot of the parts broken off we couldn't find but next spring we can look better along the fences. That one, though, is such a slanted break we thought we'd easily find it."

"The ones you found, went back together okay?"

"We weren't sure on some so we couldn't glue them back lest there be a mistake. Those where the stone was snapped cleanly off the base; several like that."

"Well, you're doing a good service; epoxy you said?"

"Yes, it doesn't match color wise but at least the parts are together."

"Someone will be very grateful, Miah," Uncle Harold said, "and that drought may help the American farmers to get sold some of our excess farm crops like, corn, wheat, and soybeans, if we can wish some good to come from a drought."

"I'd sure miss biscuits like these if drought ruined our wheat. I'll bet they're pretty worried over there in China and Russia over that drought."

"Likely they'll need to buy food, that's sure."

"My, I hate to hear of any country going short on food. Whether communist or not, we should help them."

"Not just give away food, though, Aunt Edith, not as long as they have money to pay."

"Sure but a typical business tycoon would gouge them on price."

"I'd hope the governments will agree on price. It wouldn't be like going to the store to buy the stuff."

Miah said, "Doesn't supply and demand govern price?"

"I don't think governments use that," Omi said.

"Omi, you're right as far as oleo is concerned," Aunt Edith said. "Butter and oleomargarine have been in competition all of my life, and with both of them in good supply. I've always liked them both and today I've eaten a biscuit treated to each. Oleo has a huge advantage over butter in that demand for oleo is always enhanced by oleo saying it's like butter, in appearance and in flavor, I mean. Well, butter can't say their product tastes like oleo."

"But it's colored to look like butter."

"Well, perhaps, but butter's been colored for a couple of hundred years or so. That's because Holstein butter is actually nearly white. Leaving oleo white wouldn't have been that bad, but they colored it anyway so as to compete with colored butter."

"I wish they hadn't competed in the first place," Grandma Clydis said. "One wouldn't try to make peanut butter taste like jam would they?

Or jam taste and look like peanut butter. They are separate entities, always have been and always will be; like butter and oleomargarine are and always were separate entities and both delicious."

"Can I take some biscuits to eat this afternoon?"

"Take some for Mr. Istir, too. Put oleo on some and butter on some."

Miah began loading a paper sack with afternoon provender. "It sure puzzles us," he said," where that broken part has got to. It seems to us it'd be easy to find."

Mom transferred her son's bag of biscuits to a cloth bag, the bag a dead ringer for a pillow case. "There, our workman son, that sack is not as likely to break while riding your bike."

From the kitchen window, Uncle Helio watched Miah pedal off up the road. Speaking to no one in particular, his voice sad, he said, "His mode of transportation may soon be the mode all of us use for travel if oil prices are going on up."

"I don't like buying so much foreign oil when we have our own. Like in Alaska, I mean," Anna Mae said.

"It's there all right, but for getting it into the lower forty-eight," Helio agreed.

Uncle Harold said, "They talked about a Trans-Alaska Pipeline from Prudhoe Bay to Valdez, is that near your home town in Alaska?"

"Well, no, we couldn't exactly say that. It likely will be about two or three hundred miles to the west of our Northway Village."

"Not along the Alcan Highway then? Oh, I mean the Alaska Highway, Route 2. I keep calling it the Alcan because of Anna Mae's book about the Alcan."

"I like the Alcan name better myself," Nathan said. "Uncle Helio, how are things back at Northway village? I've fond memory of going there with Aunt Anna Mae Groner and coming from there with a brand new Uncle Heliocouthe, hubby of Aunt Anna Mae."

"We've been back there twice and look forward to a trip there in the new rig. Northway Village hasn't changed too much. Still the fish camp but now more tourists and more snowmobiles and trail bikes; less dogs because the people use snowmobiles. We see more store-bought clothes than ever before. Cotton-polyester's in there too."

"What have I heard about oil storage tanks?" Luisa said. "What would they be for?"

"For jackasses," Helio scoffed. "A group of narrow heads decided to build huge oil storage tanks up on the Alaskan North Slope, at Prudhoe Bay, thinking to store oil thus delaying construction of the Trans-Alaskan Pipe Line. Not a single do-gooder seems to realize that oil stored up there becomes nearly a solid because of the cold. It'd just be a huge pile of oil maybe even as hard as those salmon we just loaded at the college. I hope they just go on ahead with the pipe line; even that may need to be heated along the way, although right from the ground oil is warm enough to flow along okay."

"Seems like a threatened oil shortage due to Middle East decisions would lead people to think we should use our own oil."

"In World War Two, another war to end all wars, the Germans used coal to make automotive fuel for use in anything that used gasoline."

"From coal, did you say?"

"Yes and the USA has many millions of tons of the stuff that could easily be mined."

"What's the hold up?"

"You got me. The idea hasn't reached the powers to be, I recon."

"Typical American is my guess."

"Perhaps not enough of the oil companies own coal fields."

"Or maybe they own all of the coal fields. I'm sorry to say, that describes American big business."

"But why not use our own fuel from our own oil fields?"

"Colonel Muammar Qadaffi knows Americans real well. No sooner does he come to power in Libya than he cuts oil production to raise the price of oil. He knows Americans are stupid enough to pay it rather than to build a pipeline to use their own oil."

"Along with him is OPEC. They've just raised prices of Persian Gulf oil knowing that's the place where America buys most of its foreign oil."

"We'd better get to mining that coal; strip mining would do it so no deep underground suffering."

"I'm wondering what the next six years will bring. Our well heeled senators and reps in Washington D. C. have passed the Federal Clean Air Act, demanding that automobile, and I guess trucks, too, reduce exhaust emissions by 90% in the next six years. It'll sure reduce gas mileage and with oil prices soaring, I guess we'd all better be thinking bicycles."

"Friends, how did our talk get to be so dismal? Let's work toward the time to tune in Marcus Welby, M. D on ABC. Let's go now to a game of baseball work-up with the kids. The exercise'll do us good."

"Isn't this the day for Masterpiece Theater?"

"Nope, that's tomorrow. And last night in case you're wondering was 'All in the Family,' that thing with Archie Bunker and Edith."

"Jean Stapleton, I like."

"But not Archie by Carol O'Conner?"

"I can't believe anyone can be as stupid as the role he plays."

"What did I just tell you about building those storage tanks? Even Archie is smarter than that. Why he's way ahead of us. He's forgone even a bicycle. He walks."

"Let's walk on out to the baseball field." Grandma stood up and reached for her baseball cap. Any comers? Cia says we're to play across the road in Mrs. Woods' big field. Nathan, come on now, the kids said you even mowed the place just the other day."

The children jumped to their feet to join Grandma. Nobody else jumped to their feet."

"Up, up, come on get up," Grandma said. "I know why we're all being so serious this afternoon and there isn't anything we can do about it except to forget it for the time being. I want to know all about that man we exhumed including who did it and why it was done, but moping here will not solve anything. Now, come on."

The game was vigorous for everyone except Luisa who stayed home to read. That action was not only forgivable but lent a note of sadness to the game. Everyone wished for her recovery yet even prayer, it seemed to them, was potentially fruitless. A standard prayer that everyone shared without saying about it to one another was: "God, her hands really hurt. Father, please help someone to come up with relief from her suffering. Amen."

Everyone was glad to see Miah ride in at the field in time to work up to bat and to have a good long session of batting. "I was thinking," he advanced as they were making their way back into the Platt yard, "that maybe his clothes may have come from Sears, Wards, or Penny's."

"Oh?"

"I asked Mr. Istir if he liked the new cotton-polyesters. He didn't know there was such a thing. He said he just goes in and buys what he needs at Wards, Sears, or Penny's. Mostly denims, he said, but other fabrics he doesn't know about. He said he's always bought at those stores. I asked why and he said they're about all the town's ever had in his lifetime."

"Monday morning I'll call that State Crime Lab," Grandma said. "Miah, thanks for the tip."

"Did you find that stone with the peculiar break?"

"No, but we think it'll be found along the perimeter fence someplace. Mr. Istir has decided to spray along the fence with weed and brush killer so then we may find that stone yet this summer."

"I wouldn't spray at all with that Agent Orange."

"No, his is a weed, grass, and brush killer; like a defoliant but not as bad as Agent Orange."

"I wondered if he didn't buy his work shoes there as well," Grandma'd stuck to her topic. "They were in fair shape, and clearly were ankle high shoes like a typical work shoe. I saw there were four pairs of holes at the top instead of hooks for the shoe laces."

"A short length of leather, what I think was leather, he may've used as a shoe lace," Edith said.

"His belt was wide, around two inches, and the buckle was utility, that is, not a big fancy affair."

The group settled around the dining table. From the sideboard behind her, Aunt Edith drew her loose leaf note book. She looked up from her notes: "Anything else? I want to record every fact, query, or concern; anything I can. We've already amassed quite a lot about his clothing."

"Let's discuss his hair and teeth. Can the crime lab determine the color of his hair? It looked brown, but maybe that wasn't even human hair that was recovered. I wonder if they could tell if it was graying or not." In shorthand Edith wrote rapidly the queries and comments under her page heading of 'Hair.'

Turning to a page heading of 'Teeth,' she said, "let me read on teeth: Molars absent, premolars absent. No sign of a partial plate found. Canines and incisors were intact but repaired; some with many fillings."

"If we just had a date, or approximate date, we could seek dental records."

She looked up from her notes. "Momma, there's no sense of us being in a fret about the hermits any longer tonight. I'm going to call the kids just to check in with them and you might stand by to say a word or so to them. I'll call Sunshine Hulda first at State."

The group was quiet while Aunt Edith dialed for her youngest, a student at Michigan State. "Hulda, hello dear. I'm just checking in. We're at Nathan and Luisa's. All is fine here." The conversation exchange was vigorous, and with Grandma Clydis, Omi, and Cia taking a turn with the older girl cousin. Aunt Edith rang off then dialed for her youngest son, Joe.

Awaiting Joe's pickup, Aunt Edith said, "That date Hulda gave is two weeks and a day from now. Momma, that date will be about right."

"I'm glad. I didn't want to rush her and you heard me say to her not to bother with house cleaning until we return; just to go ahead and move in. Helio and Anna Mae won't have been there hardly at all so no need to hurry on with house cleaning."

"Hello, Joe, just checking in. We're at Nathan and Luisa's . . ." Aunt Edith talked a while with Joe and she called her oldest, Delbert, but found that he was enduring a late obligation at the shoe factory where he was Production Foreman. Ergonomic experts were there to study flow though the assembly of the shoe, trying to offset harm that was occasionally done while attaching heels. Delbert's analysis was that the heel people were too rushed. Momma Edith talked with daughter-in-law, Pinky a while and Miah chatted a minute with Cousin Ralph. Touching with kinfolk lightened their mind burdens. Gratefully, they were all soon in the Land of Nod.

* * *

On Sunday morning Luisa, Nic, Omi, and Cia went to Sunday School. Luisa's job was to care for children in the church nursery while her own children joined others for the classes. Miah chose to sleep in that morning. "Sssh!" Aunt Edith whispered. "Let him rest." As time neared for the return of Luisa and the children, Aunt Edith checked the pot roast and Harold pared potatoes. Succotash was planned as the veggie. With the dining room table set and her braces placed handy to her plate, the family lazed around the kitchen table. Nathan said, "Luisa and I are especially grateful for the Methodist Church. Omi, we believe benefited from their Day Care. That would've helped Miah too, we now believe, as he went twice through kindergarten. How is Del and Dosia's Hi doing? Hi'd be thirteen, wouldn't he? Hard to imagine how time flies."

"Fine," Uncle Harold answered. "He's thirteen alright and his voice is changing much like Miah's. Hi's caught up his grade in school. Being left eyed and right handed is a situation one wouldn't readily believe, but the poor little fellow did see writing in reverse so he wrote backwards. Once Edith figured that out, he was alright. They gave him practice to strengthen the weaker eye. He went through his second kindergarten like a whiz. Isn't it amazing, too, that Miah had the same problem, left eyed, I mean.

"Yes, but even more amazing, the locals here at Manitou Prairie didn't diagnose Miah's problem until Edith came down here and buzzed their minds?"

"Well, thanks to Edith, but, even so, the problem is apparently rare."

"How is Del getting along?" Everyone's mind reviewed Del's history: Nathan's younger brother Del was injured in a truck tire explosion about 14 years previous. Nathan and Luisa had been on hand that day to help out. The accident occurred some three hundred miles away from their home at Leadford. Only a miracle they believed could have set the two brothers so close to one another on that fated day. Del and Dosia were trucking pig iron and a tire exploded. In mounting the spare that tire also exploded, driving a big shard of steel from the rim into Del's eye socket. In a Mack truck, Dosia drove him to the Hospital in East Jordan. The trailer tires were exploding and burning all the way. Nathan and Luisa were on a honeymoon boat trip. Just then approaching the boat dock at East Jordan, they heard sirens and a frenzy of other sounds. Following after the disturbance, they tore for the hospital and there found Del and Dosia.

"Del's doing fine. This last surgery, his doctors said, will likely be the last that can be done. They just haven't been able to completely repair the eye muscles, and there's some thirty or so of those muscles. They couldn't repair them well enough for full lateral vision to the left; his eye just doesn't turn far enough. But he's still okay, and good enough to drive legally. Young Hi rides with his dad as often as he can. Either Hi or Dosia had always ridden with him since the accident, but now that they've adopted little Virginia Louise, Dosia is thrilled to be left at home."

"Dosia's pleased that Hi likes to ride with his dad; a real budding young trucker is that Hi," Helio said.

"Little Virginia Louise is so cute; and she loves big brother Hi right along with the rest." Aunt Edith said. "And say, I was there a while back and had to look twice to see that our Danny of old wasn't at the breakfast table. Recall how Danny, whom we've called Del since his teens, but I'm recalling when he was Danny. He would put his ear down close to his bowl of Rice Crispy cereal to listen to Snap, Crackle, and Pop. Well, that morning, oh a month or so ago, when I was there at breakfast time, there sat Hi with his ear held over his bowl of Rice Crispy. It sure took me back. Well, he was showing the technique to little Virginia Louise; and so cute to see her try it."

"I'd think that it would remind you of Danny when Del was Danny, especially since Del and Dosia have bought the old family farm."

"Del sure quickly settled into adult male-hood," Aunt Edith said. "He's a good parent. And I feel like a kid again with them now reachable by walking out past that old centenarian pine and on over to their house."

"It was so sudden that Den and Naddy moved into their folk's place, but it seems their logic was like ours," Anna Mae said, "to be with Grandma Claire."

"It seems an excellent move.

"Yes, and as to Del's reaching responsible adulthood," Grandma concurred, "just like his brothers, and most like Gabe, the oldest. That's reaching responsible adulthood without serving in a war and even without serving a hitch in the military."

"It's proof enough for me that ordinary life is all that's needed. Nathan, please remember that for your boys; yes, and for your girls as well."

"Yes, do not believe the ads claiming that military, and I mean all branches, will serve to make a man, or woman, of any body into a responsible adult."

Luisa was just home from church. "I do concur," she said as she pulled a chair. In the background they could hear the sibs rousing 'Lazybones' Miah. Luisa spoke while pulling on her braces. "Ordinary life experience is all that is needed for any youngster to mature into responsible adulthood."

"Yes, I certainly agree with you on that; certainly military service isn't needed. Nathan and I're both committed to avoiding at all cost two serious factors that can interminably delay a person's reaching responsible adulthood."

"Oh?"

"Nathan has told me the story of Uncle Leonard Coffee. You recall him, an uncle to Louie and Sid Watkins."

"His was a sad case, but in the end he turned out well."

"I'd say that forcing him into military service, to fight in France during War One, did nothing to mature him. What conclusions have you folks drawn?"

"Alcohol trouble is why he was driven into the army, that or jail time. He was severely wounded in France but you are correct, neither his military service nor his being wounded drove him toward achieving responsible adulthood."

"That's because dependence on alcohol can prevent one's reaching adult maturity. Nathan said that it wasn't until nearly the end of World War II that Leonard Coffee quit drinking and then quickly matured into a responsible adult. A very good one finally, but that came after nearly a lifetime of immaturity. We're doubly concerned for Nathan's students.

"They have alcohol and various kinds of dope working together against their achieving responsible adulthood. Their experiences at college are of no avail if dope and alcohol consumption is working against the very adult maturity their folks and their professors sincerely desire to have them achieve."

"Is it really as bad as that at college? We've met a student named John and one named Carol. Both seem well on their way toward responsible adulthood."

"They are both exceptional students and, we're afraid, they are also exceptions to the rule. That is, that most students seem destined for a delay into achieving responsible adulthood."

"Hey, I'm hungry," Miah joked as he entered the room. "Should I pour the milk?"

"Have at it," Uncle Harold said, "and I'll mash the potatoes."

"Edith, cut the meat so that I can make gravy of the juices."

Following the prayer, Luisa said, "There have been other clothing stores in Manitou Prairie but mainly the typical shoppers chose, and still choose, Sears, Wards, or Penny's. I had a long visit with Alice, the mayor's wife. She came in with her grand daughter, but then sat down and visited all through Sunday School. I kept her talking on stores and she said that often through the years a new store would start up but the Men's store has been the only one to stick it out. Alice told me that, 'Men with a little money need a step up store, if you see what I mean.'"

"Good going! 'I'm thinking your way; that our victim was poor or at least not wealthy, say, of the upper crust. You know, I really do not know why I believe that."

"If we just had some dates, we could begin to get to know him."

"Luisa, what is the last name of the mayor's wife; or, actually, of the mayor, too?"

"Alice Sharp; and the mayor is Langley Sharp."

"Let's ask them for the oldest dentists in the area. Instead of waiting to see what dental records to seek, maybe one of them would recall a fellow with such a strange arrangement of teeth."

"On the subject of getting to know our victim," Harold said, "I left word at the house for Digger to expect us this afternoon. Among our other queries, I want to resolve just where the fence crossed and whether it was a property line fence."

"Starting at the intersection that Harold and I found in what we think is the east property line fence," Grandma continued Harold's thought, "and looking west as straight as we could, we guessed the fence crossed the gravel pit about fifteen feet out from where the brink on the pit is now."

"The fences may work out to be a way to get to that date; if Digger recalls were the pit wall was at some other given time."

"Digger may also know of a missing person, someone who came up missing way back. Someone, say, with teeth like we're looking for."

"Isn't it strange that Digger hasn't yet asked about all the commotion at his gravel pit, what with police cars, bucket trucks, fire fighters, search lights and all of us moving around?"

"That is strange," Nathan said. "Maybe we should call now to set up the meeting."

"Yes," Edith agreed, "his behavior is strange, come to think of it; not at all like one would expect."

"How about Mr. Merit? He may know Digger really well. After all, Digger did allow Mr. Merit and his Cub Scouts access to the gravel pit."

"That's an idea we could work on later. We left a note for Digger to expect us today."

Luisa went to the telephone. The group sat quietly while she dialed and listened to his telephone ring. Her head moved slightly toward a count of seven rings: "No answer."

Grandma was on her feet. "Now this is strange behavior."

"Let's go!" Harold spoke the minds of them all. Uncle Harold, Nathan, Miah, Grandma Clydis, and Aunt Edith rushed toward the big 1968 Pontiac.

* * *

They found a note taped to the note they'd placed on the door. "We've left on vacation. We've finally earned some time away." The note was signed, "Digger."

"I'd never of thought such would happen."

"It seems more like he has escaped."

"I just wonder what he can tell us."

"Well, after dinner I'm going in to find a fence, one that I expect to find to the north of the pit. Then on Monday we can also check property records; looking for property descriptions and property sales for this neighborhood. Let's also buy a surveyor's tape."

"Check also to see if that property to the north belongs to Mrs. Woods."

"It doesn't," Miah said. "She told us to never go back in there as the owners would have us arrested if we did."

"Talk about strange behavior; mysterious, like Digger. Miah, when did she say she'd be back?"

"About a week yet. Omi and Cia will know when to stop caring for the cats."

"Uncle Harold, you needn't buy the surveyor tape. I have a hundred foot tape from when we laid out the house before we built. Miah and I could measure from Digger's south property line up to that intersection you've found and then on to any other fence you find."

"Good going!"

After lunch and with his one hundred foot tape, Nathan and Miah drove on down the road to Digger's south property line and began measuring. Harold, Edith, and Grandma climbed a hill to above the grave and then began working their way into the woods north of the gravel pit.

* * *

In the state of Kentucky, many miles from where the group was investigating the murder, Mr. and Mrs. Digger Marl pulled into a yard off a secondary roadway. Margie Marlin Sweeney came to the door. "Why, brother, Doug, how grand of you folks to drop in."

"Hi, sis. We've taken a sudden vacation. We didn't close the gravel pit soon enough. The back wall fell in during a rain this spring. Someone found his bones."

"Oh, dear, what should we do?"

"I'll have to cooperate as the sheriff is involved. Also, but I haven't heard for sure; afraid to ask, but I think several Platt relatives are sheriff deputies from a different county. They are also investigating."

"Mrs. Woods still lives there?"

"Yes, and we've long suspected she's suspected something eerie about the woods behind her. She mentioned once that something in there scared her."

"They guess yet that your name is really Douglas Marlin?"

"No, but property records will give that to them for sure. Have you ever again heard from Larry or from Roy?"

"No, it's been all these years; near twenty, I think, and nobody has reported on Yetis, Abominable Snowmen, or other terrible creatures or any murders. Nor has any one ever found Larry's body. Larry's body would, as you know, be rather easy to identify. Larry just plain disappeared along with Roy."

"Sis, I believe that's the best thing that could happen to the poor soul; to just disappear into thin air. I've always been much more troubled that Roy disappeared at about the same time. How is old Russ; er, Senior?"

"In the nursing home. I'm his power of attorney. He no longer knows any of us. The house back at Manitou Prairie on Peach Road will fall to me. Will that cause trouble?"

"None at all. You've earned it a dozen times over."

"Doug, we'll have to allow the investigation, but let's not tell them a word more than they can pry out of us."

"Out of me, Margie, not you. I hope not to mention you at all, and certainly I'll not volunteer any information about our little Peggy and our mid-sister Bobby or of Cousin Clementine."

* * *

Back at Manitou Prairie, Harold exclaimed, "Here's that fence. Let's follow it out to the road if it goes that far, and if it does, we can let Nathan and Miah know of it." Grandma and Edith began following the fence west toward the road. Harold followed it to the east.

To the west the fence stopped at the rear property line of the home located next to Mrs. Woods'. Harold followed his part of the fence all the way to the east property line fence. He hurried back toward the others. The three were scratched, sweaty, and tired by the time they were meeting again above the gravel pit. "Ladies," Harold said as he wiped his brow with a handkerchief, "it's cooler here in the woods. I'm game for heading into it to see what we can see."

"Lead the way."

Chapter Four

PLOWING THROUGH GRAPE VINES AND fallen limbs was a test for them despite that underbrush was sparse. "The lack of underbrush in company with large trees indicates that we are into an old forest," Harold explained. "You see what under-story there is consists of young of the dominating species; mainly oak and maple in this case; and the grape vines grow up into the trees to get sunlight so they aren't so much under story as they are co-inhabiters."

"I could enjoy less grapevines and dead limbs." Edith stopped to mop her face with her damp hanky. "How long, I wonder does it take a healthy grapevine to grow," she craned her neck upward, "so high up as are these."

"I won't venture a guess," Harold said as he slapped at his face. "Mosquitoes are healthy enough, too."

"Not many of them but they're sure hungry."

"Here, spray a little more of this."

"Let's go slower. I think perspiration attracts them."

"Why all of these dead limbs?"

"Moisture, lack of, is my guess. I think were moving along over a pile of gravel; a continuation of that in Digger's pit. There's plenty of drainage so the soil is dry; dryer than on lower ground, I mean."

Suddenly they were looking into the tops of trees rather than at tree trunks. "Oh- oh!" Harold exclaimed. "We've reached the brink of another gravel pit, one that was dug in from the north side. Eventually this pit and Digger's would have joined. This long narrow hill, or esker, consists of coarse gravel left by a steam inside a glacier.

"Gravel has been dug from each end of the esker. It took a while before I noticed the esker formation."

"Wow, the ground really drops off; really steep. Esker, huh? Or just a long narrow hill of gravel, as you said, but dear, must we go back along it to get home?"

"Not me," Grandma said. "I've had enough of vines, spider webs, and dead limbs."

"Let me venture first." Harold stepped ahead, only to slide on leaves and duff, and to bash into a tree. "Oh, my," Harold called. "We can get down by sliding tree to tree. I'm coming back up to lower Edith. Momma, then I'll lower you to Edith. Get it? We'll help each other tree to tree and down this hill. It looks to be about thirty feet of elevation if we were at the bottom and looked straight up. Perhaps then it will be forty-five feet of tree to tree to get down there."

"I'm game," Edith said.

"Me, too. Children, let's get on with it."

"I'm wondering," Edith's breathing was heavy and she, like her companions, held tightly to a tree in order to take a breather. "I'm wondering how old these trees are. There are numerous ones of similar size, the larger size being, as you see, around ten inches in diameter; diameter at breast height, I mean. Mixed in are smaller trees, but the larger ones could clue us as to how long ago this face we're descending was the face of a gravel pit."

"I'm guessing the answer is twenty to twenty five years. That's judging by the growth rate of trees we planted on the farm. The soil is rather dry at home, too, but, of course that's due to our sandy soil. But I'd think a similar growth rate."

"Something happened then about twenty to twenty-five years ago that caused them to stop mining this gravel."

"Yes, and I think we'd better assume that reason to be related to that poor man in the unmarked grave."

They hadn't descended but little beyond their next grip on handy trees before Grandma called," Look!"

"My golly, if that isn't the roof of a building."

"Hey!" The sound of Nathan's voice came to them from above.

Upon the tail of its echo, they heard a mix of, "Grandma, Aunt Edith, Uncle Harold, and where are you?"

From below those above heard. "Come on down. Be careful."

Nathan and Miah had completed their measurements and using a compass a safe distance away from the line fence, had struck out to confirm that a fence did at one time cross the now void of Digger's pit. A repeat of their procedure beginning at a second line fence intersection, located north of the previous find, had led them to where Harold and the ladies had decided to venture into the woods. Broken limbs and a dropped Kleenex had led them to the brink of the second pit. The younger pair had a fun time sliding and hopping down to where they too grabbed trees for anchorage. "What's ahead there?"

"Cabin, we think, or a shack; a small building, anyway."

Grandma said, "Help us on down, you rascals."

One couldn't wait for the other once their feet settled upon level ground. They each bee lined through springy head high brush. Edith called, "Hey, an old dump here."

Harold and Nathan came in at the southeast corner of the shack. "You won't believe the stacks of wine bottles we've run into."

"There's an old bed in here," Miah had arrived at a window.

"Cook stove I see from here," Grandma said. "Miah," she said, "look for a door along your side."

"No door along this east side," Nathan reported. "Grandma; there're just these stacks of crates filled with empty wine bottles."

"No door along this side either, Grandma."

"It's here in front." The group all scrambled to catch up with Aunt Edith, arriving in time to follow into the shack.

"Must be a hermit lived here."

"You'd be right, Miah."

"I wonder how long it would take to drink all of the wine. There're hundreds of empty bottles stacked outside."

"A drunken hermit then?"

"Looks like it."

"Let's not disturb anything," Aunt Edith cautioned. "Today we must discover an easier way to approach this hermit shack. Any ideas?"

"The way seemed pretty flat to the east where I followed to that fence," Harold said.

"A fence did cross right where Digger's pit is now, by the way," Nathan said, "and the ground's still quite flat to the north and up to that second fence, the one you folks just found, Uncle Harold."

"Let's make our way out past the dump, and then stay on leveler ground and try to work our way around Digger's pit."

"That should work. The ground is higher at his pit and on up past his house, but nothing like that hill of hills we just came down."

"Well, lead on. Pop some of the brush if you can along the way. My arms are getting pretty scratched."

"Like Edith's, mine are too."

"It's like the pair of you to not think to wear long sleeves," Grandma joked.

"I'll lead out," Miah said.

"Take Me Home Country Roads," Uncle Harold began warbling that latest John Denver song.

Others picked up the chant. Ahead Nathan and Miah snapped brush in easing the route. "It's clear that the hermit didn't use this route or the route down that steep approach we made," Nathan said.

"You guys are doing good to get us out today," Edith said.

"Yes, and let's plan on using this trail for now," Grandma said. "We can perhaps discover the main, or other, routes in later. That way we won't disturb anything. Otherwise evidence could be lost."

"We don't want to frighten Mrs. Woods, either."

"Nathan, if it seems not too impossible, let's also skirt around the Digger home as well."

"His hill gets steeper to the south but if we cut more easterly we can walk around that hill and out to the road. The last part would be along a farm corn field located off of Digger's property."

"Let's do it."

"I'll agree we should keep clear of Mr. and Mrs. Digger Marl's house," Aunt Edith said. "I wonder if we haven't already begun to worry the Marls."

* * *

That evening talk began during a commercial of a program they were watching; and the program was promptly forgotten. "You know, I can't help thinking about a film we saw about Butch Cassidy and the Sundance Kid. It's the hideout part that I see in my mind," Harold explained. "It's as though the hermit was hiding out. That's why the hermit shack is hidden deep into a woodlot."

His comment perked Miah's interest. "Why two? Like Cassidy and the Kid, can you mean? Isn't there just one hermit?"

"Yes, and the one body," Omi said. "If they were at one time living or hiding out together, there'd be the two hermits; that is like Cassidy and the Kid."

"That's intriguing," Aunt Edith said. "I hadn't thought about that particular connection between the hermit shack and the grave we found. Certainly, Omi, there would have been two and one of those two may be our victim."

"But we only saw one bed."

"Yes, a big old bed; homemade, not a store bought job."

"Big enough for two to sleep on it?"

"Perhaps. I wish we'd looked longer."

"Speaking of longer," Grandma Clydis said, "and wider, too, that bed now in my mind seemed oversize in both those dimensions. Why, sleeping crosswise, it'd sleep several."

"I saw a wire-bound crate next to the bed with some empty wine bottles placed in it," Nathan said. "I was especially curious about the wine bottles. I'm now guessing close to a thousand of them stacked against that outside wall on the east side, and all bottles were stored in those wire-bound crates. That type of crate was used to ship fruits and vegetables when I was young. In my high school days I gathered up such crates to ship my caponettes to market. I can't recall seeing one of those style crates since high school. Shipping of fresh produce has been in cardboard boxes, I believe, since around 1952."

"Hey, now we're getting someplace, maybe." Aunt Edith had jumped to her feet, nearly upsetting the coffee table. "Let's say the trees we saw are twenty years old. That would have them beginning to grow in about 1951. That's close to the 1952 date Nathan came up with."

"I'm to call the state crime lab early tomorrow," Grandma said. "I'll tell them about the probability that the victim's clothes and shoes and belt may have been purchased at Wards, Sears, or Penny's. They said earlier they would consult catalogs and probably call some companies. In the morning I can present them with probable dates."

"I called the Mayor's wife while you folks were out tramping around,"

Luisa said. "You have an appointment with Mayor and Mrs. Sharp in his office at ten tomorrow. Sheriff Puller may also be there."

"Good, we can ask about dentists and about food shops dealing in a lot of fruits and vegetables. That may reveal the source of the crates and they may also remember a man who was interested in those crates"

"And about someone who sold a lot of wine."

"Goodness," Cia said, "we're moving ahead on this investigation at Concorde speed."

Nic hopped up from beside Old Sniffer. "Mr. Merit had a picture of that Concorde airplane," Nic's interest had been whetted by Cia's comment. "How fast is twice the speed of sound?"

"That's more than a thousand miles per hour, Nic. At that speed it's no wonder I'm bushed tonight." Nathan stood from the couch and stretched. "Tiger, it's about time you and I hit the hay."

They departed amid cheery good nights, and Old Sniffer moved over to the rug before the television and squeezed in between Omi and Cia. By that time the mention of speed had opened a new topic in the living room. If anyone knew who turned off the television, that person was paid no mind when Omi mentioned exploring the moon. "Wasn't that amazing how they got back? Mr. Lovell is from around here, Ohio, I think. We read about space travel at school. We saw a rebroadcast of Mr. Armstrong and Mr. Aldrin on the moon. Those in Apollo Thirteen were going to the moon when they had an explosion in their space ship. Isn't saving them something like the investigation we're doing?"

"Yes," Uncle Helio said. "Facts are gathered then thought is put to what they add up to. In that space ship the astronauts and at Houston Mission Control the techs added the facts and concluded a way to rescue those brave men from space. The same kind of thinking but on a different subject is what we're doing about the victim and the hermit."

"Investigating outdoors, I thought this afternoon of Little Big Man, like I was him and pitted against the elements and vying with the human factions at the same time. I really had fun today out with Dad and then with you folks when we found the hermit shack. I almost expected to run into Indians back deep in those woods."

"Living back in there likely required many skills used by Indians," Uncle Helio said. "Anna Mae and I need to get on back home so I can get back to trucking. We'd sure like to see that shack before we leave, say, tomorrow morning. I could carry Nic in there on my shoulders."

"I want to go," Omi said.

"Not without me," Cia chimed.

Sniffer made his way to his feet and looked at the others. Obviously the old dog was game to get started.

"Uncle Helio," Miah said, "I can go in there with you guys. I'm finished at the cemetery until it's time to mow again."

"You still didn't find that broken off part of the stone?"

"No, and that still has my attention."

* * *

On that Monday morning, the groups left early, Helio and his troop to explore around the hermit shack, and Harold's group to visit with Mayor and Mrs. Langley Sharp in the Manitou Prairie City Hall. "I popped to attention the moment Alice mentioned J. C. Penny's," the mayor said. "I was afraid the Penny stores might close seeing that he'd gone on to heaven."

"Well, I'll be. Yes, I did hear of that," Grandma said. "Age ninety-five, he passed on during the winter."

"Left sixteen hundred and sixty stores; thank goodness Manitou Prairie still has one of them."

"I'm not surprised," Alice, the mayor's wife, said. "They've always done nearly as well as Sears in this town, and that's pretty darn good, but Langley worries about every little thing to do with the town."

"I assure you, Mr. Mayor, we aren't here to worry you. I'm Clydis Groner, here with my daughter Edith and her hubby Harold James. Do not worry, sir, that we are all deputy sheriffs and are being allowed to work with your Sheriff Department and city police."

"Sheriff Puller explained all of that. He can't come in this morning but said he thought you all were as capable as he himself."

"We feel as though we've joined the team of a true expert. Sheriff Wayne Puller is a true professional. I'm sure he's told you that the case we're working on is to be kept secret, or at least out of the newspaper and off the air for the time being. A victim's body has been exhumed from a secret grave; that is, not in any cemetery. He was exhumed just to the south of Manitou Prairie and we're working quietly in our efforts to identify him and to solve the crime. It would help greatly if you could shed some light for us."

"Certainly." The mayor sat straighter in his chair. His wife leaned forward in hers.

"Mr. Mayor, you may have heard of Nathan and Luisa Platt," Uncle Harold said. "Nathan is my nephew and is a biological science professor at the college. Luisa is an accountant at Wards and she cares for the nursery on Sunday's at the Methodist church.

"Yes," Alice answered for her husband, "Langley knows Luisa very well and I explained to him how we visited about old time clothing stores of the town. Do you have dates for us to consider?"

"We're targeting on the decade from 1945 to 1955 as a starter, and hoping to narrow it from there."

The mayor rubbed his chin. "Hummm, uh, right after the wars. Let's see, now there was clothing sold in the dime store. One was down town at the time. I just can't think of any men's clothes there though. The men's store going now was going then; had suits, slacks, and that, presumed to be a grade up from the big three - that's Montgomery Wards, Sears and Roebuck, and J. C. Penny's. There was also a ladies' apparel store. The 'big three' carried men's shoes but the shoe store we have now was in business already back there in the forties and fifties.

"The shoe store always had a summer sale so if your victim was poor he still may've bought from there. The 'big three' also had shoe sales quite often though, as I recall. Were his shoes substantial or of lesser grade? By the way, Alice and Langley is fine with us."

"Thank you; we appreciate hearing Clydis, Edith, and Harold. Langley and Alice, we aren't sure yet on the shoes. The crime lab is looking at them. We understand that the type of arch support is crucial in determining the grade of a shoe. Can you think of any private shoe salesmen in town? Harold always bought from a private dealer, aiming to buy shoes to hold up a whole year at his factory job."

"Oh, my gosh, yes. Alice how did it slip my mind? Folks, I always have, ever since I came home from the Pacific, I've always bought from Glenn Mills. His shoes always go the entire year and beyond. Alice, write his address and number."

"Now as to dentists," Edith said, "and again we want to know of dentists in practice here during our decade of interest."

"Old Yank'um Woods! Darn, now there was a dentist! He'd as soon yank a tooth as to fill it again. Of course that's after he'd made his groceries several times over on each tooth until it couldn't be filled no more. Of course then he'd pull out several more so's to sell you partial plates. He sounds bad, huh? Well, I liked him. He was undoubtedly the favorite dentist in the town, and was so for years. Died in around 1950 or so. Bankers' funeral parlor would have that date, or the court house. He's buried, too, at the Lakeside cemetery just south of town a ways; and I know he has a headstone."

"I think then, we've found our dentist. Langley, we thank you. You and Alice have been very helpful."

"Oh, that Glenn with the shoes, he lives out of town now; a few miles out on the road that passes right past the front of the hospital, that's Southern Road."

"Again, thank you. We'll give him a call."

Back at the house, Grandma dialed the crime lab. She gave them the name of the other shoe company that may have sold the victim his shoes and told of the dentist along with his modus and date of death.

Harold called Glenn, the shoe man, and was invited to come on out that evening.

Harold and Edith left the house to try to catch up with Anna Mae, Helio, Old Sniffer, and with their troop of young investigators who would be busy exploring in the hermit shack venue.

Grandma Clydis stretched out on the sofa. She joined Luisa who snoozed sweetly in the nearby softly upholstered easy chair. The pair settled to snoozing right on through 'As The World Turns.' On the end table beside her, Luisa's alarm clock was aegis against her being late for work at Wards.

Chapter Five

Harold and Edith borrowed a pair of bicycles from out in the garage and rode along Peach Road to the turn into the corn field south of the Marl property. They left the bikes at the stile Nathan had constructed to cross the south line fence into Digger Marl's scrub choked field. Edith commented that they'd indeed found the best way in and out of the hermit shack arena. Harold agreed as it kept the investigators out of the Marls' hair while at the same time would spare Mrs. Woods the worry of their going and coming. After a short while they were near enough to the hermit shack to hear voices, but heard none. "Strange," Aunt Edith said.

"Hey, hello the shack!" Uncle Harold called.

No answer. They quickened their paces, in mere minutes passing the old dump with its load of rusted tin cans and glass bottles.

The hermit shack came into view.

"Hey, you at the hermit shack!"

No answer!

Now running, they burst up to the shack. They saw where brush had been lopped off close to the ground and the brush piled neatly. Now the cabin was in clear view, nicely approachable. "Hey, where are you?"

Finding no one, Edith thought to blow her police whistle. Its shrill sound reverberated through the woods. Still they heard no reply. "Edith, will you look at that?"

"Oh," she saw where the others had hung their jackets and sweaters on short spikes of branches they'd left on some trees ahead. Having reached the garments they saw that ahead limbs had been lopped at intervals on into the distance.

"Hey, where are you?"

No answer, but repeated calls and whistle toots eventually brought a response. "Over here!" Although shouted by Miah, his words came faintly to Edith's ears and to Harold's not at all."

"They're ahead. I heard Miah answer."

After a few minutes the groups hooked up. "What's going on here?"

"We found the Congo." Little Nic was prancing proudly and waving his hands.

"Congo? The Congo River, Nic, can you mean?"

"It's not needed any more," Omi said, "because they renamed it the Zaire River where it's in that new country called Zaire."

"What, the Congo?" Uncle Harold wiped his hand across his brow. "Is this a lead on the hermit, is it? I don't follow."

"Just play," Cia said, "but I guess we can name the creek, can't we?"

"Sure, I guess. But why the interest in the creek?"

"It is the Congo River." Little Nic was still prancing.

"No, not just play," Aunt Anna Mae said. "We've been having loads of fun but as a matter of fact the creek was located a lot farther away than anticipated."

"They asked this Indian how I might get in here, to the shack that is, without others knowing. Before I could figure an answer, Omi or Cia said they'd bet I'd walk in along a creek bed like in the movies where Indians made escapes. Well, why not, I said so we went in search of the creek." The last few words of his reply were lost in the splash of water draining from Old Sniffer as he emerged from the cool Congo.

Sniffer hurried up to the children and there placed them in a shower of water as he shook himself.

"Gee, Helio," Harold looked all around, trying to get his bearings. "The creek really is farther north than I'd have thought."

"Yes, but Old Sniffer seemed to know the way. Back up stream a ways it makes a turn away from the shack. It could indeed be waded. These boots are tallowed water proof and I didn't get in over the tops. A hermit could, I suppose, be so equipped, but I'd cross off the idea. I'll say my feet nearly froze in that water. As well, we didn't see any obvious landing spots or evidence of an old trail leading off; not even a deer or any other game trail did we find."

"Just the Congo, huh?"

"The Congo. The Congo." Nic was still filled with jolly. Harold placed the excited and soaked Cub Scout upon his shoulders.

"Well, old scout, let's lead this outfit back to the hermit shack."

"Did you know, Uncle Harold," Miah said as he fell in beside Harold, "that David Livingstone was exploring the Congo area when people thought he was lost?"

"Wasn't he lost?"

"The ones searching for him thought so. He was found in 1871, just a century ago, while still exploring the Congo. I don't think he thought he was lost."

"The Congo, the Congo." Nic squirmed around on Uncle Harold's shoulders. He waved his arms, one arm at a time while the other hand gripped at Uncle Harold's chin. Uncle Harold was feeling the test of distance by the time the shack venue hove into view ahead.

At the shack Aunt Edith lifted Congo Nic from her husband's complaining shoulders. Uncle Harold sank gratefully down next to the doorway and used the doorframe for a backrest.

Aunt Edith asked the group to stand outside but look in through the window and door. "There's little room inside," she cautioned, and today we want to collect information about the bed. Helio and Anna Mae, if you'd help Harold inside, he can direct your measurements while I take notes."

Harold held to one end, the stationary end, of Helio's tape measure. Helio pulled the tape out from Harold's grip. "Length is eight feet and three and one half inches." Edith recorded the measurement and began a sketch of the bed. "Width is six foot and one inch."

"Dear," Harold said, "these measurements vary some from what we say due to uneven-ness, but we'll give you our best guesses."

"Sure."

"Height at the head is thirty-four inches, that is if measured at the southwest corner," Anna Mae said. "But at the foot of the bed on that side the height is thirty-six inches. Height at the head and foot on the north side of the bed is thirty-seven inches."

"Group, what can we make of this?" Aunt Edith pinched her bottom lip into a pucker. "It's a puzzle, isn't it?"

"I was in an igloo or two a long time back," Helio said. "Now you don't see them anymore as buildings are built on stilts to protect the permafrost. But maybe way on up north maybe they still do. Well I was impressed in there as each occupant had a special place to sleep. They all slept on shelves covered with furs and blankets and each had sort of a private spot. One could almost just point to the person whose spot each one was, except couples I wouldn't know. The same pattern applies here. Two persons slept here on the bed; a smaller one, I'd say about five feet eight inches, and a giant. I mean a big, big guy. I'm talking around seven feet tall or a little more; and wide, I'd say wider than three feet at the hips; perhaps wider yet at the shoulders."

"My goodness! Why, I can't imagine!"

"One of them had long hair as I see on this brush and some caught in the bed frame," Anna Mae continued the description. "The hair was medium brown but with a slightly reddish cast to it. I can't tell whether the hair here is head, beard, or what."

"Thanks, gang. We'd better not pry more right now. We'd better get the sheriff of Manitou County in here. A guy this size could easily dispatch a poor victim."

"And then bury him up above, do you think?"

"Where is he?" Omi had a slight stammer in her voice.

"That giant? Nowhere near, kids. And my guess is that he's a long time gone; most likely dead of old age by now."

"But likely the giant hermit killed and buried the little hermit, huh?"

"We can't know just yet."

The group was silent on the walk back to the bicycles and then talked very little on their remaining way home.

*　*　*

Nathan arrived home in time to lunch with his expanded family and to bid his wife good bye as she gunned out with the big 68 Pontiac. The gang all pitched in on yard work and weeding, wanting the afternoon clear to meet with Sheriff Wayne Puller. A sheriff's patrol car slowed for their driveway just as the mower and yard tools were returned to the garage and shed. Both front doors of the patrol car opened. Sheriff Puller stepped from the right side door. From behind the wheel the group was delighted to see Deputy Fanny Gillespie.

Fanny was a link in their memories of the home town area of Leadford, Michigan. Grandma Clydis, Aunt Edith, and Aunt Anna Mae crowded around her at seeing she held an envelope of photographs. Amid hugs and kisses, Fanny managed to say she had the latest photos of her two little girls and of her mother Babe Faygard Toberton. "The girls are 11 years old," she spoke proudly, "Candice and Cassandra but they became Candy and Sandy almost at once."

"Our Omi is 10 and Cia is 8. They're nicknamed from Naomi and Phoenicia. We'd love to meet your lovely girls. Would Saturday work?"

Her smile was grand. "Sure thing," she chuckled, "I itched to bring them today, but remembered I was on duty. They're also in Bible School and in the afternoon need to memorize the next day's verses. Naomi is from the Bible. Is Phoenicia?"

"Yes, like in some Bibles; spelled with an 'o' in it. That spelling also suggests the name is of Greek origin. A Phenicia is actually a palm tree, so the word may have been quite widespread. In the Bible, Phoenicia is also spelled P-h-e-n-i-c-i-e pronounced Phen-i-cie, all vowels short except the last e. In 'Phenicie; the ph is like an f, like in telephone. That ph is thought to be Greek, as well.

"In Alsace-Lorraine, France where I sailed from, the spelling ends with an 'e' or an 'a,' and sometimes the letter 'x' is the last letter of the word. We were looking for a name that would logically be shortened to a nickname a little different."

"'Cia', it's a cute nickname. I'd heard the Phoenicians descended from, or at least split off from, the Canaanites and became great merchants that established many far apart towns."

"Yes, my husband studied on that. They invented an alphabet based on what we now call phonics, the phonetic alphabet, I've heard to foster communications port to port. There's a town called Byblos. That may have been the origin of Bible; or Book."

"Officer Gillespie," the sheriff said. "We'll be walking back in, leaving the car here in the yard. Be sure your hand-held radio is okay."

Instantly Fanny was returned to serious deputy duty, taking pains to carefully run her radio checks.

Nathan took a load of folks up to the edge of the corn field then returned the light blue Chevy pickup to the yard. He took a short cut through the gravel pit that required a rugged hill climb, in lieu of a detour, to get past the pit. He was puffing when he caught the others on the trail into the hermit shack. "What does Digger Marl have to say about all of this?" the sheriff was asking just as Nathan joined the group.

"I just dashed through his yard," Nathan said. "It looked like nobody was home. He left a note for us to find the day after you were here that other time. Said he was taking a much needed vacation. We've heard nothing from him."

"And Mrs. Woods?"

"Omi and Cia are caring for her cats. She's on vacation to visit relatives in Tennessee, at Oak Ridge. On her calendar, the girls said she's marked next Wednesday as her day to return."

"See anything of the Lance family? I need to question all who live near. No telling what they can tell us."

"The Lances, Dale and Peg, we seldom see as they both work days. I was up to their back fence the other day, locating that fence to the north of the one that formerly crossed Digger's pit. I didn't see any sign of them. Matter of fact, we hardly know them even as long as we've lived in their neighborhood."

"How about that vacant brick house located just north of Mrs. Woods?"

"A commercial company comes in to perform lawn care but we've not met the owners or workers of the company nor of the house. I haven't seen anyone over there doing lawn care yet this summer. Usually, though, the lawn's been quite irregularly tended each summer. The place's been vacant as now even from before we built our house."

"I see. Well, I'll call on the Lances tonight. You or one or your relatives could come, but I don't want but a very few of anyone to go with me. Crowding them isn't usually a good idea."

"I'd like to go, Wayne," Grandma Clydis said. "Maybe an out of town person would be less scary."

"Could be; so I'll stop in to get you, say around seven."

"Sure."

"Harold and I will be following a lead south of town, Wayne. A fellow named Glenn Mills has sold shoes for years. At home Harold has for years purchased shoes of that kind, despite that he worked at Wolverine. The work shoes he buys cost more than do Wolverines but fit well and wear well, a whole year on the job usually. Harold regards Wolverines more for outdoor duty; good for an army, he's said. We thought, however, that our victim, even if not well to do, may've found such a shoe purchase as frugal."

"It might well shorten our investigation. Mayor Sharp and I talked this morning after you'd left. Narrowing to the 'big three' stores sounds right as to clothes. Discovering that Old Yank'um Woods may've been his dentist is like finding a diamond all cut and polished. Dates our victim, too, to around where you've said. Let's for now keep that decade to zero in on, that's 1945 to 1955. Doctor Woods died in around 1950 but we'll check to confirm the exact date."

"Yes, sure. Dr. Woods, we assume is the late husband of Mrs. Woods, neighbor to Luisa and Nathan. Did the mayor find yet who has Dr. Woods' dental records?"

"Yes, Dr. Woods was her husband. Not yet on the dental records, but we'll soon know. It'll be a dentist in this small town, no doubt."

At the dump the sheriff stopped. "Kids, I didn't think to bring my tongs. I'd hoped to lift some cans and bottles out of this dump. I'll bring the tongs tonight. Then tomorrow you may want to bring forth some bottles and cans, see, and write down the product, the company, and any dates and serial numbers from the items. Leave those items you've listed in evidence bags near the dump. I only need a selection from the top, don't dig down into the pile. Are you game?"

"Sure, Sheriff, we can see some painted ones now but no paper labels. Can we start?"

"Sure, consider yourselves unofficial sheriff's deputies." Omi, Cia, and Nic settled in at the dump.

"Miah," the sheriff said. "I'll need to check for finger prints on the crate and the wine bottles located inside the shack. When that's finished, I'll need the same info from the wine bottles your sibs are acquiring from the dump, okay?"

"You bet. I'll get to it." Miah studied every move of Deputy Fanny Gillespie as she dusted for prints.

Deputy Fanny Gillespie also snapped pictures of everything the sheriff talked about or took samples of the items. She included hair samples from bed and brush and fabric samples from the bed including labels from feed sacks used in constructing the padding that was their mattress.

The sheriff and Deputy Fanny dusted around on the bed posts and frame, the wash stand, and the wood stove and kitchen shelf. "It looks like they ate a lot of game."

"Yes," Nathan said. He held aloft a leather thong with skulls threaded onto it. "I see skulls of about any kind of animal that I know to be native here including cats and dogs and several types of birds. I'd guess quail, pheasant, and ducks."

"Trapped likely?"

"Yes, and/or shot by arrow. I see some arrows leaning in that corner but haven't seen a bow."

"Poking around outside, we'd better be alert for animal traps still set; better warn those kids at the dump."

"Sheriff, you'd better come and see this," Helio said. "They had a concrete bathroom. Sniffer found it."

"Bathroom made of concrete? I can't imagine." The sheriff led the way from the hermit shack. "Concrete bathroom, I just can't imagine."

"Looks like it to us, sheriff. Anna Mae and I will be leaving you now. We must get on home today to return to work tomorrow." He and Anna Mae shook hands all around and bid goodbye. The couple disappeared up toward the dump just as the sheriff entered the assumed bathroom. From at the dump they heard Uncle Helio and Aunt Anna Mae bidding goodbye and also instructing the youngsters to keep an eye for animal traps that could still nab them and to hold Old Sniffer close to them so that he wouldn't be tempted to follow after the camper.

"We'll need to clean this out, as well," the sheriff said, "and catalog the stuff found as usual. I can't at this moment see it as a toilet even as it's a good size and shape to be one. I see no seat, for one reason, but we'll come back with a sampler to collect core samples from the floor. They can be analyzed for human wastes or from the organisms that consume such wastes. Our labs are getting pretty good at that; or, at least, it can be determined whether the sample is likely bear or dog or such. If not one of those likely creatures, then the waste is decided to be of human origin."

"Science marches on, huh, Wayne?"

"Wayne, isn't it strange the roof and door, window frame, any parts

I'd assume were of wood are completely gone here while the wood of the shack has held up well; even the roof is fairly intact," Aunt Edith spoke wondrously. "Just one more puzzle, isn't it?"

"Fire here perhaps; we likely could spend a lifetime solving puzzles, but identifying the persons who were here and the victim and working out relationships is a crucial first priority." He scanned them with his clear brown eyes. "Paramount," he said, "is to solve the murder. We must collect any and all info we can and hope we can add it all up to solve those main concerns. I'm grateful for all of your help, you folks. I've a notion to call your home sheriff and see if I might get the whole pack of you Leadford sleuths assigned permanently to me."

"We're happy to help, but Wayne, make no mistake about who is in charge. That's you, kind sir. We'll help all we can and if we're in the way at any time, please let us know."

"This investigation is going along as smoothly as most, I assure you."

The group packed up to leave with Harold, Nathan, the sheriff, and Deputy Gillespie each carrying evidence bags. Sniffer led the way up the trail.

From behind the wheel of the patrol car, Deputy Fanny waved. Then her gleaming, eye boggling, vehicle started out the driveway. "See you all on Saturday."

The Platt girls and little Nic waved until the thrilling auto was out of sight up the road.

"Grandma Clydis, do you have a dashing uniform like hers," Omi wanted to know.

"Posh," Grandma said, "why, as you know I prefer to be undercover."

"Not today," Nic said, "why, Grandma it's real warm today."

Grandma knew that Nic misunderstood the 'undercover' term, but went with him. "Say, I guess you're right, pard."

* * *

Grandma napped without those covers well into the afternoon and was spry and fresh as a daisy when the sheriff returned promptly at seven that evening. Peg Lance answered a knock on her kitchen door. Seeing past her badge bearing guests, her heart leaped at seeing the sheriff's authoritative patrol car.

"Peg Lance?"

"Uh, y . . . yes." Dale and Peg Lance had been discussing the activity around the gravel pit over the last few days and they'd recalled and rehashed visions from the past, visions they'd prayed not to remember.

"They will come, of that we can be sure," Dale had said. "We must keep straight faces and strive not to tell too much."

"Even lies, do you think?"

"Lies to protect one's own should not count as lies. Let God in Heaven rule as to whether lie or caring concern."

Peg peered at the badge-bearing guests, noting that one was old, certainly as old as a grandmother, and the other she believed was certainly the sheriff. Sheriff Puller, standing strong and sure of himself, said, "Mrs. Peg Lance, we are of the Manitou County sheriff's office. It is with gravity that we question yourself and Dale. Is Dale presently at home?"

"Yes." She pushed the door open for them. Turning, she called, "Dale, we've company."

Seated around the dining room table, the Sheriff opened the questioning by asking, "Mr. Lance, how far back of you do you own?"

"Er, uh, just to our back fence."

"The fence along the north side of your property goes clear back to an eastern line fence does it not?"

"Yes, I guess."

"And the fence along the south edge of your property, that fence does it also run clear back to that eastern line fence?"

"Yes, sure, I guess, but I don't know."

"Am I correct that a fence buts into your property about in the middle?"

"Sure, I see it there but I'm not sure where it goes."

"That means that a narrow band or strip of land half the width of your property extends from the rear of your property clear on over to that eastern line fence then. Am I not correct?"

"Sure, I guess."

"When did you acquire your building site? What year? Who did you buy your lot from?"

"1950. We bought from Digger."

"Measuring from your south line to the south line of Marl's land, the measurement indicates that the Marl's own a standard width, that's a ten acre strip off a standard quarter section. The strip of land your house is on is the width of a five acre strip. That's the width of your site is it not?"

"Yes, we've a five acre frontage."

"How do you explain that; I mean that your width is half off of the land of your north neighbor? It's as if the neighbor to your north sold land off to you folks and also some to the Marls. Do you see what I mean? Who did you buy your land from? Be sure now."

"Why, Digger, I'm sure."

"So Digger bought the strip from your neighbor then sold your site off of it to you, huh?"

"I guess."

"He bought from the Woods', did he?"

"I guess."

"Mrs. Woods owns the property to the north of you, am I right?"

"Yes, she does."

"And her place is a fifteen acre strip going all the way back to the eastern line fence, do you think?"

"I would guess so. I haven't heard."

"Have you heard of others living on the property to your north and on back of Mrs. Woods; persons other than Dr. and Mrs. Woods?"

"No."

"Have you ever been back in there, behind the Woods' home?"

"Uh uh."

"What do you know about a small concrete building back in there?"

"I don't recall."

"Then you have been back in there. When was that? Tell us about that?"

"Oh, uh, well, I thought, well recently, not way back. There was a gravel pit back in there when we bought. Not an active one, but some of their stuff was still there. Trees have grown now so we can't see anything but trees, but I recall there was a few buildings back in there."

"A small concrete building?"

"Uh, I'm not sure."

"No other buildings?"

Dale plowed his fingers through his graying hair. "It's been a good twenty years, sheriff."

"Were you well acquainted with Dr. Woods?"

"He was handy for our dentist."

"Worked on you at his office or did he work on you at home, say after hours; neighborly like?"

"Oh, he practiced some dentistry in his kitchen of a weekend or evening; in summer he'd use his closed-in porch. Just to help neighbors; neighborly, you see. Nice fellow."

The wooded area behind the Woods' home has very tall trees, the trees older than others that one sees from up front. Was that woods there when you built here?"

"Sure."

"The rows of pines leading up to in front of the woods, do you know who planted them?"

"No."

"Did Dr. Woods?"

"I don't know. There was a road there. It was the way into the gravel pit."

"Can you say how long those pines have been there?"

"No, but say twenty years, I guess. They came into view. Must have grown up till they came into view. I didn't see anybody plant them."

"Peg," the sheriff turned to Mrs. Lance. "What is your wedding date?"

"June 11, 1946. We lived in town then built here."

"Your marriage is recorded then at the Manitou County courthouse? Ma'am, what was your nee name?"

"Marlin."

"Well, thank you folks. One of us will return if further questions arise."

Having returned to the patrol car, the sheriff said, "Marlin, huh? Sounds like Marl may be a nick name of Marlin. Would you like to go with me to the court house in the morning? We've some land records to check out and we need to confirm that Digger wasn't in the first place named Digger and that his sir name isn't Marl."

"Wayne, I'd about bet Peg's a sister to that Mr. Digger, so named. I'd agree that the names Marl and Marlin are the same name. I'd like to be sure we know too, who actually owns the property the hermit shack is on. I'll come to town with you but I want to check at the banks to see if there are any accounts to Marlin, now or way back. I'll also check the telephone and utilities records. I'll catch up with you at the court house."

"It sounds like I'd better catch up with you!" He bugged his eyes for her to see. I'll bring a radio for you to carry. That could help us link up somewhere, okay?"

"Good, we usually carry one, but this trip was designed to be a casual vacation to give me time to get over Clarence's passing. It has helped, yet all through the trip out to New York City and vicinity and now here on this investigation he hasn't left my mind. It seems to be he is guiding me every step through my involvement here. But you know, Wayne, at least I know what happened to my Clarence while perhaps loved ones here went to their grave not knowing what happened to a loved one. It is imperative then, that we bring closure to this John Doe case."

"Yes, a closure. Every detail counts, even to figuring out why, of what, and when the hermit shack was constructed. Next time back in there try to see if the shack wasn't constructed of used lumber, like building by tearing down other buildings. Look for odd spaced nail holes, perhaps. I'll keep radios with you folks at all times beginning tomorrow."

"I sure will, and thank you." Grandma said.

Sheriff Wayne pulled out of the Lance's driveway. "Harold and Edith may be back home by now," Deputy Grandma said, "back from visiting that shoe salesman, Glenn Mills."

"Yep." Sheriff Wayne Puller pushed the pedal. They swooped toward the Platt residence.

Chapter Six

SHERIFF PULLER AND GRANDMA CLYDIS listened while Uncle Harold and Aunt Edith spun their tale of misfortune. Harold said, "Mr. Glenn Mills recalled the guy right away. He remembered a man with no back teeth. He found out about the missing teeth when he offered the man a taste of venison steak. The guy said he'd take it along home as he couldn't chew it but could boil it into submission. Mr. Mills didn't have the man's name or address and said that he had never had them because the man refused to reveal those details."

"He came one night when the Mills' lived in town," Edith read from her notes. "That was in 1947 because they moved out to the farm in 1949. They would buy a home and fix it up and resell it. Several times they did that through the years, but just that one house there in town is where the man showed up. He came there two years in a row. He paid for the shoes and said he'd come back later to pick them up; usually a month or so later is when he'd be back. That last time when he came back he came out to the farm because they'd said to him they'd be moved to there."

"Is Uncle Helio going to put pigs in his camper?" Little Nic stood at Grandma's knee with his bright young eyes studying her face. Their talk of the hermit or hermits and of the shoes came to a halt.

"Hey, you little dickens, you're supposed to be in bed." All eyes were on Nic. He stood his ground.

"Grandma, is he?" Grandma looked across at Nathan and Luisa who were seated behind their coffee mugs.

"Oh, I think not."

"I haven't heard about any pigs," Luisa said, and Nathan nodded agreement.

"He called up Omi."

"Did Uncle Helio call?"

"No, Uncle Del."

"Omi, huh? Nic, we'll ask Omi about it in the morning."

"Come along, Nic," Luisa buffed his hair. "I'll tuck you in. I'm sure Uncle Helio's not going to put pigs in the new camper, so don't worry." She tucked the little guy in. "You know, sport, I'd be nice to see your new cousin again. Little Virginia Louise is three now and I'd bet she'd be some fun to play with. Should I give Uncle Del and Aunt Dosia a call?"

"Gosh, yes."

"Okay, sweety." She kissed his forehead. "Night-night, now."

That next morning while Nic was listening carefully to Snap, Crackle, and Pop, Luisa's telephone call was traveling at the speed of light to Ellington, Michigan where Dosia raised the receiver.

"Hello, Dosia here."

"Hi, sis. Nic said that Del had called and chatted a moment with Omi but she's a sleepy head this morning; still in bed. Nic talked about pigs. What's up?"

"Good news, we believe. Papa Helio borrowed our truck so that he could haul pigs to Swift in Chicago. We're glad he didn't want to risk getting the new camper tractor dirty. He thought he might've dirtied it on some of the farms. So, we traded. Now Del has asked a friend to haul for him, the friend to use our spare truck. That's loads of rice from Arkansas to Ontario. He just now saw his friend Louie off on that adventure. I asked Del why he set Louie to hauling. You know what he said? 'Why waste an opportunity with a perfectly good brand new pearly white camper?' So now we're heading for the Air Force Museum at Dayton. Stopping by your place, okay?"

"You bet it's okay! Looking forward."

"I can't say just what day. We'll go first to the museum but Hi is pouring over the Ohio and Michigan maps in search of other attractions."

"Any day will be fine. How is Virginia Louise?"

"Wonderful. But I lost her for a while yesterday. I was painting the bedroom ceiling upstairs and she explored into the attic through a little door off that bedroom. The door went shut and I didn't even think to look in there. Instead, we searched high and low. Finally like Little Bo Peep whose lost sheep turned up on their own, that darling called to us from the attic. I swear, sis, some days we age alarmingly. Anyway, I'm so glad we'll have the camper. She and I can frolic and frolic; jump on the beds and such, you know, while Del drives. And say, Hi discovered the dump back in the woods. He dragged home a baby carriage and has already loaded it into the camper. Luisa, I just believe and I am tickled pink to think it was Aunt Edith's; when she was a little girl. It banged around in the family for years and years, one family to another, and finally wore out and was discarded but Del and Hi want to restore it if it's the right one. We'll know, of course, when Aunt Edith sees it."

"I'm glad your Del is a superlative craftsman and that he's works with Hi so Hi is learning."

"You may know that Del and Hi re-did our kitchen, but when next you're here look to see an area where they ran out of wall paper; quite a large area, too. Well, they simply painted that area to match the rest of the wallpaper."

"Gosh, we'll know who to consult through the years. And, by all means, bring the buggy when you come. We'll look for you on any day that works for you."

"Great! Well, I must scoot. My Virginia Louise just bombed her hand into her oatmeal looking for a lump she believes to be in there someplace."

Luisa hung the receiver. "Nic, you were right about pigs, only Uncle Helio will use Uncle Del's truck to haul them; and guess what? They're coming, that's Uncle Del, Aunt Dosia, Hi and little Virginia Louise, on a day soon with the big white camper to visit us."

Nic took a big drink of his milk. "Good going," he said.

At the moment that Nic said "good going" a rosy cheeked Aunt Edith popped into the kitchen. "Nic, you're a dear. Good going all right. Why, several more of these early morning practice sessions and I'll be ready to out croquet you young ones." Nic grinned. He'd noticed that Grandma, Aunt Edith, and Uncle Harold were out early to enjoy a round or two of croquet.

"Oatmeal with raisins is ready," she said to her guests. "Are you sure that'll be enough? I can cook eggs, pancakes, waffles, you name it.

Nathan and Miah had buttery toast along with corn flakes before leaving for work."

"Oh, oatmeal is great."

Just entering the kitchen, Grandma and Uncle Harold chorused agreement with the breakfast menu. "French toast enters my mind," Harold said. "Would you like some for lunch?"

"Yes, but I would rather hold off on that until Del and Dosia get here. They'll be exploring their way back from the Air Force Museum at Dayton to arrive here sometime this week. They'll have the camper. Helio is hauling loads of pigs into Chicago. He's using Del's truck. Then Louie Watkins is using Del's other truck to haul loads of rice for Del, hauling from Arkansas to Canada, while Del and family are on vacation."

"Hey, that's right," Harold said, "you and Dosia are both from France, the country where World War One and much of War Two raged and here in the states French toast was birthed in protest during War One. It's like winning the war over and over again each time we dine on French toast. I'm looking forward."

"Why is that?" Cia and Omi had arrived with sleepy eyes.

"Just cereal for us," Omi said. "Did I hear correctly that Uncle Del; that he and his are coming?"

"Yes, sometime during the week."

"Why would they like French toast? Uncle Harold, did it somehow win a war?"

"It was called German toast," Uncle Harold said around his heaped spoon of oatmeal, "but during World War One folks of the USA changed the name of it to French toast."

"Really?"

"It seemed the patriotic thing to do. To this day I feel proud when I eat some."

"Children, your mom is from Alsace-Lorraine France and your Aunt Dosia is from Paris, in case you need to be reminded."

"Sure, we know. Miah had to write about family stuff, about some one or other in the tree, in Mrs. Krieger's English class, then so did Omi so I'll be next."

"Next? Do you mean genealogy? The family tree, it's often called."

"Yes but she had Naomi write in a little story about some one or something in the tree. She wrote about her namesake, Naomi of the

Bible. Her daughter-in-law Ruth accepted Naomi's god; the God, the only true God as her God. Ruth and Naomi moved to Bethlehem and Ruth married Boaz and they named their son Obed. Later Obed's son was Jesse and Jesse's son was David; King David."

"My golly! Dear Cia," she reached to tap the sweet youngster's shoulder, "what will you write about?"

"Mom said that Phoenician purple dye is also made in Alsace-Lorraine where Mom came from so the dye and my name link the two parts of the world, that is that Phoenicia and Alsace-Lorraine are inter-related. The purple dye has religious significance in that it stands for death and, of course, also for resurrection. Purple is also a royal color."

"Truly remarkable."

"Was the dye extracted from a plant?"

"No, a sea snail was the source of the dye; so that's a problem. The snails were over-harvested so now I don't know how the dye is made."

The telephone jangled. Grandma Clydis grabbed it. "Hello, Platt residence."

"Clydis, the dental records are with Dr. Dentin. I'll be there by ten this morning."

"Ten this morning. Fanny, that's great. Some of us will meet you."

"It's on Ashe-t-wetta. She's a popular Indian maiden who lived here at Manitou Prairie. As soon as you turn into the drive from the south going highway, called Southern Road, that's the one to Adrian, you'll see the sign in front of a single-story brick building."

"I'll stick here with the kids," Uncle Harold said as Grandma hung up. "We'll have a hand-held radio with us when we explore around the hermit shack. The idea of a bathroom intrigues me. If not that concrete building, then what did they use?"

* * *

Uncle Harold drew sketches of what an outhouse might look like. "Obviously one isn't standing back there or we would've seen it, kids, but I hope to find evidence that they had one."

The group was just starting out with Uncle Harold astride a bicycle like the others when Miah came zooming down the hill. "Hey, wait up!" Sliding his Schwinn to a stop he said, "I'm done for the day. There was only the one area that needed mowing then we'll mow and trim the whole cemetery on Friday. I've an idea how the hermit, or hermits, got in there without being seen. I'd like us to try to go in that way."

"Can't we ride our bikes?"

"Not the way we'd be going. You could go in the usual way and meet us at the shack."

"Nic and Cia got too tired yesterday when we explored the Congo. You know, that tiny Congo."

"So did you. Guess who slept in this morning."

"Not me." Nic stood straighter. He reached to pull old Sniffer's fur. "Me and Old Sniffer will go with the men so he can sniff out the way."

The girls rode out for the corn field and the fence stile while the 'men' parked their bicycles and followed Miah. Already Old Sniffer with his tail furiously wagging was vanguard for their exploration. He'd wandered into the woods along Congo Creek by the time Miah halted his safari on the roadside overlooking the Congo area.

"We often cross the road through the creek tunnel," Miah explained, "then climb back up to the road on this side." He pointed. "Notice that even now there's less brush growing on this side of the creek. I thought about that and decided that instead of only coming out this way perhaps he went in this way; that is down this path toward the Congo."

"Yeah the Congo," Nic giggled and spread his arms and waved his hands, "the mighty Congo."

Nic and Old Sniffer led down the steep path. Miah was on their heels and leading the way for Uncle Harold.

Uncle Harold noted handy brush and sapling handholds as they descended. "I believe you're right so far, Miah."

"Now look from here, Uncle Harold. "You can't see from the road because of the bushes along the road. From here, though, we're past the bushes. You can see there is a rather open area with little vegetation except for large trees. We of Uncle Helio's safari didn't go clear up to the creek tunnel yesterday. The tunnel was in sight but we turned back when Old Sniffer began walking down the creek toward where you found us."

"Yes, I see. Old Sniffer, I would think heard our whistle and calls before you did, so he started back."

"Sure, I'd bet that's what happened. Old Sniffer walked on down the creek and Uncle Helio waded along behind. The rest of us followed along but we were away from the creek bank where it was easier going. That's when I saw we were on a more open route through the trees."

Their trek on through the woods was easy going. A large fence post came into view. "Corner post, is my guess, and there's no fence beyond it so he could've moved easily along here behind this fence. I see this fence is the back line of the property of those folks, the ones of the vacant house. Do you know their name?"

"No. We could ask my folks."

Nic and Old Sniffer had by then began exploratory steps in the presumed direction of the hermit shack.

Miah cautioned, "Wait up, Nic," and then stood taller to peer ahead.

"Hey, look ahead, Uncle Harold. That's that row of pine trees we can see from Mrs. Woods'."

"Yes, and they're in view from the Lance's place, as well. Dale and Peg Lance, as you may know, live next door to Digger's gravel pit, just to the south of Mrs. Woods. Your grandma said the sheriff asked them about the pine trees. They thought the trees had been planted long ago along the margin of a roadway into the gravel pits. This whole area back in here was once one gravel pit or another."

"We better hurry," Nic said as he stepped boldly off toward the pines. Old Sniffer was at his heels."

"Nic, wait up. What's the rush?"

"Tootsie Rolls. Omi and Cia were going to eat some when they got to the shack. I want some."

"They'll likely save some."

"I'm hungry." He kept a brisk step ahead.

They were just into the pines along the ancient roadway when suddenly Old Sniffer burst from tall weeds located west of the pine route they were traveling. "Nic, wait for Old Sniffer."

"Where you been, boy?" Old Sniffer's tail began to wag his entire body and he retreated back into the weeds. Miah followed. "Hey, a dump here. Another dump."

Uncle Harold pushed through the weeds, making an easier route for Nic.

"No bottles and cans," Miah said, "just old furniture, appliances, and stuff from a house."

"This defile is an old gravel pit that somebody used for a household dump. Let's explore it later. I'm with Nic," Uncle Harold said, "hungry for a Tootsie Roll, huh, Nic?"

At the south end of the rows of pines they looked toward the hermit shack location and saw the route as quite clear on into the shack venue. "Boys," Uncle Harold said, "I didn't have to duck much at all to keep from bumping my head down through these pines. That may give us an idea, too, as to how tall one of the guys was. Just a little shorter than me, that is. And, Miah, I'm sure you're right about his way in. My guess is that the shack's right ahead."

Within moments the concrete "bathroom" came into view and at that moment treble notes of Omi and Cia reached their ears. Nic and Old Sniffer ran ahead, but Uncle Harold reached a hand to halt Miah. "Look here, son."

"Huh?"

"Look here. Do you see? From here we're looking straight into the window and doorway of that little concrete building. I wonder if right about here where we're standing would be a good place to feed deer and other game. It'd be an easy shot with a bow and arrow."

"Or to pick off an intruder, huh, Uncle Harold. Golly, my back is goose fleshed!"

"Mine's a bit prickly, too."

Excited voices of Omi, Cia, and Nic told that Nic had met up with the Tootsie Roll bearers. Miah and Uncle Harold quickened their steps. Old Sniffer was digging a hole as the pair walked up to the others. "It's a good thing he's busy," Omi said, "as we've only enough Tootsie Rolls for the people."

"Oh, he won't mind; or I could give him a wee nip of mine," Uncle Harold said. "He's sure in earnest on the dig isn't he?"

"Must be a rodent down in there."

"Or maybe he's trying to dig up the posts."

"Posts?" Uncle Harold moved in for a close look at the dog's project. "Posts, all right. Driven into the ground for some reason." He passed a hand across his forehead then mussed his own hair before studying his fingernails. "Posts, now for what could that be? Each post has a crotch at the top, do you see? Could be a cross pole was placed across there. Hummmm."

"To hang up game, maybe. No," Miah changed his mind. "The posts would be too short for that."

"What's he digging up?"

"Nothing yet but dirt, is all I see."

"Hummmm." Uncle Harold rubbed a hand across his mouth. "Hummmm, maybe if we find a stick to place across, placed into the crotches, we might see."

Omi discovered just such a stick. "How will this do? It's even been chopped the right length."

The heavy stick of about two and one half inches in diameter had indeed been chopped to length. She and Miah placed the stick.

Beneath the cross stick, Old Sniffer kept on with his excavation.

"Yuck!" Uncle Harold expounded. He reached Old Sniffer and pulled him back, calming his protest with a chunk of Tootsie Roll. Old Sniffer readily gave up his project. He whined piteously and wagged his tail, replacing the project with a bid to win even more of the delicious candy. "Kids, were I taller, I could show you what I think we've, that is Old Sniffer has, found. Were I as tall as the giant hermit, recall that Uncle Helio estimated him to be over seven feet tall, well, if I was so tall, I could hump on the cross bar to go to the bathroom. I haven't before ever seen a humper, but now I'm seeing one. A humper is a special type of bathroom that I've heard about."

"Where?" Nic wanted to know.

"Where is what? The bathroom?" Suddenly Omi and Cia were pealing laughter. In their minds' eye they could see the giant with his rump humped back over the cross bar doing his bathroom duty. Miah saw it as well and his chuckle melded with their glee.

Soon Miah was holding to a nearby tree for support, his glee having soared to plateau just shy of ecstasy. "Old Sniffer was digging in it!" He laughed and laughed and with the others joining anew with the new vision. Even Nic was a-roar with glee.

Finally under control, Nic could say, "I wonder if we'll find their outhouse."

"Nic, we'll not likely find one like the one Uncle Harold drew a picture of," Cia said in realizing his confusion, "but let's keep an eye out anyway."

* * *

Grandma Clydis and Aunt Edith joined Deputy Fanny Gillespie in Dr. Dentin's waiting room. Fanny whispered, "Our appointment's for ten-thirty."

The ladies began a futile scan for an interesting magazine. Finding not a one, Clydis and Edith drew crossword puzzle books from their purses while Fanny, with her daughters in mind, settled with a flyer on dental care. If I like Dr. Dentin, she thought, I just might bring Candy and Sandy here for checkups. "This way please." The clock ticked exactly at ten-thirty. "Dr. Dentin was a patient of Dr. Woods through high school," his receptionist said in introduction.

"And surely an inspiration to me," Dr. Dentin smiled at them. "My goal is to be as appreciated as was my mentor." He shook hands as the introductions were completed. "I've set aside the decade of records Officer Gillespie indicated," he said, "and I'm prepared to answer specifics if that would be helpful."

"Thank you, doctor. We're particularly interested in partial plates, especially for the replacement of the molars."

"Ah, yes. I don't believe I will ever master his technique in making the sticky dental cream or the plates. He did all of the work himself, you know; and the paste was of his own formulation." He placed records before them. "If I may, I'll sort out the patients you've indicated although by no means will I limit those to you. All of the records are available to you."

Soon the ladies had the names and statistics of more than a dozen patients with front teeth but with all molars missing and of twenty-one patients with an upper or a lower plate or with both an upper and a lower plate, or of any with a partial plate that replaced molars. Dr. Dentin assured them of the continued availability of his records and the records of Dr. Woods. "Thank you, Dr. Dentin; you've been most kind and helpful."

The ladies spent that afternoon and the next full day in the court house laboriously tracking down each person. All but three were accounted for, but none were a match for the victim found in Digger's gravel pit. "We have names, addresses, interviews with kinfolk, and burial records where appropriate," Fanny said, "all but for these three that had all molars missing. I'll take the three records with me up to the state crime laboratory at Lansing; see if the techs can match one to the victim."

As Fanny was sliding into her patrol car, Luisa came to the car window. "We're looking forward to Saturday; to a visit with Candy and Sandy."

"Oh, that's right. I haven't told the girls yet as I didn't want to mix different emotions in with Bible School. That ends on Friday. They'll be delighted. Your girls are so very sweet. They tell me they are caring for Mrs. Woods' cats. That is so nice of them."

"Yes, she'll be home tomorrow. They've done a good job."

"Well, until Saturday then." The patrol car scooted from the driveway.

Chapter Seven

IT HAD TAKEN A WEEK before all four of Mrs. Woods' cats had owned up to Cia and Omi. Now on the morning of her expected return the cats vied for attention as the girls combed their fur and tied a bow of pretty ribbon onto each flea collar. The four were sitting at purring attention when Mrs. Woods stopped at her garage door. At a rear door of the car she reached in for a suitcase then leaned tiredly against the door frame. Venturing a glance at them, she was suddenly all smiles. Then at her first steps toward her pets every one of them scooted from the porch stoop and streaked to where they barreled in under the porch. "Well, I swear, those cats don't know who buys their food."

Besides looking tired from her trip, she now stood as though in disgust of her capricious cats. "We're sorry they ran away. For the first week they mostly hid from us."

"I'll see if they'll want in tonight to view television with me. You young ladies have done splendidly by them. I'm very tired just now, but tomorrow would you join me around two o'clock for a trip to Baker's Ice Cream shop?"

"Yes, fine. How was your trip?"

"Just grand. We had a good long visit and did some sight seeing; even I went down into a cave."

"Caves are great fun. We'll carry in the rest of your bags before we go."

"Oh, I'll get them later."

"No trouble." They lugged the bags, two a-piece, to the stoop. "Our dad has your Hoover. We spilled cat food and Nic picked it all up then

81

we tried to vacuum the kitchen. There was a screech, some smoke, and the odor of burned rubber. Nic carried the vacuum home. Dad had to order a new belt for it. Mom will bring the belt home from Montgomery Wards."

"If Nic is free tomorrow at two, bring him along."

"Gee, thanks." They waved from their bicycles while pedaling on down her driveway. Mrs. Woods glanced after them but quickly darted in through the kitchen doorway.

In her kitchen, Mrs. Woods looked toward the rows of pine trees that were set against the backdrop of tall trees. Since her husband's death on that indelible day some twenty-one years previous, she often looked out at the rows of pines. Sometimes after looking out at the benevolent eerie trees she would decide not to go outside. Sometimes for days she didn't go outside. Seeing naught but the pines, she squirted out her kitchen door and grabbed her suitcases, heaving them into the kitchen where they slid into a disordered heap. She closed the door authoritatively and locked it.

On this day, had she looked again from her kitchen window she would have been shocked. She would have stood in terror as she had that day long ago when first the abominable appeared. Today she would have only seen two tiny creatures, each standing hardly more than knee high to that abominable horror but her mind would see the beast no less. She would have seen that abominable giant beast that from that first day to the present screamed at her and came at her in endless nightmares.

She dragged just one suitcase into her bedroom before smashing face down upon the bed, her bed, her own bed, and where sleep took control of her. Outside her house two sprites scampered amidst the pines. Old Sniffer'd led them to the cut off path leading to the household dump. "I saw a real strange chair in here," Nic told his friend.

Fellow Cub Scout, Alvin Beach, being shorter than Nic, hopped up and down trying to see past Nic as they moved along the path. They drew to a stop, each with a hand dug into the cordial fur of Old Sniffer. "See." Nic pointed.

"Gee, yes, now I see what you've found. It's an old barber chair. Gosh, can we get it out of there?"

They rolled the chair two times over, both turns down hill. No amount of struggle and strain would budge the thing further nor could it be set all the way up to where they could try the seat. It lay on its side within a trample down of tall weeds. Sun beams glinted off its chromed parts and stuffing oozed from its once patent leather covered cushions. "I want this to be ours," Nic was emphatic, "so we'll have to cover it up with weeds to hide it."

"Sure, lest the others find it." They jerked and jerked at weeds and tossed and tossed until an igloo-shaped mount stood on the floor of the defile. The tired Cub Scouts stood amid the pines and looked back at their handiwork. The mound was obvious as was its backdrop of old stove, old refrigerator, busted wood furniture, a suppurating sofa and chair, along with a massive assortment of other household spoil. Now dead tired but not shy of determination, they moved along behind Old Sniffer, the pair drawing step by step ever closer to that mysterious hermit shack.

At the humper where Old Sniffer resumed his digging, Alvin sought out a small log and sat down. He passed a palm across his forehead then transferred sweat to the thigh of his denim trousers. "I'm glad I could come today, Nic. After we found those two bones, remember that day? Well, that night I heard my folks talking real quiet-like, but I listened really close and they talked about Mom's uncles. She said they used to live in the woods, but one day they didn't come to get the food and my dad and my Uncle Digger went into the woods but my uncles were gone. Mom and Dad whispered about a man buried so that's why we found the bones."

"Gosh, really? Well, we think a hermit lived here."

"Not my uncles?"

"I don't know, but we could ask." Nic shrugged his shoulders. "But I don't know who to ask lest they all find out."

"I'd be in trouble. I'm not supposed to know about my uncles." He stood from his log seat and scanned around and about the shack venue. "I think uncles can be hermits too. Maybe they did live here."

"Come on along trooper. I'll show you around."

In her bedroom in the gray house, Mrs. Woods stirred and moaned in her slumber. Her hand moved out as it had thousands of times before and it came to rest on the side of the bed where John had lain until with his last breath he'd said, "I love you." He was still her strength, the strength she needed to endure each day within the reach of an abominable monster who peered at her from the pines and who made clacks in the night.

* * *

Deputy Grandma Clydis Groner and Sheriff Wayne Puller sat in his idling patrol car to compare notes. "Scoutmaster Blyth Merit's wife, she is Barbara Bobby Marlin Merit. She's a sister to Peggy Marlin Lance. She's also a sister of Margie Marlin of Kentucky. I couldn't get her address in Kentucky."

"All three of them have Douglas Marlin for a brother. Digger Marl is really Douglas Marlin."

"Wait," Sheriff Puller looked up from a jotted note. "There's another sister, or possibly she's a cousin. Clementine Marlin Beach is her name."

"Beach?" Grandma moved kneading fingers across her brow. "Beach? Hey wait. Alvin Beach is a Cub Scout. He found one of the foot bones at the gravel pit. I think he planned to visit Nic today. His mother was on the phone with Luisa this morning."

"So through Alvin we've several connections, that's to say, relatives to Digger. Sure, relatives; that's why Digger let the Cub Scouts into his gravel pit even as the pit's been closed for years."

"That little Alvin Beach is so cute. I'd bet his folks are nice. Wayne, you should know that Edith, Harold and I have through the years made friends with persons of interest. I mean real friends, not faking; even love, Christian love, do you see? Gaining confidence, you see, such that the loved one opens up to us. I wonder if through Clementine Beach we could gain the address of Margie Marlin of Kentucky. The big white camper will pull in here any day now. None of us will want to drive that thing but if we had a driver we could cruise on down to Kentucky."

"We think alike, we do. You're hoping as well to catch up with Digger, a.k.a. Douglas Marlin down there, huh? Maybe I can send a deputy along with you. A former over-the-road trucker, he drives the prison transfer bus but does trucking for a fruit farm on the side. He's due for some personal time and has accumulated way too many hours toward a vacation that he doesn't want to take. I'll talk to him, maybe trick him into a vacation disguised as work?"

"Wonderful. I'll let you know as soon as the camper pulls in and I talk with Del and Dosia Platt about us using the camper. They're due any day."

"Good. As soon as I know I'll prep him as to the mission." Again he consulted his small wire-bound notebook. "That vacant house across from Platt's is owned by Russell Marlin, possibly of Kentucky. It's possibly too that he is the husband of Margie. I'll run a check on lawn care businesses, trying there also to come up with an address."

"That land behind Mrs. Woods, did you say it's owned by Digger?"

"No, by Russell, but I believe Digger bought land from the Woods' in order to move his line fence northward. That was done just before the natural death of Dr. Woods in 1950."

"As to a comment that Harold and I both made, we'd expect a body to be buried on the property not off of it. There's a story in our family wherein a father died and the family had no money so they held a funeral among themselves and buried him on the hill behind the barn. Not on some other's property, don't you see. I think Digger fooled around with line fences to baffle anyone who may've been looking for a burial site."

"Whatever his motive, the situation was easy to figure out and it helped us put the death of our John Doe as occurring prior to 1950."

"And it clues me to reason that the deceased was an owner of the property."

"By gosh, it sure does, but Russell may be alive and living in Kentucky. I'll go back to the courthouse looking for a Russell senior and a Russell junior."

Suddenly Edith's voice came in on the radio. Grandma Clydis answered. "Edith, what's up?"

"I didn't get any new info at the post office, but at the Commerce bank I found an account for Douglas Marlin and none for Digger Marl."

"You've figured correctly. The sheriff and I have proof positive Digger is Douglas and Marl is Marlin."

"It's time now for me to go get Nathan at the college; then home to lunch. Momma, I want to visit Mrs. Woods."

"I'd rather we didn't visit her today. We should give her a rest from her trip, but let's go visit Mrs. Beach. She's a cousin or a sister to Douglas Marlin. That cute little Alvin Beach is her son."

"Good going. See you at lunch."

* * *

Alvin Beach joined them at lunch. "Alvin, it's sweet of you to come to visit. Please come more often. Is your mother related to Mr. Digger?"

"He's a cousin."

"Have another slice of pizza, Alvin." Aunt Edith passed a platter his way. "You've not tried this kind. It has anchovies."

His eyes bugged. "Uh, er, well, not that kind."

"Oh, a cheddar and hamburger man, huh?"

"Gosh yes." Uncle Harold studied their guest; saw his eyes light up when a slice of cheddar and hamburger pizza flapped onto his plate.

"He likes root beer," Nic informed; "me too." Momma Luisa reached to fill their glasses.

"Where does your mom work, Alvin?"

"She cooks at the hospital."

"Gee, that's nice. And your dad, where does he work?"

He chewed quickly and swallowed. He stretched his neck trying to clear it. He sipped his root beer. "He works with iron."

"Hey, you folks, let the poor guy eat." Grandma reached to pat the grand little guy on the shoulder.

They were impatiently polite until he'd made a stab at his fourth slice of cheddar and hamburger pizza. Obviously he was full up when Nathan said, "Alvin, we have a visiting dog that loves pizza scraps if you can spare some. I see Nic and sibs are also ready with a robust repast for that Old Sniffer."

"Sure." He set a well cratered final slice onto his plate.

"Your scoutmaster seems to be a good friend of Mr. Digger. We like Mr. Digger. Is he your uncle?"

"No. Mom's his cousin."

"Say, that's right, you did say that. How about Mrs. Digger and Mrs. Merit, are they sisters?"

"Yes, she's my cousin too."

"Alvin," Grandma Clydis stifled a yawn, "after such a wonderful feed as this, a body my age seeks rest; if you'll excuse me." She pushed back from the table. "We'd like to visit your folks sometime. Are they home every evening?"

"Mom works all night but Dad is home. Mom's coming pretty soon to get me."

"Any minute," Luisa said. "Alvin, I'll miss your mom as I must leave now for work. You are a very nice guest and are welcome always. Later, I'll call your mom, maybe even at the hospital and tell her how pleased we are that you came here to be with Nic and us."

Luisa left for work. Alvin's mom came for him. Miah pedaled off to visit a friend. Nic fell asleep watching television. Mrs. Woods drove into the yard.

"Hey, Nic! Wake up. Mrs. Woods is here to take us to eat ice cream."

He leaped from the chair. "Golly, I'm sure hungry!"

The girls made an effort at polite sundae consumption but Nic didn't take the hint while he watched his sisters or their mentor Mrs. Woods. She scooped daintily and slid the creamy concoction in upon her tongue then gently moved each dab of ice cream, chocolate syrup and crushed peanuts from the spoon. Nic scooped mightily. Finishing well ahead of the others he asked, "Have you ever been back in that woods?"

"Huh?" She patted with her napkin. "Don't go near that woods behind my house."

Luckily Nic caught a gesture from Omi. Her finger placed ninety degrees to her lips served to settle him, even to raising wrinkles on his forehead. Mrs. Woods didn't catch Omi's signal but she was suddenly desperate to keep Nic and all else away from that woods. "Children, I have been very frightened on several occasions by clacking sounds from that woods. It's a mysterious place and I'm certain the owners allow no trespassing. Don't go in there because it'll cause trouble for you."

"Gosh, Ma'am, we wouldn't hurt anything back in there. Perhaps we could ask the owners."

"I will not say what all has frightened me in the past but I will say that clacking sounds in the night is not normal for any woods. Please stay away. I know curiosity is natural and that you children have plenty of that. That is good, but being harmed is not good."

"What would harm us," Cia wanted to know.

Mrs. Woods was becoming desperate; the girls, she saw, were siding with Nic. "I cannot contact the owners, but I will call the sheriff. Now that your curiosity is directed toward those woods, you are in danger, of that, I am sure. I'll ask the sheriff to investigate the woods and to talk with your parents. Please do not challenge me on this."

"Golly, Mrs. Woods, we're sorry something frightened you. We'll not rush into trouble. You can depend on us."

Chapter Eight

HOME FROM THE CRIME LAB, Fanny and the sheriff stopped in. Their hope for good news was thwarted. Not a single one of the dental records she'd carried to Lansing matched their John Doe. "I gather he did some dental work at home," Sheriff Puller said. "Perhaps some records are still there."

"Sheriff Puller," Omi interrupted, "Mrs. Woods is going to contact you."

"Oh, why? Omi, what have you heard?"

"Nic and I and Cia had ice cream with her today at the Baker's ice cream shop down town. We sat at that picnic table to enjoy our sundaes. Suddenly Nic blurted out, 'Have you ever been back in that woods?' Mrs. Woods was very upset, er, well, actually she was more like frightened and she warned us away from the woods. But she could see that we sided with Nic even if we didn't openly do that. She said that something in the woods frightened her, something that made clacking sounds in the night."

"Clacking?"

"She didn't explain but she has heard the sounds many times and they are not normal sounds for a woods. She said the owners would have us arrested for trespassing should we explore in that woods. We said we wouldn't harm anything in the woods. She said she would contact Sheriff Puller as she didn't actually know how to contact the owners. We said we were sorry something frightened her. We said that we'll not rush into trouble. 'You can depend on us.'"

"Oh, also," Cia added, "she said other things frightened her but she didn't want to tell us about that."

"I brought home a new belt for her Hoover," Luisa said. "Sheriff, isn't this a good time to return her repaired Hoover to her?"

"She sounds frightened and desperate, wanting to protect the children, but also I believe she's asking for help" Aunt Edith said. "Momma, let's go to her tonight. We'll go on another day to visit Clementine Beach."

"Yes, it is time. Wayne, I'm sorry and you may think me daffy, but I think this job calls for ladies only. I have a feeling she'll open to us girls, and I mean to Edith and me."

"Sure, give it a whirl. Fanny, let's head back. I'm late for supper."

The purr of the ornate patrol car exiting the driveway was hidden beneath the shrill wheeze of the ancient Hoover. Nathan handed the brute over to Nic and he rushed around on the rug before the television giving it a thorough vacuuming. Uncle Harold stood ready with a rag damp with sewing machine oil. Luisa and Miah looked impatient watching Nic and watching for the ends of commercials so she could signal Nic to cut the power. Any second now she guessed Mary Tyler Moore would be speaking her woe or Ted Knight would be bragging about his prowess as an announcer. Mom's hand was in the air ready to chop the cut sign when the room suddenly echoed silence. "Works good."

"Grand old machine." Uncle Harold polished with his oiled rag. "Lovely. Look at the color in this sweet old thing."

"It's sure an eye boggler," Grandma said. She carefully wound and secured the cord.

Aunt Edith carried the beautiful relic in her arms like a sack of potatoes as the pair set out on their visit to Mrs. Woods.

She moved a fluffy cat with its yellow ribbon away from her face then craned to see past another cat that was posed upon the back of the sofa. That cat wore a green ribbon and was haughty as usual. She saw the gracious pair ascending her driveway. Atop the television from where it seemed to relish the set's vibrations, a blue ribbon cat rolled to firm its belly to the vibes. She caught the roll of the cat and laid her eyes for a moment on Ed Asner. The man was her reason for watching the show, he bearing a remote resemblance of her John, but her eyes merely grazed the screen on their swing back to the window. Her guests were nearing the top of the driveway. Her heart began a pitter-patter. She glanced heavenward in praise of God. God in his benevolence had sent angels to help her. The guests moved out of her sight from the easy chair. She stood from the chair tumbling the red ribbon cat that had been perched on her feet. That dear cat always most graciously warmed her feet. With her step toward the kitchen door her hand reach down to caress the red-clad foot muff. The red rushed to knead against her legs on her dash to answer the door.

"Mrs. Woods. I'm Clydis Groner and this is my daughter Edith James."

"Oh, do come in. I'm Cary Woods. Cary, if you please. I've heard so much about you ladies from the girls. Such sweet girls, and I'm afraid I have harmed them and little Nic, too."

"No harm. They think the world of you. As to names, Edith and Clydis will do for us."

"Let's sit around the dinning room table. There's hot water. I'll make some tea."

Small talk ensued during the tea preparation and serving. Seated behind her tea, Cary said, "During most of my life I've been afraid of the woods."

"With good reason, my dear, but we're here to assure you that all danger has passed. But first I must perform some preliminaries." She switched on her two-way radio. "You may know that we are deputy sheriffs from Kent County but here on an assignment to resolve the source of terror from the woods." She spoke into her mouth piece. "Sheriff Puller, Groner here. How do you read?"

"Five by five, deputy. Where are you?"

"Edith and I are at Cary Woods' house sipping tea. Do you have instruction?"

"You might ask into dental records."

"Roger, we'll get into that. We'll call your office in the morning, Wayne. Have a good night. Groner out."

"Good going. Puller out."

"I recognized his voice from when he was on TV running for office. I'm thrilled that we could from right here hear his voice."

"Marvelous, isn't it? Wayne Puller is a very good sheriff; one of the best we've worked with. To keep it simple let's address him tonight as Wayne. About a week ago Wayne was called to Digger's gravel pit on an urgent matter. There is no longer any danger what so ever from the gravel pit or from the woods behind this house. Wayne is sure of that, but, Cary, there are several matters that require resolution. Cary will you tell us what of the woods frightened you and for over what period of time?"

"John always slept sounder than me. I'd hear clacking in the night but couldn't see anything and when I awoke John we couldn't hear any clacking; clacking had stopped. When John was waiting release from World War Two we had this house built on land I'd purchased for us. John was coming here to begin his own dental practice; not in with someone else, you see. 1946. Our son had just finished his bachelors and he took the job at Oak Ridge, Tennessee. He is a PhD now. That's when we moved in and it's when I first heard the clacking. John came home from the practice so tired that he never heard the clacking. His practice was an overwhelming success. He worked long hours in town and saw patients here in the house on many an evening and weekend. Then suddenly my wonderful John died."

Clydis dabbed tears with her napkin. "A wonderful man is such a blessing. I grieve, too, the recent loss of my Clarence. Cary, I'd like to sit close by you and cry and cry until peace consumes our souls."

"Taking action can often offset, too, a missed loved one. Love too," Edith said, "will protect one from evils. I always look to Harold when any crises threaten. Did other fears arise from the woods after John was in Heaven?"

"I have always stood by John. He is my strength to endure no matter that an abominable monster leered at me from the pines."

"Your John never saw the abominable creature?"

"No, that abominable creature came after God had claimed my John."

"The clacking, was it a steady clack-clack-clack or did the sound vary in meter and volume?"

"Variable, not always the same loudness nor tempo."

"Okay, we think we know what caused the clacking but will need to check it out. You didn't hear clacking this year did you?"

"Uh, no."

"Last year?"

"Nooo, well not for quite a while."

"Years? Years have gone by since you last heard the clacking?"

"Yes, I believe so, but I often hear the clacking in nightmares that seem so real that I don't know when I last actually heard the sound."

Clydis looked up from her note taking. "Cary, please describe the abominable creature for us."

"I've only seen the top part of him, but tall, I think; very tall and hairy. Long reddish hair. I could not see the eyes but caught glints from them through the hair on his hairy head and face."

"You're doing fine, Cary," Edith said. "Did the creature speak or make any sound at all?"

"No, just stared." She rubbed her hand across her face and lips, her eyes studying her guests. "I heard the abominable many times in my sleep. Horrible sound, but I don't know any more if I heard it when I saw it sneaking along in the pines."

"From how far away? How near did he get to you?"

"The pines, always by the pines. Sometimes peering out at me, sometimes just moving steadily along. It was always near dark that he appeared."

"We think we know that the creature was a very large and tall man. Cary, there really was such a person living in the woods, but not a Yeti or an Abominable Snowman as has been reported elsewhere; a very long ways away from here. Yes this was a person, a very large person who wore a beard and had long, long hair. We believe the man left the woods some fifteen to twenty years ago, perhaps longer, and that he never came back."

"Sheriff Wayne Puller and Edith and I and Harold, Edith's husband, have been many times into that woods while you were away on vacation. There is no risk, no danger at all from the woods, but there surly was danger in a time past so no doubt you were justifiably concerned. Our investigation of the area continues and we'll keep you informed as developments finalize."

Cary Woods sat with wrinkles wrung deeply into her forehead. "Cary, we know you are still concerned and as anyone would be. We are so sure that no danger remains that we have allowed the Platt children and others of our large family to go into the venue of the hermit shack."

"S . . .Shack? Hermit?"

"Yes, there is a shack back in there and it has a huge bed in it, but not occupied for tens of years. The huge bed is certain confirmation that you actually were seeing someone. We have a lot more to figure out, dear, but for now do not worry and do, and I mean 'please do', ask questions as they come to you."

"I'll rest better tonight."

"Yes, it is getting late for old souls like us. We'll be going, but Sheriff Puller, you recall, asked us to ask you about dental records. Are there any dental records, patient records here in the house or elsewhere that you know about?"

"There are some boxes of John's. Why do you need his records?"

"There is at least one person besides the huge hermit that lived at least part of the time in the woods. Remains of a normal size person have been found and dental records are valuable resources to be used in identification."

"Someone died?" Her eyes had grown large and her knuckles whitened in her grasp of the tea cup.

"Yes, a very long time ago." The lady deputies now wished they hadn't asked for the dental records as the request had led directly to a frightening situation for Cary.

Clydis said, "Cary, do you mind if I spend the night? On your couch would be fine. Throughout most of my life Clarence had been with me as John was with you. Both gentlemen still are in some ways beside us, but I need someone alive, someone to lean on. My other daughter and her husband have moved in with me back home at Leadford and I am so grateful. And I must say, Cary, that I am jealous of you because of your cats. The cats look very comforting. May I have one to warm my feet tonight?"

"Oh, my yes." She held her hands as though in prayer. "Oh, thank you, dear. Thank you."

* * *

Candy and Sandy Gillespie arrived just after breakfast on a bright calm Saturday morning. Omi and Cia had just finished putting away breakfast dishes. Nic had his ears tuned to Sesame Street and didn't look up as the four girls galloped through on their way to the croquet court. In the yard Deputy Fanny Gillespie sat behind the wheel of her patrol car. Aunt Edith was in the passenger seat and Grandma Clydis sat in the rear. Having explained to Sandy that the red ball was always Aunt

Edith's when ever she played, Sandy agreed then whacked the red ball to begin the game. In the patrol car the ladies grinned, delighted the four girls were enjoying one another. Pulling her eyes from the game, Edith said, "Fanny, I guess we're no farther on his ID than before."

Fanny had driven in from the Lansing crime lab late the night before. She radioed Edith to report that none of the records found in Mrs. Cary Woods' closet matched the victim they'd exhumed from Digger's gravel pit. "We were too hopeful," Fanny said, "is why we're so glum this morning."

"Yes, finding that all of the records from her closet had initials instead of names gave us hope in that one record carried the initials R M. The initials may have meant 'Russell Marlin' who we are suspecting is our victim." Whack! One of the girls had tried for a long roll. Glancing their way, the ladies saw that Omi strutted toward her distant orange.

"Our land records reveal that Russell Marlin owns the vacant brick house and the woods behind Mrs. Woods. That Russell Marlin, R M, hasn't been seen in years and is believed to have moved to Kentucky."

"That R M? What are you saying?'"

"Sheriff Gillespie is checking to see if there wasn't a Russell Marlin senior and a junior." They heard a moan of disappointment from the court. Looking, they saw that Candy had managed a long drive that bopped Omi out of line for her hoop. "Your Candy's quite an athlete."

"They don't give up easily. However we've encouraged and awarded good sportsmanship."

"Luisa and Nathan have too. It'll be interesting to see what develops here."

"Hey! I've a notion." Edith's near squeal snapped heads to her. "His billing records or payment records; we whacked them aside in our bee line for the dental records."

Fanny called in, "Myself, Clydis, and Edith will be at Mrs. Woods' hoping the billing and payment records may yield clues that we need."

"Good, I was about to radio you. There was, or is, a Russell Marlin senior and a junior. Both are believed to've moved to Kentucky. When is your meeting with Clementine Beach?"

"This afternoon. She's bringing Alvin out to play with Nic and has agreed to visit with us around a cup of tea."

"Great. I heard just now from Harold. A call came to him a few minutes ago, just before you radioed me, a call about the camper. That camper is due in on Sunday forenoon. Plan to roll early next week. I've asked Deputy Jack Trip to come in this afternoon to plan strategy for that Kentucky run."

"Great."

"Good luck at Mrs. Woods'."

"Ten four. Gillespie out." Clack! The ladies looked to the court, and were surprised to see Cia standing proudly behind the end stake.

"I wonder how she managed that!"

"Ladies, let's hurry on with the work and then hope to watch another game with this four. I'll admit I'm worried. This may be the closing reign of me, old Red Ball Edith. My word, those girls can play!"

The lady deputies were surprised to see the dining room table completely cleared and that tea water boiled as Mrs. Woods ushered them into the house. "I saw you, Mrs. Gillespie, across and hoped you ladies would stop in. How may I help?"

"We need to paw around in more of the boxes."

"I've slid them out of the closet. Completely emptied the closet, actually. It's time I exercised that gleaming old Hoover."

"Great, but may I look first for any clue or item of interest that may remain in the closet? We clue hounds often look to the last speck in our desperation for evidence."

Fanny looked, crawled around, dusted, and whisked but came up with only a single paper clip from the closet. "I know this may seem over much, Cary, but had I not searched I would have been worried even to dissecting your Hoover. Thank you for your patience." The Hoover shrilled its duty as the ladies settled around the boxes they'd lugged into the dining room.

Not moments had elapsed before Fanny announced, "Golly, these are all of the financial records, both from his office and from here at his home."

"My word!" Clydis flipped through her notebook. "Here. Here are the Names, well initials, of the dental records from here at the house. Let's sort those out first."

"How many?"

Clydis counted, "Eleven from this house. I've listed them here by dates, but to isolate them from the whole, give me a minute. I'll arrange them alphabetically." The pair idled and sipped tea seemingly at ease, but with inner turmoil fired by impatience. "Here; copy this list down."

The Hoover wound to a stop and Cary carried it into the living room where it would await the terminus of their dusty paw at the records. From the kitchen she heard the list being read, and entered the kitchen to see the others furiously writing. Cary took a seat at the table with the others. Fanny dug into the first box of records.

Having extracted each record they sought, Cary who had merely been listening to them and following their activity, exclaimed, "There's only eleven. One of the records is missing. John said once that he had twelve; an even number to care for here at home."

"My Word! Cary, you would make an outstanding crime investigator."

"Not really." She sat straighter in her chair. "I just happened to catch it."

"Hey wait, there's only one R M record here." Edith scanned her notes. "If there is, or was, an R M senior and a junior, then an R M record is missing; missing from the dental records as well as from the financial records."

"The date on this R M that we do have is well within our decade of interest. I wish he'd have recorded the age of the patient. We don't know whether father R M or son."

Edith moved the paperclip on the R M record she held, the better to read every speck of writing. "Paper clip!" Clydis fairly yelled it. "Paper clip. Each record is held with a paper clip."

Fanny whipped out an evidence bag and tossed in the paper clip she'd recovered from the closet. Edith drummed her fingers a moment before turning to Cary Woods.

"Cary, I take it that you always lock your doors while you're away?"

"Yes, always."

"The girls had a key to facilitate the care of these beautiful cats. Through the years, have you had others care for the cats while you were away?"

"Well, yes. At times that was a nuisance for me. Early on children of the Marls' cared for them, but one day they were all grown and left so the last time, I asked Digger to do it. As usual I visited my son at his job in Tennessee."

Already Fanny was busy dusting for finger prints. The boxes and all records from the boxes were dusted. "Ladies, my prints are on record; yours too, Edith and Clydis. Cary, I'll need your prints as well. Any other prints I've managed to lift could belong to Dr. Woods and others who had legitimate access to the files. "Make a note ladies that I have removed the R M records, both the dental treatment records and from the financial records. Use might be made of it at the Lansing crime lab." She radioed in: "Sheriff, we have only one set of R M dental records and also we have only one set of R M financial records. Cary says that her husband had twelve patients he saw here at the house. Only eleven records are here."

"Deputy, it's your day off. I had a wife once. I'm telling you, my dear, that days off are necessary. I'll send Deputy Jack Trip to Lansing if necessary, and with his siren walloping all the way. As soon as you can, you get home to your family."

* * *

Deputy Fanny Gillespie lunched with the Platt family. Around one o'clock Fanny left for home with Sandy and Candy. Edith had taken a moment to plot with Harold and Miah and they left straight away on a mission. In the echo of their departure, Clementine Beach drove into the yard with Alvin. Nic met Alvin in the yard with a bear hug and they went off promptly to explore the creek.

"It's the Congo," Nic spoke expansively; "we haven't been along it from the road to our yard. We don't know what monsters to expect in there."

"Why don't we go work on our barber chair?"

"Can't. I heard Uncle Harold and Miah planning to go do something in the pines so we'll have to wait 'til they clear the coop. My sisters went with them to do the project in the pines so we'll need to lay low, old explorer pard."

"Well, okay then, pard; it's to the Congo." He squared his shoulders then reached a hand to a rear pocket. "I have my slingshot, but what monsters are around the Congo?"

"Any kind you see, old scout."

Mrs. Beach watched her son leave the yard with Nic. "I know what the visit is about," she said to the lady deputies, "and I wanted to be sure Alvin was out of hearing. It's about those bones."

"Yes, and you aren't implicated in any way, we assure you. Come have a seat." Edith stood with a pot of fresh coffee. "I've had an over supply of tea thus far today so I made coffee."

"Sure, thank you, and creamer and sweetener."

The ladies stirred their beverages, placed their spoons on their saucers, not speaking for an additional moment; then, "Clementine, I don't know whether you'd heard yet about the body that was found at the gravel pit."

"Alvin was excited about trading 'an old bone for a geode,' he said. I guessed the bone as human and that more were to be found."

"What prompted you to venture such a guess?"

"History, or perhaps lore, folklore; family folklore. Before we moved here my husband Charley asked that I not repeat family rumors, those pertaining to the Marlins. That information was to be discussed with him and not passed on. Squelch the rumors, in other words. We talked last night and he said it is about time to lift the shame and fear and that he would come with me to see you. I said that if I find myself in trouble I would get right home then set up a different meeting. Charley and I agree. This matter should be resolved.

"We moved here because of his knowledge of metallurgy; not only for the local foundry, but for several others where he is a consultant; as far north actually as the East Jordan iron works. I've heard enough through these five years we've lived here to know that something awful happened within the Marlin family a long while ago. Now it seems that that awful something was murder.

"Several of my cousins live around Manitou Prairie as you probably know. They like me are of the generation following the troubled years and have little fear of legal reprisal. My cousin Peggy Lance called me after you and the sheriff had been there. She and Dale are afraid to say anything and they think as I do that Douglas is the one we'd wish to tell it all to you. Douglas, Digger as you know him, has fierce family loyalty, wanting not a single word uttered against any family member living or dead. I think the rest of us feel the time is now to get the mess into the open and over and done with.

Edith wrote swiftly in the shorthand she and Momma Clydis had developed over the years. In a moment, she raised her ball point then brought her eyes to meet Clementine's.

"It was three uncles who were in the actual distress" Clementine continued, "but several cousins are involved in keeping the secret. The cousins who know most about the history are Douglas, Peggy, and Margie. I know few details. I've talked some with Bobby, she's the scoutmaster's wife and I'm sure she is quite ignorant of the affair, like me. Our cousin Margie lives in Kentucky. Cards and letters come seldom from her and never with a return address, but I wheedled the address out of Jill one time. Jill is Digger's wife. It was at Christmas and I wanted to send a card to Cousin Margie and her family." She reached into her purse. "I'm not being a traitor to my family I believe, not at this late date. It is time the truth was known. Digger would not concur with me in this, but the others would. Here is Margie's address.

"I've heard talk among the men that the 'old boy' is very ill and in a nursing home; and that he doesn't know anybody. There were two Russell Marlins. The 'old boy' must be the senior of the two."

"Yes, we concur," Edith said, "there should be two sets of dental records labeled R M; each a different Russell Marlin."

"Yes; and of the two, I believe Russell Marlin junior is your victim, the one you exhumed. Margie left for Kentucky with Russell who I assumed was Junior but 'old boy' has convinced me otherwise. Russell junior, the one you exhumed, was Margie's husband." She patted away tears. "I'm so sorry for poor Margie.

"Two uncles, twin brothers but not identical twins lived in the woods. Larry was abnormal. He kept growing and didn't reach sexual maturity. He went mean and so his brother kept him drunk to keep him calm. My cousins, nieces and nephews to the uncles, kept the pair supplied with food and wine. Suddenly it was over. I don't know what happened. But, I now guess a murder. I'm sorry I don't know details.

"Please, ladies, do not relentlessly grill Peggy, Margie, Bobby, and Jill and not Dale either. They cannot tell even if they know. Be gentile with tough old Digger. He's one heck of a man. Please don't break him into a blubbering nincompoop. He'll tell it all. I'm sure of that. But kindness, patience, compassion will be the prime movers."

No one spoke for a time. All had soaked handkerchiefs and had produced a heap of wadded sodden Kleenexes. Edith placed her arms around her friend. "Clementine, my dear Clementine, you are equal to the bravest strongest kindest person I've ever met. Rest easy, my dear friend, no harm at all will befall any of the family. Assurance of that with Douglas is our first priority. We only seek the truth so that the tragedy has an ending, a closure. A closure not just for the record, but, more important, a closure for all of you brave souls."

"We've found your whole family to be one of intelligent, caring people," Clydis said. "We as deputies seek tributes to all of you rather than any condemnations." She gently pat upon and rubbed her new friend's back. "Come now, we've a friend to visit across the way, a friend in need of closure; and then we'll challenge Red Ball Edith to a round of croquet."

Chapter Nine

Nic and Alvin had finished trekking the Congo. Alvin had a sore hand from its being slapped repeatedly by the rubber and sling of his trusty hand-made slingshot. Also, Nic had snubbed his fingernails a dozen and more times in his prowl of the creek bed in quest of stones for his marksman buddy to sling. Many a poplar tree had digs in the bark and several birds had fled the jungle. "As planned," Alvin said, "monsters see birds fleeing and so they hide so we don't see them."

"Someday I'll go this trek with a Red Rider carbine," Nic said.

"Man, there won't be monsters for miles after that. Do you have shovels?"

"Sure, for monsters?" Nic passed a hand through his dark messed-up hair.

Alvin drew a sweat damped paper from his jeans and spread the paper on a handy boulder that rested beside the Congo. "See here. If we dig a hole on one side of the barber chair and a little under it we can push it into the hole, but not a real deep hole, but that would stand the chair up so we can sit on it."

"Gosh this is a good idea. Maybe we could sneak over to see if they're out of the pines yet."

"Let's get us some shovels."

Carrying their shovels at half mast, the pair scurried across Peach Road and made a dash down the steep path to the Congo. Catching Nic's signal, Alvin hunkered down next to his friend. Together they peered through the light brush, making a study of mysterious activity ahead. "Don't move, pard, or they'll see our white T-shirts."

"What are they doing that for?"

Nic shrugged his shoulders. "Keep a-watching."

They watched Miah and the others. Miah was seated on a fallen tree trunk and had his feet in the creek. On his feet were his Dad's knee-high boots. He was leaning out over the boots to reach his hands down into the water. Omi stood nearby with a wine bottle. Miah brought his hands out of the water and handed a wine bottle filled with water to Cia who passed the bottle up to Uncle Harold. Uncle Harold stood holding a bath towel and with it he dried the wine bottle. Omi passed an empty bottle to Miah, while Uncle Harold wormed a cork into the neck of the bottle he'd received from Cia. Carefully he placed the corked bottle into a wire-bound crate, a crate like the ones Nic had seen at the hermit shack.

The interloping boys could see that groceries were in the wire-bound box along with the wine bottles of water. The next wine bottle of water was placed into a different wire-bound box. "Two boxes," Nic whispered.

Alvin shifted his position enough to better his view through the brush. "Yeah, bread and some flour and tin cans."

"And several of those wine bottles."

The curious Cub Scouts watched a while before realizing none of the workers along the creek ever did look their way. More relaxed then, they fooled around the edge of the Congo and finally ventured inside the tunnel that conveyed the stream under Peach Road. Having scampered all the way through the tunnel, they reached the starting point of their recent trek. They took time enough to scare a few additional monsters away before curiosity propelled them back through the tunnel. Resuming their former vantage point they were instantly alarmed because no one was in sight.

"Well, I wonder," Nic said.

"Yeah," Alvin bumped Nic's shoulder, "let's go see what they were doing."

From the site of the recent activity, the boys could see the foursome vaguely through the trees ahead. They set out at a dogtrot to close on them. Their shovels clattered and scraped so they slowed but were at once frustrated for again their quarry was fading from sight. They again quickened their advance.

As the pair was passing between two trees, simultaneously a shovel was wrested from each of them and a harsh shrill whisper stung their ears. "Shisst!"

"You ninnies!"

Omi whispered, "What are you guys doing here with those stupid shovels?"

Nic was annoyed. "What are you guys doing?"

"Helping to help Mrs. Woods. Be quiet or you'll spoil everything."

"What were you going to dig, worms?"

"No. Maybe."

"Just whisper. Leave the foolish shovels. You'll have to come with us, but don't make noise and just whisper."

After a few yards of stealthy advance Uncle Harold came into view. He stood quietly beside the two wire-bound crates containing food and the water-filled wine bottles. Just coming into close proximity of the boxes, the boys were startled by a body hurdling down from a tree. "All set, they're on the driveway; Grandma Clydis, Aunt Edith, and Mrs. Beach."

"Mom?"

"Yes, she stayed to visit," Cia said. "Uncle Harold, we'll go now so we can go to Mrs. Woods'. Should these little boys come with us?"

"Boys, you'll stay with us but stay back and if you hear any noises, just stay back out of sight of Mrs. Woods' home."

"What are you doing?"

"Helping Mrs. Woods. Watch and you'll see."

"Stay out of sight of us for now." Miah and Uncle Harold disappeared ahead into the pines. Omi and Cia disappeared back toward the shovels. Nic jerked Alvin's arm. The cubbies drifted back toward where they'd left the shovels.

"What's up?"

"Let's go on with our shovels. When they get on ahead we can dig on our barber chair."

"Good going."

The ladies on the driveway heard the Hoover a good many steps before arriving on the stoop of Cary's house. Edith checked the time on her wrist watch. Clydis rapped the door loudly but the faithful Hoover motored on. Edith tapped the kitchen window. The Hoover shrilled on with authority. Clydis opened the storm door and rapped the inner door hearing naught but Hoover determination. Opening the inner door, a blue ribboned cat streaked out and shot between Edith's legs before charging down under the porch.

"Cary! Oh, Cary! Yoo-hoo, company!"

A green ribboned feline shot through the open doorway, bashing Clementine in the shins on its dash for haven under the porch.

"Yoo-hoo!"

"Cary!" Clydis stepped through the kitchen, the dining room and up behind Cary in the living room where Cary busily vacuumed the easy chair. "Cary," she tapped her chubby friend's shoulder.

Cary let out a "Whoop!" and dived headlong onto the chair and plowed across it to land on her head on the far side. Her dress was to her neck in a wholesome display of garter belt, bloomers, and nylons.

Edith cradled Cary into her arms and the others took to a-righting her attire. The Hoover yet wailed and flapped its hose. Clydis reached to shut its motor. In the echo of silence Edith said at Cary's ear, "We didn't mean to frighten you. Are you alright?"

"Gosh, I'm used to scaring the cats when I vacuum. Cat hair, you know. Well, they're likely scared and all in under the bed."

"Two streaked outside at the kitchen door. Here, we'll help you up."

Gratefully standing upon her slipper-clad feet, Cary said, "I vacuum each second day."

"You keep a neat and pleasant house. We want you to meet Clementine Beach."

Had they been handy to a window they may have at that time seen Alvin and Nic with their shovels. They were sticking within the pines, showing only glimpses of their stealthy advance.

In the house, the ladies gathered in the dining room. Introductions were made.

Edith went to the kitchen and filled a tea kettle. Having placed the kettle and clicked on a gas-fired burner, Edith again checked the time on her wrist watch. She entered the dining area and took a position over by the window, with the window behind her while the ladies continued to chat. Each moment or two Edith looked out through the dining room window, finally winking at Clydis. "How pretty the view from here," Edith remarked. Clack!

Click, clacking, clack, clack, clunk, Clack!

Cary's eyed bugged. She stood and glared out the window, achieving a view as Edith moved aside. Cary's scream would've kept the cats hidden for hours. She screamed unintelligibly, "Lord, No! Help them, help them! They're going to be killed!"

Her screams shrilled relentlessly on with the others trying to understand her. Clydis held tightly to her friend. Screaming, and with her fear drawing strength due a tiger, she broke away from Clydis. Cary grabbed a broom and with that broom in hand, she slammed out the door.

"Wait, dear, wait!"

Edith tackled her in the yard, driving grass stains into Cary's nylons, shredding a knee of them. "Please, Cary, darling, it's okay."

"It's okay, dear." Clydis and Clementine knelt beside Cary and Edith.

"The abominable beast is after the little boys." Cary jerked her arms free, struggled to get to her feet.

"It's okay. The little boys are okay."

"The monster. That horrid abominable." She glared out to where she thought the monster would be.

Edith took hold of her hand. "Yes, we heard it too. I saw the little boys. They're alright."

"We must be sure." The ladies held their friend's arm, hand, and shoulder.

At the dump the boys began digging beside their own personal precious barber chair. In the yard, Clydis and Edith called loudly and waved their arms. The clacking persisted, its decibels putting roar to the heart of tender Cary. Finally Harold and Miah burst beyond the pines and into view of the ladies in the yard. "Cary, see it's only Miah and Harold. They made the noise."

"See, Cary, they're making their way to here." Having steadied their loads, the clacking grew less intense as the pair neared the ladies.

"Yes, but the little boys." She pulled free of her friends. "I don't see the little boys."

"Who?"

"Alvin and Nic," Edith said. "I caught a glimpse of them a few moments ago, before we heard the bottles clacking. I'm sure they're alright."

Down in the dump, the pair of husky Cub Scouts leaned their all into moving the barber chair, finally nudging it upright. In a flash they were up and into the seat. From the yard, their heads poked above the intervening weeds and brush. "See, I see them, they're okay."

Omi and Cia plunged into the scene astride their bicycles. "We heard them but did we miss the action?" Behind the girls, having caught the activity, Nathan was puffing up the driveway.

"We saw Mrs. Woods fall down." Omi touched Mrs. Woods on the arm.

"Yes, thank you, I'm alright."

"Did you see the little boys?"

"Yes, in the woods near the creek, that mighty Congo of Nic's. They had shovels with them."

"Shovels?"

"By then in a rush, louder clacking announced the arrival of Harold and Miah to the yard. Harold caught Edith's eye. "How was that? Did we do alright?"

"Splendidly."

"Cary, this was to be a simple demonstration of what made the clacking. We're sorry that we frightened you."

"See here, Mrs. Woods. It was wine bottles clacking together that you had been hearing."

"These wire-bound crates were used to transport food and wine from along your property line and on into the woods, ma'am. We think someone in the now vacant house set food out for the hermits. Also we think the Lances and Marls set out like provisions. You would've heard the sounds on various nights and from varying directions. Especially at night, sound carries, and in the dark it would be difficult to carry the provisions silently."

"Praise the Lord, I now know about that."

"The sounds would've frightened anyone," Clementine Beach said, "and, Mrs. Woods, my relatives would've been involved in delivering the food and wine. Digger Marl and Peggy Lance are my cousins. They didn't mean to frighten you. They were just trying to help their relatives who lived in the woods."

Cary Woods took on a no nonsense posture. She leaned from the waist while she spoke, and her chin was thrust toward Clementine Beach. "Your relatives? Really, more than one? Were they abominable?"

"They were hiding in the woods, Mrs. Woods, but I don't know why. Clydis, Edith, and Harold are detectives as well as good friends. They are trying to find out all that happened back then. I want to know more just as you want to know more. Knowing more will help all of us. We'll soon know more. As to abominable, I can't think that any of my relatives in the woods set out to scare or to harm anyone."

Mrs. Woods now smiled at Clementine and the two hugged one another.

Cia said, "Mrs. Woods," and Cary Woods turned toward her sweet voice. "I'll bet the little boys went into that dump."

"Yes, we saw them there. Let them be," Harold said. "They'll be alright."

In the dump Alvin held firmly to the control lever that when released would stop the chair. He was taking his turn at spinning Nic around and around. Alvin was swinging the chair with all his might. "Yes, I can see Nic's head going around and around."

"Around?"

Miah, Harold, and Nathan began wading through weeds and brush toward the brink of the dump.

The four ladies and Cia and Omi went into Mrs. Woods' kitchen. Having seen their loved ones, the blue ribbon cat and the green ribbon cat emerged from under the porch. They were joined by the two other cats, thus four cats competed to rub and purr amid the legs of the girls.

"You know, Cary, my very first vacuum cleaner was a Hoover." Clydis strove to further calm her nervous friend. "Two men, Hoover and Spangler invented it by improving on an earlier attempt by a Mr. Booth. I've always felt that we had one of the first Hoovers for sale. We've had a few since, always a good machine."

Nathan burst into the kitchen. "You'll not believe what those little boys found, a barber chair."

"Yes, John high schooled in Greenville, Michigan and a Mr. Meijer cut his hair. Later John bought one of the chairs. Mr. Meijer by then had started Meijers Thrifty Acres. He bought it for old time sake, I guess, but later he brought the chair here and installed it on our side porch and used it for a dental chair. In the winter he crowded the chair into this kitchen."

"Cary, I'm sure you recall that Hendrik Meijer died in 1964, but did you know that his widow, Gezina, has served as Meijers' president since then? We women are very proud of her and had her as the women's guest of honor for the Labor Day parade last fall."

"My John knew her and thought her most capable. I'm very glad for her. Did I read about some building that she was involved with?"

"Yes, the new Meijers' office building located in Walker; that's in northwest Grand Rapids; not far from us. Business has boomed as always but even more so since she's had the stores open on Sundays. She's a gifted company president; much appreciated, not unlike your Dr. John."

"Thank you. Isn't it amazing how that mention of that old barber chair has brought back pleasant memories of the Meijers'?"

"And speaking of Hendrik's old barber chair, Cary, can you recall the names of any who used the chair; patients, I mean?"

"No, not really. John said I deserved better that to be his secretary or dental assistant, but now a few first names do come to mind." She touched her forehead. "Ummm, well a Russ comes to mind, and you know Digger. He and John were friends. A few times John went with Digger to treat some friends who Digger said couldn't come to the house."

"My, your John sure was dedicated. Can you recall who couldn't come so he went to see them?"

Again the kind Mrs. Woods pressed her forehead. "I can see John clearly asking 'Is Larry in pain?' And Digger said, 'Roy says he's pretty bad,' so John went straight away carrying his mechanical drill and black bag."

"Edith and Clydis looked up from their shorthand notes. They exchange slight nods, both thinking, 'this confirms that the two hermits are Larry and Roy. Likely our Mr. Doe is certainly one of the Russells. "Mechanical drill," Edith said. "What's that?"

"I can show it to you. Foot operated, it was before the electric drill was invented. John had a thing for collecting antique dentistry tools."

"Gee, Nathan said, I'd like to see that. George Green invented the electric drill in 1875 so John's mechanical, drill may be older than that, I would think."

"I'll get it." She hurried from the room. "John just loved to show off his old things." The words trailed behind her yet she emerged with the cardboard box of relics as she was saying 'things'. She sat the box with its ancient drill on the table in front of Nathan.

"Gosh, Mrs. Woods, I'm honored." He began to carefully probe the box. "Gosh, a dentist's drill around a hundred years old." He checked its movement. "And its still works just fine." His hand shot deeper into the collection. "Hey, what's this?" He pulled a small box from amid the ancient dentistry tools."

"Oh, I'd forgotten about that," Mrs. Woods said. "It's another keepsake of John's. He said that the invention of candies and cookies was necessarily a prelude to his making a living at dentistry."

"Cookies?

"Animal crackers. They were invented in 1902 and came on the market at Christmas time. They were wrapped in that white paper and the excess length of string was so that one could hang them on a Christmas tree."

"By Uneeda Biscuit, I see, but now Nabisco. I'd heard someplace that Nabisco invented the Oreo cookie, too."

"I was jealous of some of the kids at school," Aunt Edith said, "when they flaunted their Oreos. Around 1910 or 1912, and yes also by Nabisco, but I always had superior cookies baked by Momma or Grandma even if at the time I wasn't aware of my great fortune."

"John always liked cookies and hard candy; both bad for the teeth so he limited himself and he brushed regularly. The gravel pit family, John said, had similar appetites but didn't brush so their molars went bad. That family, my John said were in Roosevelt's programs so they had that history in common with him to talk about besides cookies and candy. It's nice to have neighbors with interests in common, but friendliness is more important; like you folks. Yours weren't in the WPA or perhaps you haven't even known of it."

"Oh, yes, back in the 1930's, "Edith said, "even into World War Two. We knew several that were in the program. Gratefully we made it through the Great Depression and recovery what with our farm produce to help. Works Progress Administration was a good title for the president's program although few knew what letters W-P-A stood for."

"John's father was a dentist, and very public minded. He wanted to do good for people. He worked in Roosevelt's WPA as a dentist."

"In the WPA; why, I hadn't heard of such as that? You say the WPA had dentists?"

"Yes and other skilled workers such as teachers. Not all WPA workers repaired roads or laid sidewalks. When my John was young he worked in a branch of the WPA called the NYA, the National Youth Administration. It provided work for young people. John believed that the NYA, along with his father's public mindedness; contributed to John's work ethic and to his desire to help others."

"He was a fine man and a fine dentist, Cary, a man after my heart."

Mrs. Woods patted a tear. "John said the previous gravel pit folks, who owned the gravel all in behind us where the woods now is, some of those men were in the CCC. Had you heard of the CCC, of the Civil Conservation Corps?"

"Oh sure, it was another good program of the depression era."

"I knew some men in that," Cary said. "They planted billions of trees, built dams, aided wild life, and did projects to correct or prevent erosion. John said that the previous gravel pit owners had benefited by their CCC experience, judging by the fine rows of pines they planted."

Mrs. Woods reached to tug Nathan's shoulder. "Was there really only hermits back in there?"

"Yes, two," Omi answered for her dad, "one big and one little."

"My brave John went in there with that drill you have there," she said to Nathan. Her statement sounded like a question, and it brought Nathan to attention:

"Er, why sure, why, he was a good dentist and someone needed him. It may not have been dangerous because a person in need is often more tolerant, but John couldn't have been sure of that. He was a brave person and a fine dentist, Mrs. Woods. I feel as though I'm getting to know him just by this box of artifacts. Folks who knew him were very fortunate."

"Was keeping it a secret all these years something like the Pentagon Papers?"

"Who? Omi, you don't imply my John, do you? Why, he didn't keep secrets. I'd bet he didn't know about there being hermits or abominables. I'd always hear them in the night after John was asleep."

"Well, I mean keeping the whole thing a secret even from Dr. John."

"The men we call hermits may not have thought of themselves as hermits," Grandma Clydis said. "They may, however, well have thought themselves fugitives; somebody with something to fear so they kept hidden. In that sense of hiding something incriminating, they were like the Pentagon Papers affair, but the Pentagon Papers reveal much greater intrigue. That Tonkin Gulf incident was a hoax, or Casus belli. That's a made up event that provokes or is used to justify war.

"The Pentagon Papers were written up months before it supposedly happened. Those Papers were discovered by Daniel Ellisberg and they described the Tonkin escapade. That was deception and that's bad. Our hermits, or fugitives, didn't apparently stoop to such deception. They lived as quietly as they could in the woods; not wanting trouble nor to recruit cohorts."

"Mrs. Woods!" Nic's high voice cleaved into the kitchen. "Come and see!"

"What?" She led the group exiting the kitchen. "What's to see young Nic?"

"Hi, Mom," Alvin was surprised to see his Mom still among the others. "Do we have to go now?"

"In a while," Clementine said. "What have you to show us?" She reached to smooth his blond hair.

"Barber chair." Nic's voice chorused with Alvin's. "See, over there. Miah and Uncle Harold helped us get it over by the pines. See it? Can we keep it?"

"It was in the dump," Alvin spoke as if to make sure she knew it'd been discarded.

"Sniffer found the dump then we found the barber chair. Can we keep it?"

"Dale Lance carried items out to that defile after Dr. Woods died. He's been good through the years helping me with such as that." The little boys were dancing like marionettes as she pondered. "That old barber chair, you say? Yes, but who'd want such a thing?"

"Merry-go-round chair." The little boys danced about and clapped their hands. They rushed back into the tall weeds and brush, disappearing all but their squeals: "We can keep it!"

"It's ours!"

"We can keep it!"

"We can probably strap it onto our refrigerator truck," Nathan mused. "I'm glad we bought that thing to help us with moving. But first I'll see if there's a reasonable route out of there." He followed into the weeds and brush after the boys."

Clydis took Cary by the arm. Clementine took her place at Cary's other side. They headed toward the kitchen, aiming to bid their goodbyes. Edith waved her goodbye then jogged along trying to keep abreast of Omi and Cia peddling bicycles.

Finally the youngsters darted on ahead and Aunt Edith stood puffing in Cary's driveway. "When will I learn of my age?" she said as Clydis and Clementine caught up to her. "I should know better than to try to keep up but I wanted to ask them not to play croquet just now. I said 'Let's just let the over forties have a game together.' What a relief when they said 'okay' and streaked on ahead. Come on girls, we've a court to ourselves; and that's good. Those girls are good players so with them none of us would have a chance."

Chapter Ten

BEFORE BREAKFAST ON THAT NEXT Sunday morning the huge gleaming white camper pulled into the yard. Having anticipated that event, Luisa had French toast batter ready to dip bread into and she had her largest griddle heating atop her electric porcelain-topped range. Aunt Dosia and little three-year-old Virginia Louise led the charge from the camper into the house. "Hurry," Nic called, "we're having French toast to win the war." He stood with Old Sniffer.

Hugging to Nic, Sniffer pranced. His tail thrashed and his drool was friendly.

The womenfolk ignored Nic's French toast interjection and swooped past Old Sniffer on a dash toward the visitors. Virginia Louise was buried within a bevy of female cousins, aunts, and a grandma. "Hurry, we gotta eat French toast to win the war." Poor Nic, no one heard him. He stood a moment with his finger touched to his chin then he and Sniffer burrowed into the bevy to get a look at Nic's youngest cousin.

Having squirmed in under Aunt Edith's arm, Nic stood astonished and proud. The tyke was beautiful. She stood around three foot and Nic was proud that even with her golden curls piled upon her regal head, he stood head and shoulders above her. He reached to take her hand and she squirmed out from her relatives and into a side-by-side dash with him to the table. They hove into chairs side-by-side. Sniffer slid to a stop beside their chairs. "French toast is war bread to win the war."

She giggled and turned her smiling oval face and glittering blue eyes toward her mother. Momma Dosia smiled and nodded her approval and

Virginia Louise turned back to her new cohort. "I'm from Scandinavia." Her grin held a poise that signaled she was expecting a reply.

"I'm from Manitou Prairie. We live here."

Again that merry giggle pealed from her sweet face. "Gosh, oh golly, do they eat French toast?"

"Sure, and so do Scandinavians, I think. It's to win the war."

"We brought a baby carriage."

"I got a barber chair we can ride around on."

"Golly!"

"Uncle Harold," Luisa said, "well you offer grace? These kids are starved, I think."

Uncle Harold offered a simple prayer that Luisa capped with: "Hi and Miah are occupied and can be served later so we can begin. Cia, where is Aunt Edith?"

"Out with them at the camper. Hi brought something and Aunt Edith squealed when she saw it."

"What?"

"An old baby carriage," Uncle Del said," Hi found it out in that family dump on the edge of our woods."

"Oh, that's right. Dosia did say you folks would bring it."

"Baby carriage." Grandma Clydis pushed back from the table. "I'll be right back. I must see this."

Moments later Grandma Clydis and Aunt Edith toted the relic into the dinning room. "It is! It surely is!"

"I'd thought so," Del said.

"What's it for?" Virginia Louise asked but went immediately after her next chunk of syrup-dripping French toast.

"It's broke," Nic told her, "but we can ride in the barber chair."

"I'm just thrilled," Aunt Edith said, "to find my old baby carriage."

"To ride in, huh?" Omi said, "like when you were little?"

"I filled it with toys and drove them all around the house. Once when Aunt Naddy, then a little girl like Virginia Louise, came over, Momma helped us fill the carriage with pot, pans, spoons, and such so we could take the load outdoors to play in the sand."

"Probably no children rode in it until it was passed along to our house," Uncle Del said. "We'd coast down hills; the roads both had a hill that began to go down right at our driveway as you know. Papa put the springs back onto it. Scary ride then sometimes."

"Children, your grandfather Clarence removed the springs originally to lower the basket so I could see into it and to load and unload my treasures."

"When Gabe needed it for May when she was little, he took the springs back off so she could see inside like Aunt Edith once did."

"I wonder if Gabe still has the springs," Uncle Harold said.

"No, we do," Hi said, "Papa thought we should bring them along."

"Well, family, eat up big," Nathan said. "Right after breakfast we have a 1905 or older baby carriage to restore."

"Did we win the war?" Nic grinned over his cleaned up plate.

"War, yes," Virginia Louise said.

"War? What are you kids playing?"

"Win the war, did we?"

"War?"

"World War One," Aunt Edith said. "During the war German toast was renamed French toast, and yes, dear Nic, we won the war. Nic, your Uncle Harold was in the war. We who stayed at home relished French toast just to spite those Germans whose fault it was to have the war. We won alright."

"Now we would, too," Nic declared, "with ray guns and laser guns."

"You bet, old scout, and we'd eat French toast a-doing it."

Aunt Edith pushed back from the table. "Who is for croquet?"

"Against Red Ball Edith? Uncle Del said. "Why, Aunt Edith, there's just no time for that for us guys. We've a carriage to restore."

* * *

The men, that is the Uncles Harold, Del, and Nathan met with a firm surprise. After breakfast was concluded and the dishes done, they'd joyfully entered the shop. The shop was located along one side of the garage and in summer it expanded to take in the entire garage interior. Uncle Nathan walked right into a makeshift workbench, the bench consisting of a pair of sawhorses with an old door spanning them, and he was bumped by Hi who was busy sanding the rusted frame of the ancient baby carriage.

Uncle Del, too, was halted by the bench and before he could speak, his son Hi said to Miah, "We'll need to re-enforce the frame here, as you said. It's rusted to pretty weak." Hi didn't seem to notice that the uncles stood handy.

"Like we thought. Okay, let's try brazing this coat hanger wire along it." Miah stood with welding goggles positioned on his forehead and with a pair of heavy pliers in each hand. He was busily straightening coat hanger wire. With his mind so occupied, Miah didn't even notice the uncles.

The uncles stood gaped.

Finally, Uncle Nathan said, "How about the wooden parts? Will you need all new wood?"

Uncles Del and Harold looked keenly at Nathan and their eyes went on to scan the boys. They completed the scan with a smile on their faces. "You might ask Aunt Edith what color the marvelous thing was in the beginning," Uncle Harold said.

"Maroon wood and wheels," Hi said.

Black frame," Miah said, "and the lining cloth was a color somewhat like garnet. The wood, remarkably, seems to be sound and we'll epoxy it back together with some of the glue that we were using to repair cemetery stones."

"A little of the wood will need to be replaced where the frame bolted to it." Hi said. Throughout their discussion the boys seemed to be discussing the restoration between them, ignoring the uncles.

"What of the wheels?" Uncle Nathan's query seemed to be in desperation, He was struggling with the other two uncles to keep himself into the restoration. Pain and pride both subtend the son's arrival to manhood.

"They were half buried in the sand," Hi said, "and they're no good; can't be repaired."

Miah added a comment to his cousin's sad report: "But we hope to fit wagon wheels to it; take them off the Radio Flyer, but the axles are different size so we'll need to shim them."

Uncle Nathan leaped to his chance to be involved in the thrilling project. "List the size wheels, axle, and tires," he said, "and we'll try to find some buggy wheels for you. You're doing a super job, boys."

"Great," Uncle Harold said. "If we can be of any help, let us know."

The uncles knew to a man that they were not to be consulted, that their young men, no longer mere boys, had taken manhood positions.

Outside the shop, Uncle Del said, "Well, at least I'll be busy a while. I'll be busy showing Deputy Sheriff Jack Trip about driving the new Mack camper."

They'd arrived at the croquet court by the time Uncle Dell was speaking and now again stood agape. Totally ignored by the striving ladies, the men gaped as Luisa delivered a good smack to her green ball and it streaked over to bash Red Ball Edith's trusty red out of line for a hoop. She didn't hear "Good shot," uttered by one of the men. She did hear "Drat!" uttered by a determined Fire Ball Edith. The three uncles turned away and remained unnoticed by the fired up croquet players, each with an eye on the orange as Clementine clacked it past Red Ball Edith's stalled red to take the center hoop.

"I'm meeting Deputy Jack Trip sometime before dinner," Del said.

"Sheriff Puller says he's a good trucker," Nathan said. "He trucks for a fruit farm and some for the county and some for the state. For the county and state he does prisoner transfers by bus, but Sheriff Puller said he'd do that if necessary while Jack's down south with you folks."

"You know, what I look forward to the most is our arrival back home with lights flashing. Deputy Fanny Gillespie called and asked if we'd like to trade for a patrol car to drive back home. You can bet I sure said a delighted 'yes' to that."

"Say fellows," Nathan said, "after we walk all over our four acres here, there's good fishing in the pond next door; big bass in there. If the day gets hotter, they take a popper like it was their worst enemy."

"Sounds great to me," Del answered his brother.

"Uncle Harold, I've some poppers for a fly rod." Harold grinned. Nathan poked his brother Del's shoulder. "You may wish to try them too; little brother."

"You know, now I believe the day's grown hot enough to have right at it," Del said.

"Lead us to those poppers," Uncle Harold waved his arms, and he smacked a fist into his palm, making like he was ready and anxious to play ball.

* * *

The bass tore at the poppers, throwing their glistening willowy bodies clear of the water in a shower of excitement only to crash back into the pond for a sinewy warp of the slender supple fly rods. They fished a solid hour before Harold called, "Hey, I recognize this fish. I've caught him before."

"Yes, they seem to like being caught. The bigger ones have seen us real close up a number of times. We prefer to eat smaller ones, maybe a foot long or so. Let's keep those about a foot long for a fish fry. Keep the bigger fish only if they're badly injured. We've some bluegills on hand in the freezer so let's attempt to collect enough more fish for a fish fry supper."

"Sounds like good work to me, brother. I'll do what I can before I must leave to be with Deputy Trip."

"He coming out here, did you say?"

"Yes, real soon now."

"He'll bump his siren if I know Jack Trip."

They were still fishing when he bumped it.

Nathan called from the pond. Jack entered the scene. "Howdy, Professor Platt, Claudia says hello."

"Hello back to her. Jack I want you to meet Uncle Harold and my brother Del from Ellington; about fifteen north of Grand Rapids."

Jack shook hands around before again focusing the professor. "Claudia's in residency now up at Butterworth in Grand Rapids. She thanks you again and her mother, I'm sure; God bless her, and I concur. Prof, you gave her the start she needed. She's whizzed right on through to becoming a plastic surgeon."

"Great, she's very special; one of the top students we've had. You have every right to be proud. I know Liz is looking from heaven with approval. I hear you're ready to vacation in Kentucky." Nathan nodded toward Del.

"Well, I may not go." His statement snapped them to attention. Jack grinned, and said, "I may just remain here and try for fish like I'm seeing."

"Jack," Del joked, "the biggest in there seem to like people so well that they want to come ashore now and then for a closer look at us." We've had to toss the buggers back in a half dozen times it seems.

120

"Well, friend, check me out on the camper then loan me that fly rod."

"Sure thing. Come on, that camper's a snap to drive. It's just a new Mack truck with different covering. Deputy Fanny said you'd trade me a hotrod Plymouth patrol car for it; a Barracuda, maybe."

"Cuda'd be fine but they only sprung for hot Plymouths; but you'll like the power under the hood, all right."

"Jack," Nathan called as the pair started away. "Have you eaten?"

"No, not real hungry."

"We'll set a place. Then, after lunch you can help catch some supper. We were late at consuming an overlarge breakfast so it's likely a soup and cracker lunch"

Indeed his truck driving lesson took but a few minutes as Jack required no actual instruction, his expertise being obvious the moment he slipped into the bucket seat behind the steering wheel. The ladies and Omi and Cia, along with Nic and Alvin had enjoyed vegetable soup while the driving check out was occurring. Cary Woods and Clementine Beach were also on hand for lunch. Luisa had left for work at Wards before Jack Trip's arrival so the men and ladies were served by Edith and Clydis.

At a call for coffee, Edith and Clydis joined them at the table and the group began discussing the trip to Kentucky.

* * *

"I understand we're going to Kentucky to acquire the positive identity of Mr. Doe that youins found, but I'm wondering now if we haven't three men to account for. The sheriff mentioned Larry and Roy and also a Russell Junior and a Russell senior. Might it be one of the Russell men whom you've uncovered."

"Yes, we've arrived at that same conclusion, Jack. This journey may clear up that detail," Harold said. "We think that Margie of Kentucky was the man we found's wife."

"It's sure sad to think what could've happened back then. I pray we can help her situation." His hand rubbed lightly across his cheek. "Well, as I see our trip, we'll go down into Indiana to Fort Wayne then slant into Ohio; then through Ohio to Kentucky. This route through Indiana is a little out of the way but I like the roads that way the best. It'd be about thirty out of the way at first but then a slanting road on into Ohio.

Covington's the first town we'll hit in Kentucky," Jack Trip explained and pointed. On his map he'd drawn a line and drew circles around various points. "Covington's right across the Ohio River from Cincinnati. Cowboy Roy Rogers is from Portsmouth near Cincinnati and there's the Delta Queen show boat near Cincinnati, but I didn't know how our time would be so best we pour on through into Covington; maybe could visit some sites in the lower Ohio area another day. For now," he moved a finger along the line he'd drawn on his map of Kentucky, "it's a roll of around 170 miles to Lexington, but I'd rather we went to Paris instead."

"That'd give us the longest leg of the trip the first day," Aunt Edith confirmed, "and I see your idea of Paris." She pointed to where he'd circled it on his map. "See here, Momma. It's a small town."

"I see, but why? It's a little out of our route."

"You ever been to Moscow," Jack asked. He had a grin on his face.

"Why, of course not. Have you?"

"Yep; it's a small town near to Jackson, Michigan. I sent a postcard from there to my family. Postmarked in Moscow, do you see? So why not from Paris; even if Paris, Kentucky? We could send cards to Luisa and Dosia; and me to Claudia."

"Gotcha, pard." Uncle Harold pat Jack on the back. "And that'll leave the short run for that second day, that's the run into London."

"Yep, and a postcard from there." Jack was beaming.

Jack went on to say, "Sheriff Wayne has contacted the London Village Police and the sheriff. They'll have the route marked out on a county map as to how to get on into Margie's place,"

Deputy Grandma Clydis said, "Even then, they say, we may have a time of it." She read from the sheriff's notes: "Cross the South Fork of the Rockcastle River then follow the winding road, a two-track, on up Raccoon Mountain. Keep watch for a fork in the road and take the fork that is bordered by a rock cliff. Drive around the cliff and we'll see their place; an unpainted clapboard ranch-style house but the only place thereabouts to have electric wires serving it."

"Jack, we'd better rent a car from London. It doesn't sound like a route friendly to Helio's gleaming new camper."

"He's right, I'm afraid," Aunt Edith said. "I'll call Wayne to set that up."

"Also," Uncle Harold said," ask about a safe place to leave the camper; er, uh, like right at the police station, maybe."

"Or at the car rental. But let's not bother Sheriff Wayne about a car rental or the other details right now. Let's fret over that later, maybe not even until after we get there." The others wondered what Deputy Clydis Grandma Groner had in mind, but knowing her, they didn't ask for an explanation; instead they were content to wait and see.

At day break Manitou County Deputy Sheriff Jack Trip seated comfortably in his bucket seat. The big white camper rolled from the Platt yard. Kent County Deputy Sheriff Aunt Edith Groner James occupied the bucket seat on the far right of the spacious Mack cab. She held Jack's marked up map in her lap even though it was still too dark to read it. In the middle bucket seat Kent County Deputy Sheriff Uncle Harold James nodded and Aunt Edith checked to see that he had his seat belt buckled. In the far rear of the camper, in the living room/bedroom, Kent County Deputy Sheriff Grandma Clydis Groner lay flat on her back on the sofa/bed with an afghan pulled to her chin. She dreamed sweetly of a day long ago when toddler Edith first pushed her baby buggy.

Grandma Clydis cuddled deeper into the warm afghan and smiled in her sleep. Her dream'd revealed the baby buggy heaped with toys and with toddler Edith pushing her treasure around the house. Her smile reached grin status in focusing the dog named Sniffer, foundation dog of a long line of Sniffers and Snifferettes leading to the present Old Sniffer. Sniffer'd remained ever watchful of the buggy with its pusher, a tiny wavy-haired toddler named Edith.

Little could Grandma know that in the Platt garage, located on Peach Road south of Manitou Prairie, cousins Hi and Miah Platt had present-day Old Sniffer ever watchful as they labored to make Grandma's dream come true; and maybe with an added attraction, that of buggy rides down the hill west of the house.

* * *

The cousins, having seen their relatives depart on their important mission, settled back to continue work on the restoration of that very buggy Grandma Clydis was dreaming about. Finally, they attached the buggy's basket to the frame by way of the black newly painted springs.

They stood back, each with a hand to an aching back, and marveled at their accomplishment. For want of wheels, she was ready.

But the wheels were lacking, ordered at a bicycle shop, but lacking. They scratched their heads.

Having worked most of the night, they went into the house and plopped into bed.

Outside the Platt home the robins chirped and the earthworms squirmed and, ignoring both bird and worm, Professor Nathan Platt hurried to his light blue Chevy pickup. He was leaving about an hour early to meet his summer classes. Before the classes, he'd a stop to make at the bicycle shop in town. The man had called the evening before to say that the wheels were in. Nathan hadn't told the boys, or anyone else, wanting the wheels to be a surprise. He guessed that Del and family would be leaving for home that day and was thrilled that with the wheels the restoration would be completed on time.

The boys stirred in their sleep upon hearing the pickup drive into the yard. "Boys, wake up!"

"Get up, you sleepy heads."

They emerged with their hair a-scatter. "Huh, what's the rush?"

"Eat first."

"And comb your hair."

"Hey!" Nic yelled from the garage. "What are these?"

No time for breakfast, and with their hair still a-scatter, the cousins darted into the garage on a bent to translate Nic's excitement. In just a short time, Nic was getting his very first white-knuckled ride in a baby carriage.

The buggy coasted down the hill to the west of the house. The bumpy yard wobbled and bounded the buggy which was aimed toward an old door that was emplaced as a bridge across Congo Creek. Nic yelled as the route ahead bugged his eyes. He hunkered down into the hurdling buggy. He held tight, his eyes closed tightly as the buggy shot across the creek and onto the grass beyond. "Whoopee!"

"Whoopee!" Omi and Cia came running.

"My turn!"

"My turn!"

The cousins wished they were not too big for the buggy – then again, they stood proud. They'd not imagined they'd fit the buggy but stood proud that many others could.

"Alphabetical!" Cia shouted. "Let's choose alphabetically."

"Oh, you would," Omi said.

In a moment Cia screamed as the buggy streaked toward that precarious door spanning the Congo. Omi stood next in line to have her bravado tested. "Not so fast, please." She had barely time for a modest screech before the restored turn of the century Sears and Roebuck special hurdled over the Congo and scampered out into the yard beyond.

"I'm calling Alvin Beach!" Nic tore for the telephone.

"Hurry, let's call Candy and Sandy Gillespie!" Omi and Cia tore for the house.

The cousins stood in the yard beside their restoration. Hi rubbed his hand along the rim of the basket. "Smooth," he said. "And she didn't break. Cuzz, we sure did good."

"You bet," Miah said, "and, Cuzz, how about tackling that old barber chair that Nic and Alvin found?"

"I'm with you, Cuzz. We'll have that thing as torturing as an astronaut's centrifuge."

"Yeah, a real neck snapper. Uh, and, say, old Cuzz, that thing's big enough so's we can ride in it!"

The cousins rushed back into that garage which was their workshop. In moments the old chair'd been hoisted onto the workbench.

Meantime back in the big white camper Grandma Clydis Groner arose. Luxuriously she showered and dressed a-fresh; even to a splash of Coco Chanel's # 5. The mirror revealed to her that she was 'the apple of the eye' that she felt like. She grinned at her notion then turned to make her way forward to the spacious cab. As she was moving toward the truck cab her mind became firmly fixed to her dream of the buggy. With her mind so fixed, upon entering the cab she was taken aback. "Oh!" Her hand went to her lips. "Oh, gosh," she looked confused, "now I see."

"Momma," Edith leaped from her seat and Deputy Trip's carefully folded map went airborne into the windshield. "Momma?" She held her Momma. "Momma, what is the matter?"

"Oh, nothing, dear. You've grown so, that's all. I so love you and that old baby buggy."

"Sure, Momma." Edith looked across at Harold, her eyes asking what she should do, asking what is wrong with her Momma. Her arm around Momma, she led the sweet lady toward the vacant bucket seat. "You'll be alright, Momma. Good view from up here."

"It's just the buggy," Momma said. "I dreamed about the buggy, that buggy you pushed around the house. Oh, Edith, how I do miss your father; and, well, I guess I also miss your childhood."

She pecked Momma's cheek. "I do too, Momma, but really, we can enjoy their childhood and it's as good – maybe better."

"Better," Harold chipped in. "Watching the kids, we can relive ours again and again. I wonder how those stalwarts are coming on the buggy restoration. The boys have sure proven their mettle."

"Each 'the apple of the eye," Grandma said, "just the apple of the eye."

* * *

That 'apple of the eye," Jack Trip ventured to say, "by the way, comes from the Bible; from, Psalms. Psalms 17:8. It's a real old saying and refers to God's treating someone as special. So to say; it's like His saving each special person, each apple of His eye, from eternal damnation."

"My gosh, Jack, you sound like a preacher we had way back who was part Indian."

Jack Trip chuckled. "Well, I'm no part Indian and only a small part preacher. I talk as often as I can with the prisoners. Don't mind me, please, if I get wordy once in a while. I just couldn't resist that 'apple of the eye' phrase. There's another part to that verse: 'hide me under the shadow of thy wing.' That's like protection from one's enemies. So God protects those 'apple of His eye' folks while they're here on earth."

"More power to you on wordiness, Jack. Let us hear more from time to time."

"Jack, how far to Indiana?"

"We'll eat lunch there. We cops know facts that tend to turn up now and then, as you may know. Well, I thought up some facts while planning this trip and I've thought up the right place to spout about each of them. You'll be pleasured, my friends, to dine in a town made famous by Mr. John Dillinger."

"The John Dillinger? Really?"

"Jack, you push this shiny white tub on down the road. I'm getting hungry."

Chapter Eleven

"**J**ACK, YOU'D BETTER TELL US now about John Dillinger. I need a topic to stave off my hunger." Harold made a show of holding his tummy.

"No, not old John Dillinger. No sir. He's for lunch. Think up another topic. Like ice cream, maybe."

"You rascal," Edith feigned annoyance. "Now you've begun a rumble in my stomach. My golly! What can we talk about? Is it far to that Dillinger's?"

"Closer to ice cream, I'll say. I noticed a sign back there. Now I see an ice cream restaurant ahead on the right."

As they pulled into the apron a sign to their front announced, "Invented 1786, we have the finest selection of flavors."

"What ever could they mean by "invented?" Grandma asked. She sounded somewhat annoyed.

"Troubles me as well," Edith said. "Come on, we'll ask."

"Invented what?" Grandma demanded even before the restaurant door closed behind them.

"Ice cream." The man beamed at them from behind the counter. He wore a white long-sleeved shirt, a white apron, a white hair net and a white chef's hat. "Name a flavor, we have it."

"Ice cream invented in 1786, how do you know that, young man?"

"I don't, but there's record of it being sold in New York City at that time. It's the oldest mention of ice cream I've heard about so we put it out front. Look over the flavors, folks. Have fun while you're here."

"A dip each of chocolate and white in a bowl."

"I'll have two dips, all white in a bowl."

The man looked discouraged. "Did you want to look over these flavors?"

"Two dips, one white and the other strawberry in a bowl."

The guy looked about to cry. "We have sixteen different flavors"

"Triple dip cone," Harold said. "Make it one each of pineapple crunch, Oreo spatter, and moose droppings."

"Now we're talking!" He commenced a whistle as he dipped.

Handing their order, he said, "Where you folks bound?"

"Kentucky, but first our driver has promised we'd eat shortly, just into Indiana."

"He won't tell us where that'll be, but says we'll learn about John Dillinger while we eat."

"That public enemy number one? I thought he'd died; gunned down in Chicago."

"Yes, he's the one."

"That's a sad story, but well now, as to Ohio. I can tell you where to look around Akron because I'm from that area, but you likely won't come near to it on the route you're taking; Ohio, then on to Kentucky, you said."

"Yes, that's the essence of it. We'll slant over into Ohio a ways below here and then finally go to Raccoon Mountain near the town of London, Kentucky near almost to Tennessee," Harold said. "Say, kind sir, how about Kinsman? Do you reckon we'll pass near it on our route?"

With his right index finger he scratched under the band of his white hat. "No, now – but I have a map."

"No need, Jack said. I know it's way to the east, nearly into Pennsylvania. Harold, who do you know there?"

"Clarence Darrow, of the Scopes Trial. Louie Watkins, a friend of ours, told me about it. He likes to visit places he's read about. Reads insistently. Darrow was born there but the trial was in Dayton, Tennessee. I did look that up. We won't come any where close to that place on this trip. That Scopes who the trial was about just died, Louie read in a newspaper. That's how the topic came up." He felt a cool drip of ice cream trickle onto his hand. He halted his part of the conversation and licked away at drips and then ran his tongue around his whole triple dipper, but he'd chatted too long and the wonderful dips were avalanching out of control. He bit a huge bite off the top dip.

Edith giggled. "Sure, big boy, you and your cone." She rattled her spoon in her dish.

"Better this way." He glommed onto another huge chunk that finished the upper dip.

Jack Trip looked calmly up from his under-control bowl of dips. "I see you're on the baseball team." Jack was focused upon a color Kodak print of a baseball team. It hung in clear view of customers and showed the proprietor in the front row.

"Yes, we're the Hobokeners. We named us after where the first baseball game was ever played. That first baseball game was played in Hoboken, New Jersey in 1845."

"A big league, is it? I'd bet just by that picture that the Hobokeners are the champs."

He grinned, "Usually we are."

"You sure know your history," Harold said. "How long have you been away from Akron?"

"Actually, I came here with my folks in 1949. Dad had dreamed about a shop like this while in the war. I'm their only child so the business came to me."

"Think back, kind sir," Edith said, "as far back as you can since you moved here. Think of anything really exciting that happened; that is besides your ice cream business."

His right index finger again explored under his hat band. "Well, er, not much ever did happen here, just a steady business, is all.

"Something that made the newspapers; think now, what was it?"

The finger paused along his hat band. "Well my folks actually did see it. Me, too, maybe, but I recall it more from as they told of it." He wiped across his forehead. "They'd not want me to tell about it as folks kind of thought they were batty and that's bad for business."

"Come now, we aren't going to blab the story around."

All eyes came to rest on the white-clad man and, alternately, on Edith. Finally he blurted, "Yeti. They saw a Yeti but it wasn't in the paper. They only told about it to the police, er, sheriff."

"In 1949, was that?"

"More like, I'd say, more like '51 or '52. I was pretty young at the time."

"I find this very fascinating. You are a fascinating man. Tell us what you recall. And I must repeat that we don't blab. We're merely interested."

"Well it happened here in town in, like I said '51 or '52. A friend owned a grocery just down the street. A huge hairy creature broke in, smashed the front window. They called the cops but before they got to that store the monster dived out through the broken window. My folks said it was carrying several whole tubes of lunch meat under one arm and some wine bottles under the other. The lunch meat, you know, in the big tube, the kind the grocer cuts slices from to fill your order."

"Sure, I see."

"Well, this was likely the only sighting of a Yeti that tried to wear human clothes. And it's the main reason they didn't let folks know about it. Whacky, you know, and folks may say, irresponsible; real bad for business."

"I can surely see their point of view on that," Edith said.

No one heard the last few words of Edith's comment as at that moment the building shook and a diesel Amtrak locomotive roared past with its klaxon burring. A train lover, Harold reached the plate glass restaurant window in a single bound.

He craned his neck after the train. At last reluctantly turning from the glass he found himself nose to nose with the white-clad proprietor.

"Er, sorry, I can't resist those beauties either. In my youth that would've been the Wabash Cannonball."

"Amtrak and the Wabash Cannonball, you say, and on the same tracks. It's funny that I hadn't connected the two of them. We have recently returned from a truly enjoyed Amtrak excursion to New York City and to the sights and stops along the way. Wabash Cannonball; I wonder if we weren't riding along the same route as that famous train."

"I don't usually do what I'm going to do now," he said, "but having met a fellow train buff, I'm going to. Follow me." He took Harold's arm. "It's a lot to carry." The man and Harold disappeared into a back room of the restaurant. In a moment they returned huffing and puffing like the steam trains of old. Each held an end to a scaled railroad track, the track measuring some five feet in length, the whole being clumsy rather than especially heavy. Attached to the rails was the strangest train engine they'd ever seen. Attached behind the engine were a barebones engine tender and a flat car. Wood-carved people wearing dress-up traveling clothes were positioned on the flat car.

"As I've said, I'm a railroad buff; in particular I live Wabash Cannonball. Its story is a long one and, indeed, does include rails now guiding various Amtrak trains. Moment please."

He reached to switch on a record player. Roy Acuff's twang filled the room. He lowered the volume, explaining, "That's the original Wabash Cannonball song; written by A. P. Carter in 1940; and, of course, you recognize Roy Acuff. He sings of the western routes and also of the New York and Peoria branches. Later versions of the song changed western to eastern and substituted 'victory' for 'Dixie'. The later versions also included Chicago because the line expanded to serve Chicago for the World's fair or some such, early in the century. The Wabash Cannonball trains went all over, but the original route and the famous one went right past out in front here. This model of a train engine is important because it not only began the Wabash Cannonball trains, it sort of began railroading altogether in America."

"Really? Gosh," Edith eyed the flat car, "everybody had to ride out-of-doors."

"Yep, the engine was small, with only two drivers." He pointed, "The drivers are these two big wheels here; one driver to each side, see?." He continued, "Also, see, there was no cab for the engineer and fireman, and no whistle, no bell, and no spark arrester. This was in 1838 and people came to gawk at it, to laugh at it, and to wonder just what it was for. They couldn't visualize a use for it seeing as how at that time in history they were enjoying an efficient canal system for travel. Few saw this puny, funny little engine as a rival of the canal system; like the Erie Canal, for example."

"Your workmanship here is wonderful."

"Thank you. My ambition is to replicate the Wabash Cannonball engines. My next project, however, is a somewhat sad one. It'll be a model of the last of the Wabash Cannonballs to pass through here. That was in 1970. Amtrak took over in 1971. Later I'll build a model of the last Cannonball steam engine; around 1947, I think that would be."

They left a generous tip upon exiting the neat little 'Wabash Cannonball' ice cream restaurant. In the camper, Clydis said, "I'm not wondrous as to why we talked trains, but dear, what prompted that line of questioning about break-ins and hairy monsters," Clydis peered at her daughter.

"Apparently Roy and Larry suddenly left from the Manitou Prairie area. We're on our way to Kentucky to find out more, to help solve the hermit shack mysteries. Could not Roy and Larry have made the same trip?"

"Well, yes, and the route Jack has mapped out is a rather logical route to take; assuming they knew where to go, that is."

"Larry, I gather, probably couldn't find his way but Roy more likely would know the route."

"Let's ask, look, and listen for hermit/abominable news all our way down. Edith, you may have revealed another chapter for us."

"The guy only mentioned Larry, or a creature that could be Larry. From now on let's whenever we uncover more about the so called Yeti, let's visit the sheriff's office or a state or city police post seeking all the detail we can get."

Their talk continued briskly. Jack didn't interrupt when he saw they were entering Indiana. Shortly Jack let off on the throttle. "Hudson," he said.

"Huh, Hudson where?"

"Indiana. Hudson, Indiana is that John Dillinger town I spoke of earlier. He robbed the Farmers State Bank here back in 1933. He got away with $1337.00."

Jack Trip pulled to the curb and stopped. "It's the way he did the robberies that caused folks from Chicago, here in Hudson, and clear on into Detroit to like him. The Great Depression was in full force at that time. Typically people had money in the bank and the bank lost that money. People weren't upset that Dillinger robbed a bank that'd already robbed them. Another thing and I believe this to be true, he'd go into a bank and remind the banker that the money was insured, so no sense making a fuss over a temporary loss.

"There was a restaurant here in Hudson, and I'm told this is the one, where he'd stop to eat. I mean before he robbed their bank. I'd bet he didn't stop here after that, but I think he could have, and in safety. Whenever he stopped here people would crowd into the restaurant to get a look at their hero. Outside, say where we are now, they could admire his car, said to be the most powerful car in America. It looked like a regular Cadillac car but had been bullet proofed and had added power. No police could catch that car nor would police bullets penetrate it. He always wore a bullet proof vest as well."

Jack led into the restaurant.

Noon hour rush was two hours away as they took their seats. Noting the time, they ordered breakfast. Along with ordering they requested a visit with the restaurant owner or manager. They had begun their meal when a nervous middle-aged man approached the table. "I'm the manager," he informed them. "The owner's in Fort Wayne buying supplies. Is there a problem?"

"Oh no, certainly not," Harold said. "All four of us are deputy sheriffs from Michigan. Running across the trail of Mr. John Dillinger, we find exciting. Could you share an anecdote with us? A look at his personal life perhaps. We'd like a better understanding of why folks liked him."

"Well, I'll say that you folks have probably learned all of the basics of Dillinger, but there's a tale told from time to time, oh, say just often enough to keep the tale alive. The story goes that he picked up a woman hitchhiker in that armored Cadillac of his. She was hitchhiking because she had no money and she wished to go way over to near Toledo to visit her sister. He took her right to her sister's door. Later he picked her up to drive back here to Hudson. He was a perfect gentleman through it all. He had impeccable manners and was a good conversationalist. None of us doubt but what he was all of that."

"Kind of a Robin Hood, then?"

"You bet. And to think he was gunned down outside a movie theater in Chicago. Such as that just doesn't make sense to us."

"Thank you for the story," Clydis said. "If you could, we're also asking whether anyone knows of an abominable snowman, also called a Yeti, seen in this area; seen about twenty years ago."

"Yeti, do you mean, yeti? Hummm, now let me see. I'd have been still in high school. Hummm, now say there was one seen, but not here, and they called it an abominable snowman, or, at least an abominable creature, not Yeti. Fort Wayne is about forty miles south of here. We offered that newspaper for our clientele to read. They about wore out that paper as everyone wanted to read about it. The Fort Wayne sheriff expressed doubt that it was a Yeti or any like creature and many people loudly protested. With an election coming, that sheriff made no further big issue of his contrasting opinion."

"Sir, you've been most charming and helpful, and the food was excellent. We hope to stop by again."

In the big white camper Jack made his final up-shift into cruise. Clydis tapped his shoulder. "We've telephone books for major cities like Fort Wayne. I'll place a call there as soon as I think it'd be a local call. I want to talk with that sheriff and/or read the incidence report."

"Gotcha. Good idea."

They settled into a forty mile roll for Fort Wayne.

Passing through Auburn, everyone wished they had time to visit the museum. "I heard they have Bonnie and Clyde's car there."

"Oh, really," Edith acted surprised. "Their Ford in there with the Auburns, Cords and Duesenbergs, huh?"

"I'd heard."

"Dear," Edith admonished, "let's keep the excitement narrowly focused to the Hermit shack venue."

"Party pooper."

"Maybe on our way back north."

"Don't you forget."

Already Jack Trip was becoming accustomed to the genial banter his companions batted off one another. It was refreshing and it used up time that could otherwise drag.

Roadside signs were already beginning to announce their vicinity to Fort Wayne. "Clydis," he used the intercom.

"I'm with you."

"Closing with Fort Wayne. You have that number?"

"Yup. You look for a telephone booth."

She made the arrangements for their visit and after a short drive they pulled in at the county sheriff's department. "Good thing youins called ahead. I'm Sheriff Broadbeam." He shook hands around. "My clerk is down stairs fingering for the report. I'm the second sheriff since the sighting you're asking about. That sheriff who actually made the report, I'd not met. He's passed on."

"As you know, a written report doesn't fade its memory. Besides the incidence report, talking with you about it will be fine."

The intercom crackled. "It was in '51. Long report here. I'll be right up."

"Officer, madam clerk, this is Sheriff's Deputy Edith James from Michigan. Take a few moments longer, please. We want to know if there was a grocery break-in about at that time."

"Roger."

Chatting resumed. Hearing a crackling sound, their ears all cocked toward the intercom console. "Eureka! Sheriff, there was indeed such a break-in. I'm coming right up."

The reports were confirmation that the encounter reported to them by the ice cream man and by the manager in John Dillinger's was accurate. Whole tubes of lunch meat were taken, along with cheese and many bottles of wine. One of the wine bottles was found inside the store with its neck fractured off. Some spectators were in concert with the sheriff; stating they'd seen items of human clothing on the monster.

"We'll get a report back to you, Sheriff, as soon as we can. We're following an evidence trail that may lead into Kentucky. That abominable may indeed be a human. With luck we'll encounter the monster's relatives on Raccoon Mountain near London, Kentucky.

Back in the camper, Edith said. "It seems to be only about Larry, not Roy. No mention of Roy. Only just Larry alone. I'm worried about Roy."

Jack pulled in at an ice cream shop. "Well, let's get settled down if we can. It sure doesn't look good for Roy."

Despite the calming effect of ice cream, their stop was brief. Harold's query, "Aren't we running late?" prompted them to pop back into the camper.

"No, not running late," Jack said, once they were under way. "We're about eighty out from Manitou Prairie and have around one seventy to go yet today. That's to get us into Paris near to Lexington."

* * *

Back at Manitou Prairie, Professor Nathan Platt had rushed home from his classes. He wanted to be on hand with Luisa to eat a meal with them and to see their guests off for home. His eyes feasted upon a treat as he swung into the yard. Hi was going around and around hollering, "Faster, faster, I want to feel my neck crick and my head spin!"

Miah was beginning to tucker. He gave a final mighty heave that cousin Hi, indeed, felt in his neck. Omi and Cia took over swinging the barber chair. Finally, "One more push is all you get." The girls were also tiring.

The barber chair drifted to a stop. Hi was nearly thrown from the chair as Omi sardined in under him.

Cia wailed, "Hey, I wanted to be next!" "Ten pushes," Miah said. He began whirling his sister in the chair.

"Well, I'm counting, and I'll be next."

"It's Nic's chair," Omi countered. "See if he wants to be next."

"No, he's to wait a turn. Hi and Miah fixed the chair, anyway; not Nic."

"Fine job boys," Nathan was, indeed, proud of their efforts.

Just ready to enter the house from the garage, Nathan was nearly bowled over by Nic and Sniffer charging for the garage. "He can come! Alvin's coming this afternoon!"

The cousins had taken the chair apart to clean and lubricate its joints, being particularly alert to lubing the rotational mechanism. They took care, as well, to disengage the lock lever which otherwise kept the chair from free rotation.

Upon reassembly, the chair swung very well. Nathan could see they'd bolted the chair to a base constructed from a large shipping pallet. He was grateful for their good sense.

Reaching for the kitchen door, the professor was again nearly bowled over. Luisa and Aunt Dosia each carried a self-fabricated cover for either the seat or the back of the chair. Constructed of upholstery material, they expected the covers would wear well. At the least the covers would prevent further loss of debris from the seat cushions. "Ten!" Cia stopped pushing.

"I'm next." She crowded into the seat in such a rush that Omi lost her balance and ended at Luisa and Aunt Dosia's feet.

"Omi, help put these covers on then go brush yourself off. Seat padding is stuck all over your shorts and blouse." Luisa handed Cia from the chair. "Brush off your shorts. You'll be the first to ride on the new seat covers."

Wondering where his brother Del might be, Nathan went on into the house. "Hey, Del!"

An imp clad only in a pair of blond panties tore straight at him but didn't see him. Her head was turned back toward the bathroom.

"Virginia Louise, wait! Get your clothes on!"

Thump! Uncle Nathan caught her with his knees and forearms. "Whoa!"

"Not red, Uncle Nathan. Not red."

Del rushed into the scene carrying a miniature pair of red Levis. "Hold her. Don't let her get away, Uncle Nathan." He was laughing, his pride obvious.

"No, not red." She tried to pull free of her uncle.

"To think I volunteered for this, her bath and to get her dressed, while they made the seat covers."

Nathan knelt with his niece. "Say, I have a red shirt I could wear. You and me, we'd look good together; both with red on."

"The red not mine. Nic's."

"Do you mean you're old enough to wear Nic's clothes? Why that Nic better be careful or all of his clothes will fit you. He will be without any clothes on. Gee, sweety, I'd sure like to see what we look like together, both of us wearing red. How about it? The red jeans really are not Nic's clothes anymore. These red jeans are yours because you're big enough to wear them."

She looked around at her dad holding the red jeans. She darted over to him.

Del, Nathan and, freshly clad, Virginia Louise entered the garage just as three sheriff's patrol cruisers pulled into the yard. Candy and Sandy Gillespie hopped from the rear seat of one of the cars. Seeing the quests from where she stood in the garage, Virginia Louise ran over to the restored baby carriage.

The carriage had a doll and other toys inside, the toys to include blocks, a baseball mitt, a yo-yo, and a jump rope. She pushed the buggy proudly toward Candy and Sandy. Their eyes upon the barber chair, the girls tore past Virginia Louise. Virginia Louise stood with a hand on the carriage and with her gaze far off toward guests who had ignored her. She puckered to cry. "Well, what have we here?"

Officer Fanny Gillespie knelt beside the carriage. "This is wonderful, you sweety. May I see your dolly? Gosh, what a pretty dress she has."

"I look like Uncle Nathan."

"Sweety, why is that? Where is Uncle Nathan?"

"Red." She pulled at the bright red Levis.

"Oh what pretty jeans." Fanny could see ahead that her daughters had joined the group at the whirling barber chair. "May I help to get your carriage inside? You can help me set the table."

Glancing over a shoulder, Deputy Fanny saw one of the cruisers exit the driveway. That left two cruisers in the yard; one for Fanny to use in returning to work. The other cruiser was for Del Platt and family to use in returning to their home at Ellington, located three miles north of Leadford, Michigan.

Chapter Twelve

LUNCH WAS OF SANDWICHES, CHIPS, tossed salad, and Jell-O because Uncle Del Platt needed to avoid eating heavy before tackling the long one hundred-sixty mile roll back to their home at Ellington. They'd just settled into the meal when: "Dosia," Louisa'd put down her bacon-lettuce sandwich and now addressed her sister-in-law, "when you were telling me over the phone about Virginia Louise locking herself in the attic while you were painting the bed room, I was reminded of a similar debacle."

"Oh." Aunt Dosia also set aside her sandwich. It wasn't like her sister-in-law to suddenly decide to tell a story, but all knew that such could be a delight to hear. Lunch slowed a pace for everyone and some stopped eating altogether as Luisa began, "In a house before this one, there was an attic off our bedroom upstairs. It had a tiny door but one could scrunch through to set in old clothes and spare blankets and such; the usual attic accumulation. I was expecting Omi at the time and with an arm load of blankets, I squeezed through the little door into the attic. The ceiling was so low in there, one couldn't stand erect and boards covered only a small portion of the rafters of the dining room ceiling. I hadn't expected little Miah to follow me into that tiny attic. I reached to set my armload down and heard the little door close. The only light came through the crack around the door, but I could dimly see Miah.

"I squeezed past him and pushed the door. It was latched and there was no release inside; no way to open that door. Well, I didn't want Miah to wander on into the attic to where I couldn't reach him nor did I know but what he might fall through the ceiling once he stepped off the boards, so I held him. He was quiet and I could dimly see his frown. I finally decided to try a naptime story and that led to nursery rhymes. Soon I had pulled together a bed for him in a box where I'd thrust away most of the stored clothing. Finally he was sleeping.

"I went to work on the door; rattled and pried and jiggled. I was getting cold and I needed the bathroom. I found an old kettle for that then went to work again on the door. It just refused to open. I bundled in a blanket and decided we'd just have to wait for Nathan to get home.

"It seemed like hours – it did actually, the whole affair, take nearly three hours. There was a rap on our door. I couldn't believe it at first. I listened. Rap-rap-rap, rap-rap-rap. I yelled, 'Who is it!'

No answer.

'Who is it? Please answer! We're locked in the attic!' Finally I heard, 'The Watkins man.'"

'Come up stairs!'

'What?'

'Come in the house and come up stairs!' Finally, I heard him downstairs. 'Come up stairs. We're locked in the attic!'

'Coming. Coming.'

I heard him on the stairs. 'This way. We're locked in the attic.'

He opened the door and I slid Miah, still asleep in his box, out to him. 'Gosh, gosh,' he kept saying. "I thanked him. I explained what happened, that is with the door. He hurried downstairs and away without even asking if I wanted to buy any Watkins products. I'll tell you, we soon removed the latch altogether from that darn little door."

Chuckles began around the table and escalated to titter and ha-ha. "It worried me all through the story as to whether it was a sad or funny story." Uncle Del said. "But the way you ended it caused my guffaw, Luisa, even knowing it was a frightening worrisome experience for you."

"Thinking back on it as humor has helped me to weather that particular episode."

"Now as to our little door," Aunt Dosia said, "dear let's check to make sure it is easily opened from within."

"You bet, and thanks Luisa."

"Good idea," Fanny said.

With Luisa's story adding glee to the meal, lunch went smoothly toward dessert. Just into a reach for strawberry Jell-O, Deputy Fanny answered a radio call: "Corner of Bankers and Lake. I'm rolling. My

ETA, five." She'd come to her feet while on the radio. Catching eyes with her daughters, she said. "Amish buggy and a Harley motorcycle. I do wish they'd plain off the top of that hill, such poor visibility there. Girls, have fun. I'll be back later."

She zipped out the door. Tires squawked on her big Plymouth. With lights flashing and the siren piercing the mid day air, she streaked for the intersection.

"Gosh, now I don't want to leave for home until I know about those people," Aunt Dosia said.

"I'm sorry I have to run to work," Luisa said. She hugged around and pecked cheeks and foreheads, wished them a safe journey home, and then with her arms still in their leather braces, she left for the cash office at Wards.

Hi said, "There's not a huge rush to get home anyway, is there?"

"Uh, no," Uncle Del agreed, "but I sure will look forward to squawking that big black and white when we do get a-going."

"Hi hasn't had much chance to even see the hermit shack." Miah placed a hand on his cousin's shoulder.

"Sandy and I haven't even ever seen it," Candy Gillespie said.

Old Sniffer whined from over by the door, signally he was game for adventure.

Del, honey, leaving here by two o'clock should work out alright, I'd think."

"Or three, even," Del said. "You go on ahead with the kids. Me and Nathan'll be along after we try out the barber chair."

"Now you're talking!" Nathan placed his napkin beside his plate.

The men's visit into the hermit shack venue was delayed while they helped Virginia Louise to the garage with the baby buggy. The men took their turn in the chair, grinning at the experience and at Virginia Louise as she pushed the baby carriage around and around the barber chair. Finally Luisa and then Virginia Louise, on Dosia's lap, had a turn on the whirling sensation. Hi and Miah'd watched a few minutes then took off ahead of the others. Their plan was to descend into the hermit shack venue by way of the steep wooded slope just south of the shack. This was the route taken by Miah and others when the shack was originally discovered.

After watching Miah and Hi's departure, Old Sniffer stuck anxiously beside Nic and Alvin. The sagacious old dog knew something was up and didn't want to miss out. He stayed with the little boys even when Omi, Cia, Candy, and Sandy left on bicycles. The girls'd decided to approach the hermit shack by way of the fence stile south of the Digger Marl place.

The barber chair whirled to a stop and Virginia Louise was transferred to her dad's shoulders. Nic and Alvin led the way across Peach Road seeking the down-path to the Congo. They'd already begun the trek through the woods toward the pines by the time the adults and Virginia Louise left the Congo down-path. "Hey, wait up you guys!"

Squeaky voices reached the callers: "Old Sniffer ran on ahead!"

Nathan, Del, and Dosia began calling Old Sniffer but they and the boys didn't see the dog for a time. Meanwhile, Nathan led them to the margin of the pines to point out the dump. "Old Sniffer found this dump, I'm glad to say. That old barber chair was sure a good find."

When the concrete 'bathroom' came into view, Nathan said, "Old Sniffer found this, too."

"What is it, a bathroom?"

"We know now that it wasn't a bathroom. Mrs. Merit told Luisa about that. "Mrs. Barbara Bobby Marlin Merit," he explained, "is the scoutmaster's wife and is a sister to Digger Marl. Mr. Merit is the Cub Scoutmaster for Nic and Alvin. This little concrete structure was the company office; made of concrete to protect the payroll and also they stored explosives in there. We've found a humper, or rather, Old Sniffer found it, a type of outdoor latrine. It's over yonder a ways."

The adults popped to attention, and lent their ears to the sounds of laughter. They recognized Hi and Miah's ha-ha due to the mix of boy and adult male octaves, and the squeaky glee of Nic and Alvin was unmistakable. Del lowered Virginia Louise from his shoulders to his arms to keep her clear of overhead branches then led the charge toward the laughter.

"It's the humper, ha-ha-ha, he's digging in the humper; the bathroom."

"Why is he? Hee-hee-hee," Alvin wanted to know.

"Likes it. He likes it!"

"Hee-hee-hee!"

"Ha-ha-ha!"

Sniffer, come out of there!" Nathan drew the old dog back by his collar. "No telling what you'll run into in there. Yuck!"

"Do you mean that's an old humper latrine he's digging up?" Aunt Dosia asked in a tone of disgust. "Del, please keep him away from there."

"Kids, bring that tape from the cabin; the tape the sheriff used to cordon off the boxes of wine bottles beside the shack."

"Yes, he said he was done studying the wine bottles."

Old Sniffer was tied to a tree by a twelve foot length of yellow cordoning ribbon. Omi slipped him half a Babe Ruth candy bar. He chewed into the bar a chomp or two then wolfed it down except for running his tongue searching for the last fragments. Cia rubbed along his neck hairs, marveling at the silkiness where a short while ago the neck'd been naked and raw due to his trying to regurgitate a swallowed pot holder. The hair had grown back to as long as a three-day-old beard on a man and the new hair was lighter in color and silkier than the rest of his fur. The new hair also took on a russet hue. Old Sniffer moaned his pleasure at the attention he was getting from the girls. "Funny that's a different color there," Candy said.

"Didn't you say the big hermit had reddish hair?" Sandy was curious. She reached to stroke the soft russet fur.

"Yes, that's right," Omi said, "but we're sure there's no connection. Ha-ha."

"Sure, I know. Still, he reminds me of the hermit somehow," Candy said. "Mom calls that, like my reminder, a hunch. She says not to labor over it but to let it simmer on the mind. Sometimes then, right out of the blue, the whole assorted connections will add up; then she goes to work on the new idea."

"Like a detective, huh?"

"Yup, she's training to become a detective."

"Gosh, she could get famous."

"You know that man that was buried? She told us about that because she said we'd soon get the story anyway from being around you guys. Well, she said to dad, 'That belt was around two inches wide and the buckle was utility, not a big fancy affair, so he was probably an ordinary working man.' Also, she said that one could determine his waist diameter by measuring to the most stretched belt hole. That kind of talk sounds like real detective talk to us."

"Sure, it really does. Gosh, a detective mom."

"You won't be able to get away with anything at all."

"Gee, I hope she . . ."

"Oh, don't worry," Omi said. "No parent can ever know everything."

"I wonder why Old Sniffer's digging got me to thinking about the hermit," Sandy said.

"And Old Sniffer's reddish fur caused me to think of the hermit's reddish hair," Candy said. "Sis, we'd better tell mom about these hunches."

The group explored the area and discussed as much as they knew about the hermits. Soon they discovered that two in the afternoon had passed. Miah and Hi walked along with the four girls and with Virginia Louise getting a turn at piggy back on each of the young men's shoulders. As they neared the stile and the bicycles, Candy Gillespie remarked, "Did you know that Edith Wilson, wife of President Woodrow Wilson, rode a bicycle along the corridors of the White House?"

"Really?" Omi took a look at her friend. "Gosh, how do you know that?"

"Oh, she wrote a report on presidential anecdotes," Sandy answered for her sister.

"Yes, for government class. Mrs. Law said that in every presidency the government should see to it that much is known about the president's family. It was fun to learn about Mrs. Wilson. It's remarkable that Teddy Roosevelt's wife was also named Edith. Sandy wrote about the Edith and Edith."

"Did you notice that nearing the bicycles reminded you of Mrs. Wilson and Mrs. Roosevelt? Is that a clue or a hunch?"

"Clue, because I knew the connection. Not like the big hermit where we don't yet see the connection." The girls started for home on their bikes.

Hi hopped over the stile.

Miah held tighter to Virginia Louise and stood up to the fence stile where he passed Virginia Louise across to Hi's shoulders. They heard the girls, their voices growing faint in the distance. "Miah, do you suddenly think we've taken the long way home?" His head nodded longingly after the girls.

Miah reached up to catch hold of Virginia Louise. "Sweet little cousin, we're going to let you walk for a while. She held alternately to a hand of Miah and Hi along Peach Road.

Virginia Louise began pulling away from Hi as they neared the Platt driveway. When well into the driveway, he released her. She ran ahead. They saw her dart into the garage.

When the cousins arrived they saw her proudly pushing the baby buggy around. And as they neared the buggy, she began to point out her treasure collection.

"Hi, why'd we restore that thing?" He looked with pleasure at his tiny cousin and the buggy.

"Why, Cuzz, I'd say for Grandma and Aunt Edith and, er, no, just wait. For her, that's why we did it." He moved over to touch his sister's golden hair and he pat her on the shoulder. "Let's put it in the car, Sis. Let's take it home. It's yours."

The black and white rolled from the yard with Miah's well worn clandestine issue of Penthouse snuggled under the floor mat in the trunk. Hi sat in the rear seat, the seat nearest that thrilling issue. Three-year-old Virginia Louise was also in the rear seat jumping around near her big brother. As well, her brother had said, she was riding as close as she could be to her baby carriage.

* * *

While the powerful Plymouth black and white cruiser purred north with the Del Platt family the big white camper continued its cruise to the south. Del thought about talking about that Kentucky mission while he drove toward home, but didn't get around to the topic before turning into their driveway at Ellington. Continuing south, the others with the camper arrived in Paris, Kentucky near dusk where they pulled in at a filling station.

The camper drank fuel enough to have the station owner believe his name'd transformed to Rockefeller. He folded their stiff green bills into his pocket. "Sure, why heck yes. Plenty of room to the side there after I pull away that old truck. He eyed the women while talking with Jack.

"I'll help with that move," Jack Trip said. "I can steer the truck. Do the brakes work?"

"Emergency does. I'll go slow. Fellow gave me the truck so I keep it for parts. One don't know but someday somebody with an old Ford may need a part or two. It'll be just as handy out back. I'll tear a little at first out back as I must keep ahead of ya going down a hill."

"Wait for my signal before you tear ahead. I'll want to be sure I'm in low gear."

The old Ford was chained to an aged GMC and the move started.

Suddenly –

"Jeepers!" Jack yelled as the GMC disappeared.

The Ford tore ahead like a rocket with Jack stomping the useless brake, prying the emergency handle and grinding gears trying to achieve a low enough gear to stop the juggernaut. That 'down hill' the guy had mentioned was a virtual cliff! Despite all his frantic moves, the Ford threatened to overtake the grinding, hollowing GMC. Mr. Rockefeller poured on the coal. He crossed a lawn then tore toward the tree line growing huge ahead.

At the last second he veered the GMC out of Jack's line of charge. The Ford cleaved on past, snapping the chain free and sending Jack several yards into the woods where the Ford came to decorate a tree.

In a daze, Jack made his way out of the woods to find Old Rockefeller sitting behind his steering wheel. "Good place for that darned old truck. Climb in."

Before climbing in Jack looked ahead to the precipice they'd just hurdled. Can't climb that, he thought. Gingerly he climbed into the GMC. "How?"

"Four-wheel drive. This is our raccoon hunting truck. It'll climb anything."

He put the willing beast to the hill and poured on coal. All disappeared ahead but the rosy clouded evening sky. They were headed for the moon when suddenly the powerful old beast slammed down onto the level station apron. "Told you, by gosh." He slapped his knee. "She'll climb anything."

"I'm a believer," Jack said as Harold joined the two and they headed toward the door of the establishment; which they now decided was a gasoline station/general store. Jack asked as they stepped inside the place, "Now which way from here is the post office?"

"Down a block on this side. Opens at nine." The man wasn't looking at Jack and Harold as he spoke.

"And a restaurant?" The man was busy ogling Clydis and Edith; as they could see.

He said over his shoulder, "I got eats for sale all right."

"Good." Jack wondered how they could use the man's obvious proclivity to wantonly admire ladies to their advantage. A quick glance across told him Clydis and Edith were thinking in concert; and Harold sent Jack a subtle wink. "Say, do you have a checkerboard located by a potbelly?"

"Sure. Come over after while." His feet were prancing. "Bring them others. Good looking women, they are."

"All taken for life, I'm afraid."

"No need to clean up then." But all of the group could see that he hadn't given up his notion regarding the 'good lookers'. "You all come when you want." The man seemed to be wringing his hands.

Jack and Harold grinned at seeing him dart for a rear room, likely his living quarters, just after they left the station/general store. They grinned, guessing that he was to, indeed, 'clean up.'

Jack and Harold came over to the gasoline station/general store after wolfing down a couple of sandwiches and a healthy swig of sugary iced tea and took a seat on a backless kitchen chair, one to each side of a barrel, the barrel topped by a crude square section of plywood. A sign, 'Crackers 10 cents,' was printed on the barrel and a well worn checkerboard sat atop the section of plywood. "I'm called General, by the way," the man said. "After general store, get it?" General had changed his shirt and slicked his hair.

"Got it. Now, well, General, after this first game, you're welcome to play me, the winner," Harold said.

General didn't turn from where he was peering out the front window. "Those women coming over?" He glanced, hopefully, over at the checker players. He spoke back at the window. "Why, I got cards, too, and dominoes. Even could light up that potbelly."

The checker players seemed to pay him no mind. "Well, I'll light the potbelly." He banged at the potbelly's lighting. "You tell them ladies I had a potbelly, did you? It'll be nice and warm."

"They might be back. They need to go to find a public telephone."

He rubbed his hands together. "Oh, say, now I got a phone. No charge for local."

"It'd be a couple of long distance."

"The phone's back there. I'd show um but I wouldn't listen. They can shut the door and I'd be out here with you. I got an oil stove back in there; nice and warm. Gets chilly here nights."

A glance told the checker players that General was near to panting. "I'll go tell them," Harold said, but he stayed tight to the checkers. "King me, by golly." He said over his shoulder, "General, get ready to play. I'll be but a minute here."

Jack was ready to get the show on the road. "Go now, darn it. I concede, and he's ready now."

"I'd rather an undisputable championship, but as you imply, the time is nigh."

At the camper, Harold said, "He's panting. It'd be dominoes or cards."

"We'd vex him more with cards."

The three entered the station/general store. "My, it is nicely warmed in here. You keep a fine store, kind sir. May we use a telephone?"

He pranced around like ants were at him. "This way. I keep it in my living quarters."

In a moment, General emerged. The men saw the door close behind him, and they saw him flinch at the firm sound of the door's closing. "Have a seat here, General. I'm all warmed up now."

He hesitated; the seat would place his back to the door that had just firmly closed. "Say," he said, "I'd prefer the other seat. "Easier to watch for customers what with that mirror on the far wall back there."

"Sure." Harold took Jack's seat. Jack began a casual survey of the store's commodities and prices.

General had a cackling style of laughter. Despite his bore at the closed door to his quarters, he was winning (through no obvious effort of his own). Finally the door opened and the ladies entered the room.

"We reached both Wayne and Dewy John down at London. The men knew that Wayne was Sheriff Wayne back at Manitou Prairie and that

Dewy John was most likely a police chief or a sheriff down at London. "We had a good visit," Edith said, "and Dewy John even said 'yes, some time ago,' when I asked if any Yeti, or similar creature'd been reported in his area."

"Sounds like we're on a correct course," Harold said.

"How about a game of rummy," Jack said. "General has it nice and warm in here." He spoke just as General slapped his kinged black over a half dozen of Harold's haplessly placed reds.

"I'd say the General's ready for cards." Harold beamed over at the ladies. General thinned himself as he stood from the checkers. "Rummy's fine; or there's poker."

Clydis poked her chin. "Poker, I'm not good at."

"Golly, me either," Edith said. "We've nothing to bet anyway."

"Oh, no problem. Match sticks, even. No problem. A friendly game. I'll show you."

Harold said, "Jack, then will it be rummy for us?"

"Rummy, you bet." He took a deck of cards from the counter and carried them over to the plywood table top.

Chapter Thirteen

IT WASN'T LONG BEFORE GENERAL casually mentioned, and in a voice so low Jack and Harold barely heard, that playing for match sticks was dull. "You've learned fast," he kept his voice low. "We could bet items of clothing if you care."

"Huh?" Clydis rapped her knuckles across General's nose."

He reared back. The rap wasn't hard enough to bloody his beak yet General stayed far into his chair and he looked puckered to cry. He pleaded in a loud whisper, "But two against one and you're good players and we'd stop the game whenever anyone wanted it stopped."

"That Ford truck was your truck."

"Huh, why, what?" He held his nose, peered at Clydis.

"There's an ordinance here inside the town limits that one can't keep an old disabled heap parked in the yard."

He rubbed his nose. "Don't matter to me."

"You can keep up to three of such vehicles at a place of business that does automotive repairs. So you dragged that old heap here."

"Yeah, for parts, so what?" His frown was now cutting deeply into his forehead. "Who are youins, anyhow?

"We want to play poker, to learn about it from an expert as you seem to be, but you've been dishonest about the old Ford truck so how can we trust you at this poker game; this clothing game, I mean?"

"Oh, I won't cheat and stop whenever we want."

"That was your truck," Edith said. "We know about city governmental regulations so we'll likely know whenever you're lying, but at cards we may not know that, so I'd rather not play." Edith began to rise up from her seat.

Clydis pushed back as well. "Me neither. I've changed my mind."

"Wait. I'll be honest, really."

They sat back down. "We want to know you better. Where do you hunt raccoons?" Clydis reached his shirt sleeve over a bicep. "I maybe would like to go with you to learn about hunting such wily creatures or even some bigger, more dangerous ones." She held to his sleeve. "Are there Sesquatch out there?"

General looked to be nearly in tears. He'd hoped so dearly for the card game. "Well, I hunt about anything but prefer raccoons. Sasq . . . What was that?" He plowed his palm across his forehead. "Uh, well by gummy, Dicey Robert was with his pa and they saw one if it's what I think you mean."

"Big Foot, or Yeti, she means," Edith explained. "The Abominable Snowman; or you may know it as Big Foot."

"Oh, sure," he looked relieved. They, at least, he guessed, were staying. "Dicey Robert and his pa didn't have any gun handy so they stood still as a stump and the thing went on off down a cut. We went back there, Pap and Dicey Robert and his pa and me. We heard um, but never got a shot."

"Lately, or say a time ago, say when you were a boy; back when you first began coon hunting? Was that when? What were Dicey Robert and his pa doing? Were they working a still?"

"The still's not there no more but Dicey Robert said the thing broke up the place and it carried off some jugs of moon."

"I'd bet you weren't scared of Big Foot; were the others?"

"Why, no; not with twelve gauge. We carried twelves when we went in to look."

"We want to go and see where Dicey Robert and his pa saw that Big Foot and where you heard the Big Foot. Get the other coon hunters rounded up. They're to come, too, and also Dicey Robert and his pa."

"His pa died last winter; pneumonia."

"We want to see Dicey Robert anyway."

"Yes, we do. So, General, we've only time for a quick hand of poker because we'll get up before daybreak to go with you fellows and try to scare up Big Foot."

"Sure." He grabbed the cards, shuffled, and dealt furiously. "We can ante such as socks and such," he explained. "I'll ante my right sock."

"Hey, this is kind of fun." Edith anted a shoe and Clydis stood partly up from her chair and sucked in her tummy and thrust out her chest while removing her belt; which she anted.

General's eyes nearly bugged from his head!

The bugging soon turned to a squint. In mere minutes the ladies had him shivering, his naked torso jiggling whitely, his hair mussed into Appalachian facsimile. "We'll be over to get you up sometime near morning. You and your pards and Dicey Robert bring your twelve gauges. We hunt with revolvers."

"Huh? Er, sure." His hands plowed his Appalachian peaks into landslides. "Who are youins?"

Clydis flipped her deputy sheriff's badge from a blouse pocket. Her move bugged his eyes and returned deep furrows to his brow. "Deputy Sheriff Clydis Groner," she introduced. "We're all deputy sheriffs from Michigan. We're going to forget about the old Ford truck and about your advance upon my daughter and me, but you'd better be bushy-eyed and squirrel-tailed to go Big Foot hunting in the night; and I mean this very night, and I mean you and your pards and we sure do mean Dicey Robert, too."

"And tell your pards we're not after shiners. None of you nor Dicey Robert needs to worry. That moonshine work's disgusting to us when there's Big Foot to hunt."

At three in the morning four battered trucks and a converted hearse boiled from the station/general store and poured down the highway toward Red Horse, a small town located south of Lexington. Edith drove the ancient hearse with Clydis, Harold, and Jack aboard. Harold occupied the jump seat and served as navigator although he didn't know the route. It was, however, no chore to keep tight up behind the others. Barreling along in the GMC, General led the pack to his turn-off into a labyrinthine mire of two-track trails, hills, curves, mud slides, and brush, finally landing them in a clearing. The vehicles stubbed their tails together, aiming their headlights into the primeval forest gloom. "We wait here," General said, "until somebody hears one and snaps his lights back on."

Quiet settled over the scene.

In the trucks the husky Big Foot adventurers were tilting fruit jars of lightening.

In the hearse the deputy sheriffs, one then all, fell soundly asleep.

On the hood of one truck white elephants danced, signaling a bearded hunter to rouse up and blare his truck horn and switch on his high beams.

Instantly, the other trucks roused to that same fevered pitch, transforming the forest into a starkly glaring nightmare into which not a creature stirred. The deputy sheriffs piled out of the hearse. Deputies Jack Trip and Clydis Groner wore gun belts, his with a pair of western-style colts, and hers was a pearl-handled thirty-eight special. Edith and Harold carried note books. The Michigan deputies made a careful scan of the starkly lighted forest – and saw nothing but trees.

The deputy sheriffs, in pairs, each with a gleaming badge displayed and with a notebook ready to record comments, and with one in each pair armed, began a visit to each truck. "Kind sirs, please tell me just what you saw or heard that night. The truth now; you're to tell me about old Big Foot."

Behind the wheel of a rusted Chevy four by four, Dicey Robert sat with a half filled pint of shine; the other half of the pint was in him and wanting out. Dicey Robert belched grandly just as Edith and Harold appeared at the truck's open window. "Dicey Robert, you are the hero here. General implied you're a brave cuss. I wish you'd have got a shot at that Big Foot."

"I was a boy then but I'd have when I saw it but it scared us some, smashing things, and so we couldn't reach our twelves. Pa sure was mad. He turned to his partner seated in the passenger seat. "Recall all that, Phil John?"

Phil John brought his chin up off his chest. "Yep, cousin sure was mad, all right, what with it breakin' up stuff and stealin'.'"

"It was in the daytime, I take it, and a run was just finished."

"Yep, we was jugging it."

"Good thing you know your moon business. Making daytime runs, I mean, so nobody sees your fire. Work all day in the heat then a monster comes and buds in. Dicey Robert, I see why your pa and you were ticked."

"Phil John, recall what Dicey Robert's pa said about what it looked like, and what it sounded like. Now, Dicey Robert, you listen to see if it sounds like what you saw and heard."

"Red hair and maybe eight feet tall and strong. Threw a half full barrel right into the worm and ruined it. Ran off with two gallon jugs tied together with rope."

"Gosh All Mighty! Dicey Robert, did it tie that rope, do you mean?"

"Pa did. We tied jugs together for transport so then at home we dumped moon into pints."

"Knew your business, sure. It just took two jugs then, huh?"

"Uh, yep."

"How was it carried, er, in one hand or, say, over a shoulder?"

"Shoulder. Like pa always carried."

"It carried like a man then?"

"Er, well, uh, yep."

"Carried anything else, say, in its hands?"

"Big stick and a dead animal in a hand; waved that other hand like when it was hurrying away."

"Running?"

"Yep, real fast. Dived for our twelves, but it was gone."

"Wearing any clothes?"

"Huh?"

"Big Foot. We'd heard that some of them try to wear people's clothes."

"Naw, now I don't recall so."

"Sure wish we could have seen one this night. I praise God if you got that still fixed and went back to making a living, Dicey Robert. You are a good guy, and thank you for the help. You, too, Phil John. You've both been real straight about all of this."

Deputies Clydis and Jack with two hunters approached Dicey Robert's rusted Chevy four by four just at that time. "About ready to take off," Jack said. "General's to open his store and station and others gotta eat and get to jobs. General here recalls when Murray Don gave out a holler sounding like old Big Foot."

Murray Don stood beaming. General moved away from Murray Don and over toward Deputy Clydis.

Edith said, "Let her go, Murray Don," and old Murray Don let out a whooping holler that shook the tree limbs, and right in with that holler General let out a howl like as if he were peppered by rock salt!

In the next instant Jack had General pinned to the hood of Dicey Robert's rusted Chevy four by four and he clicked hand cuffs onto that whimpering General. The rest of you can go," Jack said. "And thanks. And we won't never say a word about nothing but that you helped us try to get a look at, or a sound of, or a shot at old Big Foot, you all hear? So go on now to your business, and thank you once more."

He yanked General away from Dicey Robert's truck hood. "You're going to have a hand cuffed to the roof rack of your GMC. I'll drive."

"But, I didn't —"

"You did."

"Just scared so I bumped against when Murray Don hollered."

"Deputy Clydis?"

"Molesting! Throw the book at him!"

Back at the gasoline station/general store Harold ran the business while the others loaded the rig in preparation for departure. General sat with a leg cuffed to a leg of the potbelly. The group was soon ready to depart. General looked at them with bugged eyes and a furrowed forehead. Clydis walked over to General and unlocked the cuffs. "You touch me and I'll bash you to a pulp."

His whimper was genuine.

"I'm letting you go only because there's not time to fool with you because we must stay on the trail of Big Foot."

As the big white camper pulled away they caught a glimpse of him. Still seated, he was, on the floor near the potbelly.

"A big stick and a dead animal in one hand," Edith said. "Recall that we found arrows in the hermit shack but didn't find the bow. That could have been a bow and a homemade quiver of arrows he carried."

"My thought, too," Jack said.

"And still no mention of Roy. I'm in a worry about Roy."

"Me too, and all of us. And, well, I have a thought, too, about what to do when we get to Raccoon Mountain," Harold said. "It's like Deputy Clydis cautioned about before we left home, to wait till we get here to see about what to do about the camper so's it wouldn't be scratched. So, I'd rather we didn't go to the local law officers first. Better that we approached our quarry without them. It's only us that know what we want to know about. Specific queries, I mean, not the usual interrogation."

"Right on. And on the telephone with Dewy John, I couldn't say exactly when we'd arrive there; said we'd been running into needed information from time to time on our way down so it may take us a while."

"Good, so let's get on with the camper as far as we can; then plan to walk on in."

"Yes, and let's make frequent stops. Try to pick up more Big Foot stories and find out the way onto Raccoon Mountain and on into the Margie Marlin Sweeney place."

* * *

It'd been several days since Mr. Istir sprayed the weeds, grass, and brush along the perimeter fences at the Lakeside cemetery. His mind on the recent visit of Hi and his family, Miah zinged around the grave markers with a gasoline-powered weed whacker. He was making noise enough even to drown out Mr. Istir who was mowing nearby with his thirty-eight inch deck Simplicity. Thinking of Hi led Miah's thoughts to review the pages of Penthouse, the clandestine magazine he'd passed on to his cousin. His thoughts were such that a quiet grin softened his face as he trimmed around the markers. Suddenly his grin transformed to a gape and a, "Huh? What the?" His trimmer line'd tangled into an obstruction. "What the – well, I'll be!" Never before had his line tangled into a perimeter fence.

He turned off the trimmer and pulled out his jackknife to cut the line free. "Well, I'll be."

Mr. Istir had said that spraying may enable them to hunt thoroughly along the fences for more parts to grave stones. "We may find that real slanted stone yet this summer." The stone with such an obvious break had vexed them because it should be easy to find but wasn't.

Miah now saw that weeds, grass, and shrubs were indeed beginning to die. "Well, I'll be." He began pushing about the rank growth along the fence, looking earnestly for that particular section of a broken grave stone. Before a minute had passed, Mr. Istir was right in there beside him, both in pursuit of that wily stone.

They made along the fence like bulldozers leaving not a single fragment of vegetation unturned. Finally they were soaked in sweat and so tired that Mr. Istir plopped to the ground, and with Miah right beside him. "No luck."

"I just don't understand it."

"Well, we've found quite a few, anyway, so tomorrow let's glue more of them back together." All along the fences there now laid a scatter of the found stone fragments. "There's glue left, I take it."

Miah sighed, "Yes, sure, Mr. Istir, the baby carriage we restored took very little glue. I'll bring the glue tomorrow."

"Miah, I just don't understand where that obvious chunk is." Mr. Istir caught his breath. "Where next can we look?"

"I think we should dig out the dump." Over many years old flowers, flower holders, and other debris had been dumped in a far corner of the cemetery. Miah looked worried, having thought of the dump and caught a vision of the task he'd described.

Mr. Istir moaned, "Naw, now we aren't a-going to. Too much to do. At least now we'll get more stones restored before the glue gets all stiffened and useless. That's why I decided to spray; to get full use of the glue before it gets all hard in the can." He rubbed across the top of his sweaty, thinly haired head. He flapped his battered Detroit baseball cap back on and creaked to his feet. "Now we've done good, Miah. We really have. I'll see you tomorrow."

They both knew that avoiding the cemetery dump for the time being was only to put off the task until later. Miah shuddered as he mounted his Schwinn.

He coasted into the yard at home and dragged himself from his Schwinn. Old Sniffer walked up to him and licked his hand. Miah dropped to the lawn and hugged and patted Old Sniffer in appreciation. Cia sat down on the grass beside her brother. Her hand came to rest on Old Sniffer. She ruffled his fur, saying, "Dad and Nic are away this afternoon to take a colleague of Dad's to Detroit airport. Sandy and Candy are coming for supper. Omi and I are trying to cook mac and cheese, and mushroom green beans with French onions. How about garlic toast to go with? Can you make it?"

"Yes, easier than I've been through today. We looked and looked but never did find that chunk of grave marker we sought. It's sure a puzzle."

"Their mom's coming, too, to look around some more at the hermit shack. Sandy and Candy had a hunch about it the other day. They're trying to act like a sheriff detective like their mom. She's training to be a real detective sergeant. Detectives play their hunches, Candy said, and the girls want to play their hunches with their mom."

"With better luck than the hunch Mr. Istir and I had, I hope. It's really tough when one's hunches don't play out, I'll tell you. Why, we sure didn't find that missing grave stone piece along the perimeter fence." He mussed his hair. "I'll say it's tough."

"Well come on. It's getting near time Mom'll be home from work. Dad, Nic, the Gillespies, they're all due here right soon."

Supper went very well; each dish was relished until all dishes were emptied. Omi, Cia, and Miah were sitting proud and content. The experience had revitalized Miah and he pranced as the group prepared to leave for the hermit shack. Nathan carried a few fold-out camp stools under one arm as they set out.

It was acceptable by then to walk out through Mrs. Woods' yard to skirt the barber chair dump and to enter the hermits' old route to the shack. They'd enter that old hermit route at the end of the pines and mere yards from a view of the concrete 'bathroom'. On the way up Mrs. Woods' driveway, the larger group began to fragment, the youngsters easily outdistancing the adults, but near the head of the driveway a third group cleaved from the first. Candy and Miah had drifted back to form a group of their own.

It had happened so smoothly that Miah's heart didn't begin its race until he found himself indeed alone with her. She'd begun a casual conversation with him as the group climbed the driveway, a conversation about his work, about how his day had been, and his steps had slowed to match hers and so that away from the others he could hear her better. It had all been soooo smooth!

He'd not felt his heart in his chest before.

She'd not felt so giddy before.

Both being glad, they stayed together, the pair getting a grin from Mrs. Woods. The pair was as well getting smiles from Luisa and Nathan Platt and from Mrs. Fanny Gillespie who followed some paces behind them; that group even slowing their steps to give space to the birds and bees.

Throughout the group's fragmenting Old Sniffer had kept his loyalty to young Nic of the lead group. Nic walked close to Sandy Gillespie and Sandy's mind began a review of that previous visit; that visit where she'd expressed her thought: 'I wonder why Old Sniffer's digging got me to thinking about the hermit.' "A particular hermit," she now said aloud.

"Huh?" Nic said.

"Wait, you guys," Sandy cautioned, "we'd better tie old Sniffer lest he dig again under the humper."

"Sure," Omi said. "Cia, run ahead to get the yellow cordoning ribbon we used before." Cia ran on ahead.

Suddenly Old Sniffer bee lined from beside Nic. "Get him! Get him!" They knew he was on a dash for the humper. "Get him! Cia, hurry!"

"Sniffer, get back here!"

Already dirt was flying out from between the legs of Old Sniffer. Miah and Candy rushed into the scene. "Sniffer, No!"

Miah dragged him back. Candy knelt beside him and held him, her eyes in a search for Cia. "Cia, hurry with the ribbon!"

"What's the problem?" Luisa asked as she, Nathan, and Fanny Gillespie entered the arena. "Is he into trouble?"

"It's his reddish fur," Candy said, "here on his neck where he'd rubbed away his old fur. On our last visit the reddish color reminded me of the hermit at the same time that the humper reminded Sandy of the hermit. Our hunch is that the two reminders are related to the same hunch. Mom, what do you think?"

"I'm sure they're related," Deputy Fanny agreed with her daughters, "but we'll need to mull them over before we'll learn what they add up to." She unfolded a camp stool. "I'll just rest here a while." Cia rushed in with the ribbon and promptly Old Sniffer was tied.

Their curiosity tweaked, Luisa and Nathan began to poke around in the excavation dug by Old Sniffer. "It's no problem," Luisa said, "there's no yuck here." She reached to snap a small root that projected into the hole. "Just rock, dirt, and roots here."

"It'll please the kids to keep him tied while we mull over their hunches," Deputy Gillespie said, "even as we know there wouldn't be any recognizable excrement in that old humper after so many years."

The kids meandered off to explore. The adults were thrilled that Candy stuck with Miah as they entered the concrete building that was formerly thought to be the bathroom. Fanny's voice held a whimsical tone when softly she said, "Funny, isn't it how things work out?"

Luisa pushed litter away around and ahead of Sniffer's dig. A solid object appeared at the edge of his hole. "What the heck is this?" she said. "It hurts my hands to try and move it."

"Rock, I guess. Let me see." Nathan dug to get his fingers under the edge of the rock. The rock pulled free. "Huh? You wouldn't have guessed that it'd have squared edges?" He sat the rock aside.

"Surprising object to find in the hermits' presumed bathroom," Luisa said.

Luisa and Nathan sat on camp stools near Fanny. It was peaceful in the woods and they took to idle chatting. Their children's excited voices served as background to their friendly chat until – "Edges! Squared!" Luisa jumped to her feet. The odd shaped heavy stone slipped in her aching hands. "Nathan, help." He reached to take the clumsy thing from his petite wife.

"Here. I have it."

"Nathan, look at it!" She ran toward where they'd seen Candy and Miah headed. "Miah! Candy! Miah, hurry! Come and see! We, Old Sniffer, found it!"

Miah slid to a stop next to the oddly shaped stone. At once he knew. "That's it," he breathed. "That's that chunk of grave marker that Mr. Istir and I've been hunting."

"Candy, call Sandy, playing your hunches really paid off."

Chapter Fourteen

Their first stop that next day in the big white camper was in Winchester where Jack had spotted a public telephone booth. Jack and Harold started to drive on down toward a store/restaurant displaying a hamburger sign and advertising country smoked ham and RC Cola.

"Hey, wait!"

"Come back."

"This phone doesn't work."

They climbed back into the camper and rode down to the restaurant.

"Nice outfit," a chubby man said. "You been to Alaska? Could've told you that telephone yonder don't work. Fellow got mad and yanked the wire off. Company isn't here yet though it's been days now. Alaska, you say?"

"Decorated like Alaska, all right," Jack said. "Friend of ours lived in Alaska years ago. Now he and his wife travel to there a lot. We've borrowed it for a Kentucky vacation."

"We want to travel some back roads now that we're here," Edith said. "We're collecting any stories we can about Big Foot. One was seen, they say around here some twenty years or so ago. Did you know it?"

"Why, yeah, come to think on it, there was. Folks couldn't agree it was a Big Foot though. Some say it was, but others doubt that such a creature would drink."

"Oh, liquor, do you mean, or wine?"

"Yep. Store sold liquor and wine also beer down the way a piece from here. In the night their guard dog was killed. Stabbed. They didn't find what stabbed him. Dead was a prime German Shepard, you'd just know it would be. Some suggested by an arrow that went clean through and nicked and left a spatter of blood on a table leg, but nobody saw any actual arrow. Clevis William Cars, my cousin, owned that store and he owned it wasn't no Big Foot seeing's it filled a basket with wine bottles and took off. Cousin said that's too smart to be no Big Foot but others saw that huge hairy creature toting that very basket and they sure agreed it was Big Foot as no man was like it; tall, wide, hairy, I mean."

"Does sound like a smarter than thought before of Big Foot, I'd agree. Kind, sir, I need to use your telephone. I'll leave money because some calls will be long distance."

"Sure."

"You saw it, did you?"

"Naw, just my cousin told me about it."

"I see." She turned to Harold. "Harold, order a hamburger with everything for me and an RC; same for Momma. Jack, find out where the police or sheriff's is located. Momma, you come and listen in with me."

Wanting family news first, Edith dialed the Platt number at Manitou Prairie.

"Hello, Luisa here."

"Luisa, how is everyone? We are fine. We've been uncovering numerous stories of a Yeti, or Big Foot, down this way from Indiana to down here in Kentucky. We think it is more likely Larry, the giant hermit that was seen along our route to here, but about twenty years ago. We –"

"Us, too," Luisa interrupted. "We've hermit news. Old Sniffer helped us find that broken grave marker that Miah and Mr. Istir have been looking for. You couldn't have guessed that we found it in the big hermit's humper."

"Humper? Really, right where Old Sniffer's been insistently digging?"

"Yes, right about on top of the ground but it was covered by duff. It wasn't buried deep. The dog would've run into it had we let him at his digging. Deputy Gillespie was with us. She's letting us keep it and to clean it up but not to loose track of it, to know at all times where it's at because it may be evidence."

"She's going to be a mighty fine sergeant detective. By all means keep an eye on it. There's evidence here that Larry, that huge hermit, is the creature folks are calling Big Foot, and he's shown signs of violence. We're worried about Roy, the smaller hermit. The only signs we've found along the way point to Larry and Larry alone, never to Roy. We are nearly to the Sweeney place. We may just find out about Roy there. He may even have been there along with Larry."

"I certainly hope so. We are all fine here. Del called here last night from his home at Ellington. That was after we'd found the chunk of grave marker. He said the local deputies said he couldn't drive around in that sheriff's cruiser. Del wanted Fanny's number, hoping she'd help clear up the matter for him."

"I hope so on that. I wonder what the beef is, anyway."

"Fanny said Sheriff Puller will call Bertram Benson, the Leadford town marshal and he's also a sheriff's deputy, you may know, to inform him that Del is on a secret special assignment, but the details can't be revealed just yet."

"Oh, that's cute. Good of him to help Del's parading. Well, Luisa, we just called to touch bases. A so called Big Foot raided here and a watch dog was killed, some believe by an arrow, and a supply of wine was carried away in a wicker basket. Other similar stories along the way have us thinking we're dealing with Larry. Keep good track of the stone. Also, Luisa, we'll ask Sheriff Puller to collect those arrows in the hermit shack as evidence."

"Sure thing, Aunt Edith, "and you should hear about little Virginia Louise. She's so proud to have that baby buggy. Dosia and I are just thrilled, believing we're getting a look into your antics when you were tiny. Oh, so cute."

Grandma Clydis interrupted, "Cute, cute, cute little dickens, I called Edith back in those days."

"That phrase fits perfectly. Nathan's summer classes are done next week then we'll drive up to visit them; may even drive that big cruiser back to here, Nathan said."

"Did he and John decide on the meaning of soul, the soul in a religious sense; that is what soul originally meant, what it met in the first place before many additional meanings were attached to it?"

"He says, no, but they're close."

The ladies rang off then Edith phoned Sheriff Wayne Puller to bring him up to date. "Good idea going directly there," Wayne said. "Report in to Dewy John later. I talked with Dewy John, joking about not wanting to get a scratch on Helio's new camper. He said that Hal Sweeney is a trucker, an eighteen wheeler and drives his truck home and parks it in his yard between runs. Jack should have no trouble driving right on in to there. I didn't tell Dewy John just when you'd get there so that way we can do as you see is best. Going right on in there and surprising the Sweeney's and Marlin's unannounced sounds best to me."

Edith's call to the local police chief, Chief Bubba Benny, set up the group's look at the local Big Foot report of more than twenty years ago. Bubba was quite surprised, "You'll studying history, are you?"

"Really does sound like that, doesn't it, Chief? Ha-ha. But we're trying to assemble a story that extends from Michigan to Kentucky by way of Indiana and Ohio. All the way it looks like that Big Foot may have actually been a man. Our evidence may close many yet open cases. That's our hope."

"Well, I'll dig that report out for you; have it in an hour or so. But say now I'll bet you are correct. I do recall something about a bow and arrow used here in town. No evidence to prove that, but my cousin, he's dead now, but his nephew runs the place, well his uncle told of arrows stolen from a hunter's supply store down there in Richmond. The same story, actually in that some saw a Big Foot right down town in the night that night. Of course they were drunk, yet who knows what they did see. I'll have Chief Willis there, he's my cousin, pull that report for you to read if you stop in at Richmond."

"Gee, thanks, Chief. We'll eat some hamburgers here at this good place then come on down to you."

"Michigan, you don't say." They were at a sporting goods store in Richmond, Kentucky talking to an aged gent who'd worked in the store ever since boyhood. "I know your state right well. Why, Stubby Overmire was my favorite Detroit Tiger back in 1943. I saw him play a time or two when I'd go by train up to visit Grandma Luella Jean. Yep, this was the store broken in that time. A window was broken and arrows taken and a whole box of twelve boxes of Smith Brothers cough drops. Those black ones, you know. We still carry the Smiths because they may be the oldest kind of cough drop and we carry other patent remedies, too, as hunters are out in the cold at times or they eat too much or some drink so we sell

Alka Seltzer and Pepto and such. Good business here and only broken into just that once when I was little more then a boy."

"A Big Foot, we heard. Did you see it?"

"No, that was Deputy Calvin Lights that said he did, saw a big hairy creature but Calvin he died some fifteen years back, sorry."

"Well, your telling it is near as good as Deputy Lights telling it so we thank you a lot, kind sir."

On their way again, Jack announced, "There's more of those old signs."

"Yes, look ahead on our right, you two." Edith and Jack were referring to ancient Rambler automobile signs, the signs displayed in a manner reminding one of modern Burma Shave signs. Early in the century the Rambler automobile company set out signs, each sign an advertisement for Rambler but to enhance longevity of the signs, each sign stated direction and distance to a given town and/or to services available at that place. The signs had out lasted even the original Rambler cars and were a blessing as the adventurers moved along the back way in the big white camper. According to that Rambler sign, Berea's about two miles ahead," Jack said.

At the grocery in Berea Clydis ordered Bisquick, and patted her own back as she did. "Edith ran out of Bisquick yesterday," Clydis declared, "and we would've been stumped had I reached for it today as our biscuit supply is diminished.

"Now, Momma, Bisquick would be on my list as well. I've used it insistently since it was invented back when Delbert was a babe. I can't recall any other baking ready mix product before it or any product since that's been any better."

"Aunt Jemima may have been first," Clydis said, "but that's just pancakes, I'm sure. There's none better than Bisquick for biscuits."

"I'm wondering how you can sound like Yankees talking yet talking about the number one food in these parts," the store clerk said. "Why, folks here couldn't go a day without biscuits."

"We either; and do you prefer cut or drop biscuits?"

"Haven't heard of dropped. Indeed, you must actually be Yankees."

"Dropped is my daughter Edith's specialty. Instead of rolling out, she drops spoonfuls on the baking sheet; resulting in an entirely different treat even from the same mix as cut."

"Why, I'll sure try that some time. Do youins add a spate of extra shortening?"

"Oh, my yes. I cut in oleomargarine galore."

"Me too. I wonder that biscuit making hasn't by now healed our wounds from the Civil War."

"Well, unfortunately moonshine has also helped to heal from that war; lot of shining done up north now as well as here. That got started during prohibition when a lot of alcoholic beverage entered Michigan from Canada. Canada manufactured only export liquor and Michigan getting it illegally whetted some appetites for illicit drink. So we've had stills to this day. All of us here are deputy sheriffs from Michigan. I just hate it back up home when we've been obliged to bust up a still."

"Gee, well, I'd guess you'd have to."

"Moderation is not harmful but the busting up results every time from somebody who went way beyond moderation and became down right obnoxious."

"Like here it's the same."

"I'd not wonder that." She passed her list across to the clerk. "Could my daughter go around and try getting these items? It'd save you a walk and we've need to ask you some questions while we're here."

"Uh, sure." The clerk's forehead had instantly furrowed. "What?"

"Oh, not about you. You're alright, wonderful actually. We've stopped in here to buy staples as it was handy to settle both our needs; that is to buy supplies and to ask about Big Foot. We'd heard about a Big Foot raiding this very store back about when you were just a child. Do you recall any of that trouble? We've been investigating Big Foot reports from Michigan, Indiana, Ohio, and now here in Kentucky."

"It was awful here. My folks kept all the newspaper clippings. I'll get them for you."

Clydis and Jack sat down to read the clips while Harold and Edith completed the shopping.

The clips told of a Berea man found dead in his grocery. His skull was crushed by a slam against a door frame, his injuries were a dead ringer to the damage done to the person they'd exhumed back in Michigan. Their eyes followed around the store. "Whew," Jack murmured, "all that just for some tubes of lunchmeat taken and a ten pound chunk of cheddar cheese."

"Gosh, what monster are we dealing with?"

* * *

In the late afternoon the white camper rolled in at the tiny town of East Bernstadt, located just short of the outskirts of London. Their arrival was too late that day to pull in at the Sweeney's. A roadside stand was positioned nearby. They decided to eat there of whatever was available from the camper refrigerators as supplemented by fresh produce. Soon they were munching melon and peaches, and in the company of the proprietors. "Just picked today," Harold expounded, "my, one can sure taste a difference, all right."

"Just the two of you to raise all of this, huh?"

"And nine youngins all totaled, but two are too young and three have married and moved into London. In London two've gone into factory work and one's a mail carrier. There's enough work for the rest of us, all right. We can call our oldest, Jeff Alan, for you. He delivers mail all through the area around Raccoon Mountain. Actually he sees about everyone in a whole big chunk of the Daniel Boone National Forest every day. He can draw you a right accurate map to where to camp tonight and where to go tomorrow to find your folks."

"We check in with home base about every day. We'll pay you amply for the use of a telephone to make two long distance calls."

"Happy to oblige."

She called Sheriff Puller and then dialed the Platt home at Manitou Prairie. Miah answered the telephone: "Hello, Platt residence."

"Miah."

"Oh hi, Grandma Clydis. What's new?"

"Miah, I just talked with Sheriff Puller. He told me that Deputy Gillespie would be there with you. Have you found anything on that chunk of grave marker?"

"Mom and her washed it real clean and now it's drying on a cookie sheet in the oven. There's some words written on it that we can't read yet, but we're sure that one of the words is probably Marlin but the last part of it is on the chunk still at the cemetery. I want to go to the cemetery with a flashlight to see what it says. Mrs. Gillespie has some special paper and a big chunk of graphite to rub on it so whatever is written on the stone will be clear on the paper as the paper is more readable than the stone is."

"Hello, Clydis, Gillespie here. Miah is right. Definitely the marker inscription is M-a-r- and part of an l we think, so we're leaving now for the cemetery."

"Will it take long?"

"No, a few minutes."

"I gave Miah this number. Call back if within an hour."

"Sure will. Nathan wants to talk to you."

"Grandma, explain to me why it happens that one arrives at an important answer in the middle of the night. It came to me what soul is and when I came up with it I knew also that John also knew. Well, John called here before I was even dressed this morning saying he came upon it too. In the classroom we, without looking at each other's work went each to a chalk board and we both, completely independent of each other, mind you, we each wrote exactly the same thing. 'Soul is the mechanism by which we know that God exists.'"

"Wait, I'm writing."

"Be sure it's the God, spelled with capital G; our God the only God, God of the universe. Grandma, we're just thrilled. Soul is the mechanism by which we know that God exists."

"Surprised me, that definition. I'll tell it to the others so we can mull it over."

Luisa and Fanny said to keep you talking until they get back. It won't be long. She's using her siren and I hear it getting louder. They're on their way back. Uncle Harold knows what us few that ever read Darwin's book learned about the attributes that make us humans. Darwin wrote that to be human the being believes in God and the being has a soul. Darwin could see no way that these attributes could have arisen by means of an ascending organ scale; not by evolutionary processes is what he was saying. That ties in with what John and I concluded about soul. Well, here's Fanny."

"Clydis, the inscription definitely is Marlin, May 9, 1897, but we can't make out the first name. It measures to be seven letters. We'll get to the court house tomorrow.'

"Good, we'll see the Sweeney family and likely the Digger's as well tomorrow morning. You call Wayne yet tonight on the grave marker. He's as antsy as the rest of us."

"Okay. Good night, dear."

"No, put Nathan back on."

"Hi, Grandma."

"Does Darwin cite any evidence as to when the first humans appeared; that would be, I'm thinking, the instant they first were granted a soul by the Creator?"

"An enormous pile of details are missing from Genesis, as we know, yet we've no iron clad proof that man appeared by any means other than as stated in Genesis. Darwin couldn't think of just when the human first appeared but he said that if any beings knew of God they would act like they were aware of an Omnipotent Creator."

"Like what behavior?"

"Burying the dead with artifacts for the journey beyond. This began all over the world, we believe, around 60,000 years ago. Much more work needs to be done on the topic, of course. For example, that data point would include both Neanderthal and Cro Magnon man, both believed to've buried their dead with tools for the journey beyond and some believe that the Neanderthals didn't survive; kind of iffy to think God would have allowed the demise of a whole race of soul bearers."

"Gee, that sure gives us thought to ponder," Aunt Edith said.

"Thanks, Nathan," Grandma Clydis said. "Good night, you all."

Dark descended on the Kentucky travelers as they pulled to the roadside in sight of a stream near the foot of Raccoon Mountain. Stopping beside a man on a porch, they were able to confirm the nearby stream to be the South Fork of the Rockcastle River. Somewhere along the narrow road that crossed the South Fork they expected to come along beside of a rocky cliff face. The next opportunity after that to turn to the right should take them to the Sweeney home.

The next morning Jack had no trouble driving along the narrow hilly winding way in the camper. Abruptly after the last right hand turn they plunged into the Sweeney yard. Jack pulled to a stop beside a Peterbilt tractor with an attached refrigerator semi trailer, a reefer, so called in the trucking trade. A 'Kentucky Meats' logo decorated the reefer and an electric wire connected the reefer to the house. The house was powder blue in color due to a fresh siding of aluminum. It was a modernly-styled ranch house. From photographs they recognized Douglas, a.k.a. Digger, Marl and the slightly built woman they took to be Margie Sweeney. They were seated on the house porch holding pink lemonade in large glass tumblers.

Those on the porch watched alertly while the big white camper disgorged its four passengers. Their scrutiny continued as the strangers approached. "How do?" Clydis greeted. "We are four deputy sheriffs from Michigan. You must be Douglas and Margie." The deputies saw Digger's eyes narrow at the use of his real name.

"Yes," Margie said. In lieu of southern hospitality, the guests were not offered refreshment nor a seat on the porch. "What do you want?"

Douglas crossed his arms over his chest.

Edith said, "We are investigating the disappearance of Russell Marlin, Larry Marlin and Roy Marlin from Manitou County Michigan. In no way are we here to wreak havoc or to harm anyone. These particular missing person cases are old ones and we're assuming that no living relatives are implicated in any way. We seek only the facts that will close the file, releasing the present living relatives from the bondage of secrecy."

Those on the porch merely stared at their visitors, Margie still held to her condensation dampened icy glass of pink lemonade and Douglas didn't shift his arms from across his chest.

The deputies from Michigan had trouble shifting their eyes from the delicious-appearing drinks to study the faces of apparent adversaries. "Douglas, Margie," Clydis continued, "we seek closure of this case for the Marlin family; for you both and for Jill, Clementine, Peggy, Russell, Dale, Bobby, and all others of the Marlin family. We intend only good will. Margie, when and where did you last see Roy Marlin?" Margie shifted her position; sat down her glass. She began a rise to her feet. "Please, Margie, our mission is to help. Please visit with me or any of us. We can visit in the camper, if you wish."

"Sis, sit down." Douglas reached for her arm.

"No, Douglas, please; I want a Christian burial for Russell." She pulled from her brother. She took a step toward Clydis. "You have found Russell?"

"Yes; your husband?" Margie burst into tears. Half way down the porch steps she ended in Clydis' arms.

"Ma'am, it was so terrible and nothing any of us could do. Please come and sit down, all of you. Douglas, wake up Hal and Jill. Bring more glasses and lemonade. Have Hal and Jill make sandwiches, and you help them."

"Sis, I . . ." Douglas looked mean and determined.

"Go!" Douglas stooped his slipper-clad feet on his way from the porch. His scowl shivered the guests just climbing onto the spacious porch.

"I think Digger will be alright," Margie said. "I've talked with Clementine Beech. I agree, you should go slow with him. We're sure he wants out of the nightmares, too, like the rest of us, but he hates to have anything bad said about his family. Also, and more so than the rest of us, Digger hates to have family affairs aired publicly." Her eyes fell upon Edith.

"Margie, we can assure you, there will likely not even be a blurb about this in a local, or in any other newspaper. We've found a body and we agree that it is your Russell. He's now at a laboratory in Lansing awaiting official identification. With what we've found out about him, your statement would complete the identification. He was, we believe, a victim of Larry Marlin. With a statement from you, the law would be satisfied and no public airing should occur. We are perplexed, however, as to the fate of Roy and Larry."

"We haven't heard from Roy since he and Larry visited here in the late 1940s. They drove down by car on a route down through Indiana, Roy said, so Roy could visit the Jean Stratton Porter home; a favorite author of both Roy and Larry. In the early 50s Larry showed up here again. He said, 'Roy is gone' and then he just walked away."

"Can you narrow down that date?"

"June of '51. About at the end of the first week of June. Hal'd just begun expanding his route from local to open highway. I was worried, didn't know when to expect Hal back. The door was pounded. It was Larry."

"Describe Larry to us."

"Frightening! More like a hairy beast than a man. I recognized his voice and his size, more than seven feet tall. He carried a handmade bow and a quiver made of raccoon skin. The arrows were like one can buy in a store."

"How did he get here, that is, walked or what? Could he follow a map?"

"Walked. I'd not considered any other way. I just knew that he walked. Both uncles, Roy and Larry, could read and write. Roy went farther in school, through the eighth grade. Larry went through the seventh. They were the same age but weren't identical twins. Larry fell behind in school and quit school when Roy did. By then Larry was already over six feet in height. And he was already strong and mean, quick to lose his temper. Larry took an awful beating socially from society. That's why Roy went with him to live in the woods. Alcohol was effective in keeping him calm.

"My husband Russell was afraid of Larry and was afraid Larry would harm someone so he wanted Larry placed in an asylum. We don't know what happened there in the woods except that Larry bashed my Russell against a tree and that killed my Russell. I went along with the family to keep the secrets."

"You are very brave and very dear. Clementine told us quite a bit. We came to love you and to cry and cry. Margie, few on earth are as brave and loyal as you. Oh, how we pray that terrible burdens may be lifted from you."

"Please go slow with Douglas."

Chapter Fifteen

Hal Sweeney was the first to join the Michigan deputies and Margie on the porch. He carried a tray loaded with a one-gallon pitcher of pink lemonade and an assortment of tumblers and mugs. Some of the mugs were teetering on a stack of Tupperware plates. Harold rushed to rescue the mugs while Hal lowered the remainder safely to the table. "Quite a load. I'm Harold and you must be Hal Sweeney."

"Yes. I'm the trucker."

Tight behind Hal, Digger's wife Jill balanced a platter of tuna salad, ham and cheese, and tomato bologna sandwiches. "Digger has decided to shave and get better dressed," she said.

"You all look grand," Edith said as she helped guide Jill's burden to the table top. "And the sandwiches and lemonade are very inviting." The ladies began filling tumblers. Margie reached with tongs to place a large ice cube in each one.

Introductions were made around.

"Help yourselves. There'll be coffee in a few minutes."

Everyone filled a plate and sat down with icy lemonade. One sip of the lemonade was enough to set the ladies into conversation. "I've never made pink lemonade," Clydis said. "We've only had it from frozen."

"This is so delicious," Edith declared, "and is homemade, I'm sure." She looked at Jill. "Please tell me how it's done."

Jill smiled. "Margie's recipe. The pink is from cranberry juice."

"Hal hauls meat and groceries from Texas into London. Then he hauls a large order in here to us. You've seen the reefer."

"The truck, you mean; the reefer is the trailer, is it?"

"Yep. In the trucking trade a reefer is the refrigerator. He hauls around a huge refrigerator."

"Sure do," Hal said. "I've a load of root crops and meat on now. We installed DC current at home here to keep the reefer cool. I'll leave here for Brownsville, then up to San Antonio and on to Amarillo. Amarillo is where I bought my reefer. At Amarillo I take on most of the beef. Then I hit Little Rock, Memphis, and London on the way home. The reefer is full during most of the trip because I off load some and load something different at each stop." He turned to Jack. "I could use another trucker for my route, Jack, if you have one handy or would like to join me."

"Sure sounds like my dreamed of work," Jack said, "but deputy work has me pretty filled. I bus prisoners and do some local trucking on the side."

"The camper you see there," Harold nodded, "belongs to a relative who trucks for a livelihood. That Mack cab fifth wheel hooks right to any semi trailer instead of to the camper body."

The men soon were engrossed in their line of chatter; as were the ladies in theirs: "To each two cups of lemon juice add one cup of cranberry juice. Then it's just two cups of sugar and nine or ten cups of water. But, of course sweeten to taste."

"Juice concentrates?"

"Well, fresh lemons, but the cranberries we put up as preserves each fall. Later we eat the berries and freeze the juice. I'd like to try using concentrates sometime."

"Gosh," Edith said. "May we practice while we're here? We'd do the fresh, which is purely marvelous. At home, I think I still have a lemon squeezer. Come to think on it, we'd also better try the concentrates so at home we'd stand a chance of getting a drinkable product, one way or the other."

"Sure."

The ladies talked and munched and sipped as though they'd been friends and neighbors for years.

The men soon chatted their way off the porch and into an in-depth investigation into the merits of the Mack and the Peterbilt tractors.

Meantime, Douglas had not appeared.

"Strange Douglas hasn't come on out," Harold said. Harold was looking toward the house. "Doesn't he dig trucks?"

"Likely cornered by the ladies," Hal joked. "Collared him for dish washing I'd bet."

"Good bet, I'd think." Harold stepped down from a box he'd used to better see the Peterbilt power plant. "Sure a lot under this hood." In lifting the box he read its label. "Stone Crabs, Pride of Florida. Hal, I've not before heard of stone crabs. Aren't we in crawdad country?"

"Well, there's some crawdad eaten here but I cross the path of a trucker of my ilk at the terminal in Memphis from time to time. We swap a little Florida crab for Texas beef. It's getting so that Margie expects that to happen every month or so."

"Say," Jack said, "on your travels did you ever hear of any Yeti or Big Foot being seen?"

"I saw one before I ever heard of one. Scared me badly."

"Where and when?"

"Right here. I drove in just in time to see a hairy creature, big tall thing, disappearing around the corner of our house. That was the first week of June 1951 on a Friday. I'd just returned from a longer run than usual. I had a reefer truck then, not a semi but I was searching out a longer route so that I'd need a semi. Well, I came home and there it was. Scared Margie as much as me. We'd just been married a short while. Frightening start, I'll say, but scared us even more when she said it was Larry."

"Larry! My Gosh, did you also see Roy?"

"No, and Senior lived with us then; Russell Sr.; we just call him Senior. Later Senior tented off where ever he was mining coal. Even he camped near here when he dug a mine shaft into a mountain side; real close, he was welcome to come in and stay with us like before, but he didn't want to. That day he heard 'Larry' he took right off in search of him. Didn't find him though he was gone for two or three days, Margie said. I'd left back out on the route before Senior got back, but Margie said he'd not found Larry."

"Senior mined a lot of coal then?"

"That was his livelihood all while I've known him but he became kind of reclusive soon after Margie and me wed. Likely that's why he camped out. I liked him and we were cordial but I seldom saw him. He'd pile his coal here for Margie to sell so she saw him more often. A coal truck from town came, too, so some was sold at the London coal yard. A few years ago his mind just began to plummet right toward the pits so we had to rest him in the nursing home."

"Is he communicative? We'd like to talk with him."

"No, more like a vegetable. He doesn't know any of us."

"Hey, you guys," Edith had just walked up, "if you're going to take the camper for a spin, you'd best get trucking. We're starting beef ribs right soon, along with potato salad and spinach greens." She held a folded paper in her hand. "Harold, here's a list and a note to do in London. Momma dialed Dewy John so he expects you'll check in, but get the groceries first so you don't forget the lemon and cranberry juice concentrates." Harold stood with the folded notes. Edith turned and walked a few steps away – she snap-turned back to him. "Dear, why don't you send Hal and Jack to the grocery while you see Dewy John? I'm worried you guys'll take too long and hold up dinner."

With Hal at the wheel and Jack in the right hand bucket, Harold was little noticed in the middle bucket as he read the note. Mainly, the 'note' was a half page of instructions for Dewy John. He was to check the incidence report of the break-in where a man was killed and also the one where a watch dog was killed to see if any other person, a stranger, was seen at or about that time, and to describe the stranger's appearance; especially his clothing and foot wear. Check to see if the date was around the first week in June of 1951. If the dates line up, Dewy John must call Sheriff Wayne Puller to have Wayne call Mrs. Woods, or others, to check on Digger's whereabouts at the time. "Have Dewy John call here at Sweeney's when he has information for us."

Later at dinner the men were obliged to compare pink lemonades to determine the best tasting. None could agree. The ladies sat beaming. "Well, I guess it's concentrates for us back home," Clydis said. "I can't recall where I'd last seen that lemon squeezer anyhow."

Edith managed to plop barbeque sauce from the ribs onto her lap despite the huge bib she was wearing. "I don't care," she said, "I'd do it all again for ribs like these."

Suddenly, the house shook!

"Earthquake?"

"Dynamite?"

"Douglas?"

"Darn, I wonder where he's at and what he's been up to."

"I'd say dynamite, all right, and from the direction of Senior's mine shaft."

The men leaped up from the table. Edith grabbed Harold. "Wait. Dear, come with me while I change. We can catch up."

In the camper, Edith said as she squirmed free of her slacks, "Dewy John called before you got back. The dates of the deaths and of seeing a stranger line up, and it sounds like Digger Marl." She stood in her pantyhose. Harold's eyes riveted to her and his hands began a reach. "The boots clinched it for me," she said, not noticing that his hands nearly grabbed her as she turned to pull on the jeans. "L. L. Bean boots." She felt him pulling at the jeans to position them above her firm buttocks.

"Derriere supreme," he said, patting.

"Derriere. French for buttocks! Dear, please stick to our mission here."

"I am, that is mine, my mission, but I'll take time off to hear about your darned old Bean boots."

"L. L. Bean. You have some like them. They are like the original boots displayed in the original Bean catalog. I've seen them all of my life. Rubber bottoms of black, brown, tan, of khaki and leather uppers; like yours. And like Hal's that I saw in their kitchen. When I commented on them she said they were standard for men in her family. That's for Senior, for Hal, and for Roy, and, as well, for Douglas/Digger. A stranger seen along the route of Larry/Big Foot was wearing just such boots and I know that Douglas, Jill said he had a pair, must be wearing his right now as she said those in the kitchen were Hal's so Digger must have his on. Margie, though, said that her Junior didn't like those boots because he said she said they made his feet smell. She said the boots did one time and she was so sorry she mentioned it. It had been a hot day or two despite being muddy. After that he began buying his boots from a guy at his house in town."

"Wow! Dear, this derriere affair will have to wait, I reluctantly agree. Did you hear from Mrs. Woods?"

"Yes. Fanny called here. Digger had always been so dependable, Mrs. Woods said, but for the time she was to go to The University of Michigan to visit her son. He was earning an engineering degree and later he began working in atomic engineering where he is now, in Tennessee. That's how she remembers the date. Digger was away the first week or two of June 1951."

"Why this sudden plunge for info on Digger?"

"I believe both he and Larry were here, but Digger wasn't seen along with Larry. Nobody has seen Larry; well, nor Roy either since Larry and now I know, Digger were here. We must get Digger/Douglas to co-operate with us."

"Well, let's go. If they're correct, then the man has just blown up something."

Off the west side of the yard they saw that a small coal pile yet remained. Passing that, they heard voices and quickened their steps. Ahead they saw that Digger Marl stood in hand cuffs; and that he was wearing the L. L. Bean boots. They rushed into the scene and bee lined for Deputies Clydis and Jack. "What has happened here?"

"Coal mine" Deputy Clydis said. "Douglas blew it up. He swung at Jack so we cuffed him."

Edith walked up to Digger. "I'll call you Digger because that's the name I first heard for you. I know most about you from Mrs. Woods and from Clementine Beach so I know you're a good man." She held a key, reached for the handcuffs. "Digger, we mean no abuse and we expect none from you. We are here merely to help bring closure for the Marlin family, closure to this whole awful issue."

Jill came up and took her husband's arm and she pressed her body against him. "Dear, we trust them. Please, they are here only to help."

"Digger, she has removed those darn cuffs. I want to agree with her that you are a good man," Jack said, "but mister, why did you blow this mine shaft?"

"Uh, danger. Support was weakened, old wood. It would fall on anyone who poked around in here. I wish Senior'd not dug it. I waited but am sure now that Senior will not need this shaft so I blew it."

"Why now?" Jack stood with his hands braced to his hips, his body leaned toward Digger.

Digger stood his ground. "You'd find it and start poking around in it. You cops are prone, you'll agree, to poking around."

"Look. Digger, we have to know about this mine shaft. If you can't help us we'll have to question Senior. An injection of truth serum there may bring him to some answers." Digger stared at Jack. That he believed Jack was shown in his narrowed eyes and crinkled brow.

"Digger," Clydis said, "sit down here on this log." She held a five-gallon bucket and she motioned to Edith. Edith moved toward a heavy crate. The pair sat down before Digger.

You folks go on," Clydis said. "Edith and I will visit here with Digger.

The group began to move away. Jill turned back. "Jill, please, it'll be alright. We must visit with Digger."

Jill and the others disappeared up the road.

Edith said, "Digger, we won't try that truth serum on anyone. Deputy Jack was just a bit riled is all."

Clydis caught Digger eye to eye. "Digger, is Larry in there, in the mine shaft?"

* * *

Back at the house behind glasses of pink lemonade and with forks busy at chocolate iced German chocolate cake, that dessert to complete their interrupted by a blast delicious dinner, Jack and Harold conversed with Margie and Jill.

"I think we can say for certain that the man we found buried is Russell, your first husband, Margie. What would you have us do now about him?"

"Bring him here for a Christian burial. Hal and I purchased four grave sites side by side. You passed our church on your way into here, before the cliff where you turned to get here. The cemetery is behind that little church. I'll have Hal on my left and to my right will be Russell and beside him will be Senior. See if you can get all of my siblings and the cousins here to the funeral. I truly miss them." Margie suddenly pressed her fingers against her cheek, pressed in deeply. "Toothache." They could barely understand her. She went into a nearby bathroom.

"Jill, will she be alright." Jill nodded, yes. "Jill, what do you think is bothering Digger so? We mean no harm."

"Family name. Digger doesn't want it sullied in any way. Your probing feels dangerous to him."

"Sensodyne toothpaste. I'm so grateful to get it," Margie said upon her return to the table. "Dr. Woods had a concoction that he made that he said was 5% potassium nitrate and other stuff. This whole family has bad molars, made worse by an appetite for rock candy. I learned bad candy habits from Russell before he died. He actually would wish for a cough so that he could chew cough drops. I grew to like them too. He'd already lost his molars so you'd think I would've learned better."

"Digger lost all his molars," Jill said, "but too late to benefit from Dr. Woods' special partial plates and his glue, so he had them all pulled and got false teeth."

"That trait, the missing molars, made us near certain we had discovered a Marlin, but, Margie, we weren't sure it was Russell until Clementine led us to you. We grieve for your loss, ma'am, and wish all could've been different."

"Ladies, we're closing in, we think, on what happened to Larry. However, we're still deeply concerned about the disappearance of Roy. Do you have thoughts on that?"

"I'll sum up the family," Margie said. "Jill, help me where I falter."

"I'd better go to Digger."

"Jill, please wait," Harold said. "I know those two deputies. They'll be back here with him, and with him much relieved, any minute now."

Margie said, "The man in the shack with Larry Marlin was Roy Marlin, twin brother of Larry. Not an identical twin, but pals since babies. Larry didn't reach sexual maturity and he just kept on growing. In the elementary grades, Larry learned to read and write along with Roy. As Larry grew bigger and taller, he was more and more ashamed of his un-development. Finally Larry became insane so Roy kept him drunk to keep him happy. Dale and Peggy Lance, Russell Junior and I, and Jill and Digger set out food and wine through the years. Also Roy went to town about every week to buy food at small markets. One was on East Street down town and another store was on East Street north of the railroad crossing. At near closing time, he could approach either store rather unobserved.

"I've never met Larry and Roy's parents. They had died, I was told before I married Junior.

"I married Russell Marlin Junior, as you know; my cousin. I loved him and still do love him. But Junior was an irascible man who fretted constantly regarding Uncle Larry Marlin. Junior considered Larry to be crazy and to be dangerous.

"Junior went to Roy and Digger to have Larry committed before harm came to someone. Digger saw Larry grab my Junior and drive his head into a tree that was beside the humper.

"Senior moved with me, the widow, Margie Marlin, to Kentucky. We stayed at first in a tourist court. I thought I'd go mad here in Kentucky. I ran across Hal at a grocery store. I married him in desperation but soon loved him; both Hal and Junior I love equally. Hal and I and Senior built this place. Hal understands and was good about the burial plots we bought in the little church cemetery.

"After Larry was here that last time, Senior was gone several days in search of him. Senior never said whether he found Larry. Senior was like in a daze when he returned to his mining coal. He was unresponsive to us and he steadily grew less able to care for himself; but he didn't want our help. Hal placed him in a care facility and Senior seemed to like that but over the years he slowly declined until now he is declined to where he sits and stares and doesn't know any of us."

"We didn't hear about Roy's disappearance until recently. Douglas said he didn't know why or not even exactly when Roy went away. Recently, when Douglas told us about it, I asked 'went away?' and he said, 'must have, there's no sign of him.' I believe he's telling the truth."

"You don't think Roy came here with Larry?"

"Yes, that first time, but then later, I've told you about, Larry was here alone. Alone, I'm sure because if Roy was with Larry, he'd have been beside him."

* * *

Back at the blasted mine shaft, Clydis said to Digger, "You know, Digger, my daughter here and I've been on your rear porch and at your kitchen door. I knocked in hopes you were home despite the note you left hanging there. Sunlight was bright on your kitchen table. The book on the table looked well worn, as though you'd read it numerous times. Until now we've not told any of our cohorts about the book. We didn't tell them about the book even though we could make out the book's title.

"The book was 'Of Mice and Men,' published in 1937, by John Steinbeck. A movie of the book appeared in 1939. Tell us about that book, Digger."

Digger had tears in his eyes. "George was okay, that is, he was normal.

Lenny was simple-minded and a friend of George. Lenny got into trouble. He killed a bunny and he killed a woman. Locking Lenny up would've been a terrible tragedy for Lenny and perhaps, but almost certainly, for many others. George killed poor simple-minded Lenny. A man said to George, 'That's all you could do, George.'"

"Digger, we can leave Larry where he is, in the mine shaft. A report will be on file about it in Sheriff Dewy John's department and in Sheriff Wayne Puller's department. Do you wish to detail what happened to Larry?"

"No. I'll never say. I'm so sorry for Senior, that the events went so hard on him. I'm sad to smithereens about the whole family affair. I'm glad she found Hal; it was terrible for Margie."

"Another detail to clear up," Edith said. "Records for Russell Marlin were removed from Mrs. Woods' closet."

"I did it, stupidly, and I did other stupid acts to try to protect Larry and the family's good name. We were, are, believe me, a good family."

"One of the toughest, loyalist, best darn families ever to grace this noble earth, kind sir. You can depend on our loyalty to the preservation of you and of your whole family."

"Digger, can you tell us the whereabouts of Roy?"

"No. I suspect Larry knew but was not able to communicate with any of us."

Chapter Sixteen

O N THEIR WAY HOME, THE load of Michigan deputy sheriffs in the big white camper were just leaving Cincinnati, Ohio. Leaving Cincinnati, their goal became the city of Hamilton where they intended to go onto U.S. 127. Their aim by noon was to be in Greenville, Ohio, where they'd feast in the grandeur of Annie Oakley memories. Shortly beyond Hamilton, however, a road sign announced the tiny town of Seven Mile. "Hey, Jack, Seven Mile reminds me of Alaska. This grand white tub will be there many times from now on. Can we pass this up?"

Jack applied the brakes. "No post office so I can't get a postmark," he muttered.

"Does Seven Mile in Alaska have a post office?"

"I'd bet it does; that is if Alaska even has a Seven Mile." He suddenly brightened. "But with this cozy little eatery looking so lonesome, we can't pass this up, that's sure.'" He pulled up out in front of 'Rozie's Kitchen.'

"Here already?" Grandma's head had nodded up from her chest. She blinked her eyes. "Greenville already? Is this Greenville, Ohio?"

Harold arrived from the living room where he'd been engrossed in a historical treatment of his heroine, Annie Oakley. "Don't see a statue of her," he mused, "and I'd thought Greenville'd be a bigger town."

"We'll arrive at her town with full tummies, dear. This is Seven Mile, about fifty below our goal."

"Alaska? Jack, you've sure got us off course."

"Blame the navigator," Edith chuckled. "I couldn't pass up dining in Seven Mile even as I think of it, I'm not sure if Alaska has such a town."

"Sounds Alaskan, and it does look inviting. Sourdough flapjacks for me."

Mid way in their meal: "Say, I have it!" Deputy Clydis declared, reaching for her purse.

"What, gold? We're in Alaska alright."

She winked but didn't reply. Instead, she flipped open her notebook. "Wayne Puller. Harold, accept a refill on my coffee. I'm going to call Sheriff Puller."

"What's up?"

"I've thought up that special assignment for Del to do while using Wayne's flashy patrol car. Del could use that powerful cruiser to transport Junior down to Kentucky."

Her companions idled until her return to the table. Wayne's calling Lansing for a release of Russell's remains. He'll also contact Judge Theta to be sure all is legally done. Wayne will call Del to set up Del's part then he'll call Leadford Town Marshal Bertram Benson to let him in on the details of Del's special assignment."

"Bravo!"

"Del will drive to Nathan's and meet us there."

Late into the next afternoon the freshly polished sheriff's cruiser was parked in the Platt yard as the big white camper pulled in. Nathan greeted them with: "Seeing I didn't get to drive the big cruiser back to Manitou Prairie, Del's invited Miah and me to go with him and Hi down to Kentucky."

Not me," Luisa greeted, "the girls and Nic and I'll go on up to Ellington. We hear that little Virginia Louise and her baby buggy are inseparable. I pine to see her and Dosia. We'll be up there when the guys get back."

"We've a loose end to mull over," Grandma Clydis said, "but we've decided to ponder it from our homes at Leadford. Fanny has charge of the case here now. We still don't know what happened to Roy."

"The sheriff called a while ago to say that a Chester Marlin lived in the area on the dates covered by that broken grave marker. He has the courthouse checking to see if that Marlin can be linked to Marlins we've encountered. He said Officer Fanny will also ask family members, perhaps one or more has done the family genealogy. We aren't even sure of the parents of Larry and Roy."

"Knowing the genealogy could hold a clue as to why or how the stone came to be back in there near the hermit shack" Harold said. "Fanny will work on it until she knows."

"Fanny Gillespie sure is thorough. I'd much rather be a Montgomery Wards bean counter. There're too many different beans in Fanny's work."

"Say, dear, did you ask your doctor about a more definitive diagnosis of your pain filled hands? I wish he'd send you to that clinic at the Ann Arbor University Hospital."

"Well, Grandma, I see your logic but who knows what will work? Some days are better and some times my jaw joint or a shoulder or a knee can hurt almost more than my hands."

Aunt Edith stood listening and her finger came to rest on her chin, but the finger popped into the air – "Moves? Did you say the pain moves around? Where have I heard about that before?"

"Well, let's eat. The guys want to get packed for going early tomorrow morning with poor Russell's bones."

"I still think 'moves' is a clue," Edith said as she absently spooned potato salad onto her plate. "Moves? Now that's a puzzle."

"Edith, you are holding up the line. Please pass on the potato salad and serve yourself a pork chop."

"Rheumatoid! I heard about that when we read and read trying to help Del and Nathan's Grandpa Delibar Platt."

"Pass those chops along, Aunt Edith."

"Rheumatoid Arthritis – 'pass the chops' – I hope you don't have that, Luisa, but if you do you need treatment right away." Harold reached the chops and they bypassed Aunt Edith to continue around the table. "Please, let's call your doctor right away tomorrow morning."

"Aunt Edith, will you help yourself to the creamed corn and then pass that along please?" Already Harold was reaching for it.

So concerned for Luisa was Aunt Edith that she finished her meal without knowing she'd missed pork chops and creamed corn. "Lovely meal, Luisa, and I'm so proud the children helped in preparing it?"

"The kids and Nathan leave me little to do as far as meal prep when I've returned from work. Typically, we enjoy quiet evenings around here."

"Coffee, anyone?" Miah stood proudly with the pot. "It's Sanka."

The adults sat stirring coffee and Omi and Cia, whose turn it was, splashed away at washing the dishes. Their tom-foolery lent background music to the table conversations until suddenly no one heard another save for Nathan who began fielding questions about soul. "Recall that Darwin wrote that the presence of soul and our knowledge of God are traits that clearly define the human. No other living thing has those traits."

"Do you think the soul first, then the knowledge of God?"

"I surely think so," Nathan concurred.

Del, in recalling an earlier discussion with Louie Watkins, said, "Yes, Darwin stated that soul could not have evolved, er, as Darwin said, could not have developed by any ascending organic scale. So when the being received a soul the being would immediately know that God exists."

"Did Darwin mean that humans didn't evolve from anything?"

"Darwin didn't know and so couldn't say."

Miah repeated a phrase he'd often heard at church: "God works in mysterious ways, huh?"

"No, God doesn't work in mysterious ways. Thinking that way is an excuse for human ignorance. Miah, now you know better."

Miah continued, "Maybe the Bible is all we know about the start of humans, though."

Del put in, "That's not enough is it?"

"For some it is, but most people need a more elaborate explanation."

"So why the Scopes trial?"

"Stupidest trial in history, "Harold expounded. "Obviously not a single person involved in the trial had ever read Darwin's book so each and every one was blabbering away in total ignorance."

"Still, Harold, the trial led to the Butler Act."

"Yes, and it was repealed in 1967. Nathan what do you really think about all of this – just prattle is it?"

"There is an enormous body of facts to the support of evolutionary theory but I've found that the same facts can support other theories as well. Two factors occur to me. One is that all living things are similar. Humans are more like dandelions that we are different from them. A plan for having life, for being alive in the first place, occurs to me; God's plan. It is magnificent that all things living live by the same basic plan. The fundamental basic factors required to be alive in the first place, these factors are the same in all living things. That's the miracle. God alone does miracles.

"My students and I work with the mouse embryo to study the cause and effects of birth defects and apply medicine to abolish or to correct those defects. We do so in confidence that we are discovering medicine to directly help any human unborn child. We don't ask ourselves why the mouse is so much like the human, we do say silent, and sometimes out loud, prayers to God in thanks that due to his plan for life being fundamentally the same in all life, we can proceed with confidence. We're totally confident that our research with mouse embryos has direct application in the treatment of human embryos.

"As far as getting a new species from an existing species, this through isolation and the factor of time, I have never witnessed any new species developing from an existing species via the isolation and time method. There are many who describe the conditions that would or could make the appearance of a new species possible, and the similarities between species are obvious, but I challenge that any have ever actually seen the event occur. In short, I, with my present thinking, cannot say with certainty where any species came from."

"Except by God, I say. And Nathan, do they let grandmothers attend college? I'd like to learn more?"

"So would I like to know more," Nathan said. "I believe God wants us all to learn all that we can. For me though, I'd rather be a kid again and be at Grandma Clydis or Aunt Edith, or at Uncle Harold's knee. It's where I've learned the most about the truly important things."

"Now you're bringing my tears," Aunt Edith said. "Good night, you all. It's time a tired old head hit the pillow."

* * *

At breakfast Grandma Clydis said, "Phoenicia, have you identified any more birds? If so, I'd like to see more pictures."

"Just one, Grandma, and my scout leader said my photo was propitious indeed. I snapped one of a Red Tailed hawk as it was about to launch at the other birds at my feeder. I was trying for a better picture of a cowbird when all my birds suddenly all went away and my camera came to focus the hawk. My Bluebird leader has it so she can enlarge it."

"Splendid! I look forward to viewing your album."

"Mom suggested that I also collect more information about my name this summer while I have the time. I'll be in Mrs. Krieger's class this fall. Did I tell you that Phoenicia is a palm tree?"

"I'll see if I've written that down. Wait while I get my notebook. I want information on all of you children's names." Selecting a page which she'd titled 'Phoenicia', Grandma Clydis read aloud that Phoenician purple dye is also made in Alsace-Lorraine where Luisa came from so the dye links two parts of the world. Phoenicia and Alsace-Lorraine are inter-related by way of the purple dye. The purple dye has religious significance in that it stands for death and, of course, also for resurrection. And purple can also indicate royalty. Grandma wet the tip of her lead pencil with her tongue and wrote 'Phenicia or Phoenicia is a palm tree.' She looked up at Cia and said, "Shoot."

Phoenicia shot off with, "Phoenicia is a coastal strip along the Mediterranean Sea and it includes the towns of Tyre, Sidon, and Byblos. Byblos means book and may be the origin of Bible, the Book of books. Phoenicians are descendents of Canaanites and may have split from the bulk of the Canaanites even before the exodus. In Acts 27:12, men sail to Phenicie (Phoenix or Phoenicia) looking for a safe port. In Acts 15:3, Paul passes through Phenicie." She poked in a good size bite of oatmeal while waiting for Grandma to catch up the writing.

"My goodness, you've sure studied. What next?"

Cia grinned broadly; thinking: Sure, I've studied. "I'll have that mean teacher, Mrs. Krieger next fall and I plan to win a smile from her. The Phoenicians invented the phonetic alphabet. By the 700s BC, a common phonetic alphabet was being used by Phoenicians, Moabites, and many others as a means of communicating commerce records and information from port to port. Did I say that Phoenicians are a split off of or are descendents of the original Canaanites?"

"Wait, let me catch up." Cia poked in another generous gob of oatmeal.

"There; now Cia, let me think. Out from Egypt, Moses and his chased and mauled those Canaanites something terrible, but you say some were split off before Moses and Joshua and the others warred with them and those who'd split off became the Phoenicians?"

"Yup. Grandma, your oatmeal's getting cold."

"When was the Bible written, the oldest books, I mean?"

"Gosh, I don't know. Grandma, your oatmeal."

"Well," Grandma touched the point of her No.2, Ticonderoga cedar wood pencil to her tongue tip, "David is credited with writing a lot of the Psalms and he is said to have died in around 962 BC. He wrote phonetically so writing was invented before that. Hummmmm, I wonder just when."

"That's sure a topic to ponder, Grandma," Nathan said as he pulled a chair at the table. At the Exodus, which is said to've occurred in about 1300 BC, there was no phonetic alphabet. Between that time and the time of King David an alphabet was invented and the oldest books of the Bible were written, or could've been written. We could guess that the Ten Commandments would've also been written phonetically. That info could help to date the beginning of writing as well as to date the Ten Commandments. And the alphabet used was of the folks Moses and his chosen were for forty years and more bent upon decimating. Ironic isn't it?"

"That David's an exercise in irony," Uncle Harold said, as he spooned oatmeal into his bowl. "First as a young man, and perhaps even an undersized one, he felled old Goliath, that oversized Philistine, with a rock flung from a sling. Then David became an armor bearer to Saul, the first king of Israel and he married, Saul's daughter. Later, Saul banished him so David spent a period of his life in exile. He returned some how and became the king of Judah and in around 993 BC, he also became king of Israel. He then coveted Bathsheba, Uriah's wife. The second son of David, that is David and Bathsheba's boy, was the wise King Solomon. Having done some bad things along the way, I'd guess he'd have some explaining to do at that Pearly Gate. None-the-less his lineage leads to Jesus."

"Say, that ties right in with my name." Omi said. "Naomi and her family from Bethlehem went to the country of Moab during a famine. Naomi had two sons; one married Ruth then Naomi's husband and her two sons died, leaving Ruth a widow and Naomi a widow. Naomi led Ruth to accept God, spelled with a capital G, as the true god. Ruth was, I remind, a Moabite; and recall that Phoenicians and Moabites were among the first to use the phonetic alphabet. Ruth returned to Bethlehem with Naomi, her mother-in-law. In Bethlehem, of Judea, Ruth met Boaz. They were wed and a son was born named Obed.

"Obed was the father of Jesse; and Jesse was the father of David; ie, King David.

"King David's lineage leads to Joseph, or to Mary; I'm not sure."

"It seems more logical that David's lineage leads to Mary."

"I'm going to ask Reverend Naveapse for clarification on that issue."

"Well, that be as it is. However, my name," Omi continued, "I looked that up when I was in Mrs. Krieger's class; my name means 'my delight.' I don't know if that refers to Ruth or Naomi or any one else, but I like to be 'my' delight; or 'yours,' Grandma." Grandma grinned.

"We've all had to take her class," Miah said. "Likely even poor Nicodemus will have to."

"Miah, what did you find out about your name?" Grandma licked then poised her pencil.

"Not much, but she gets more out of us with each new victim. Look at Cia's and Omi's compared to mine. I only wrote that Jeremiah was a prophet. In the book of Jeremiah there are several prophecies of the coming messiah, Jesus, as the messiah turned out to be. In the book where definitions are given to names, my name means 'will rise up or establish something.' That's not very clear but I guess it may relate to Jesus. I can't wonder what she'll expect of poor Nic when he gets into her class."

"Names," Aunt Edith said. "Names, now why does that remind me of the hermit shack? Have we missed something in there? We still don't know what happened to Roy Marlin."

"Hey, that fits Nic's name," Omi said. "His name means 'victory' or 'victory of the people.' Finding the answers isn't that sort of like winning a victory? I mean for the Marlin family and for Mrs. Woods, and for all of us."

"Yes," Aunt Edith said, we've enjoyed some victories, but we haven't won it all yet. What else can be said about Nicodemus' name?"

"You understand, by the way, folks, that we didn't name the children from a book of what names mean. We did give them names from the Bible and we had in mind to choose a name that would birth a nice, socially nice, nickname. Mrs. Krieger's class added the fun of what the names mean."

"I don't know as I've run across Nicodemus in the Bible," Uncle Harold said. "You folks must have read the fine print."

"There is more to Nic's name, and I found it in the Bible; ran across it by accident. In John 3:1, Nicodemus was a ruler and he examined Jesus according to the works of Jesus. Jesus satisfied him as to Jesus being a divine person; Nicodemus believing that a new birth is promised through faith in Jesus. That is to be born again, ready for heaven."

"Gosh," Aunt Edith said, "Our Nic will sure have the right words to say when he gets into her class." Suddenly her hands came to her forehead. She rubbed, rubbed hard, and her face took on a configuration that burst Nic into laughter. "Name, names, naming, what does Nic's name or any of your names have to do with the hermits?" She rose from her chair, her oatmeal untouched. "I'm going back over to that mysterious hermit shack to ferret around."

"Edith," Grandma said, "I heard Luisa on the telephone earlier. I wish you'd wait for Fanny. She's taking a test then she's bringing out Sandy and Candy."

"Which test, for sergeant or for detective?"

"Sergeant," Omi answered for Grandma. "She goes to Lansing for the detective test. Sandy and Candy want to put together a picture frame here instead of at home. They're preparing a frame for her sergeant's certificate."

"Here?"

"Here's where they are, the boys." Omi rolled her eyes in a sweep of the ceiling.

"Am I to guess who?"

"If you guess Hi and Miah," Omi tilted her head for a brief gaze at the ceiling, "you get the prize."

Grandma smiled. "The approach is different now-a-days. Your Aunt Edith ran in front of a large chunk of fire wood that Harold tossed. It drew blood on her shoulder. She sure got his attention."

Aunt Edith placed a hand high up on her arm near her shoulder. That spot still felt warm when she placed her palm there. "Harold," she said, I wish you'd come with me to ferret around the hermit shack."

"Not wait for Fanny?"

"If she wants to she can come on over after a while. I want to look around sort of alone like."

"Hummm, well, folks, if Fanny doesn't come on over, have her wait if she can so we can congratulate her on the exam."

"Hey, let's bake a cake," Cia said, as she dashed for the kitchen. Her voice trailed back from her, "What kind, Mom?"

Luisa called, "White, and with white frosting; writing in lavender." She turned back to the others, "Fanny is purely an exceptional person and lavender is my special color."

Edith and Harold left for the hermit shack. Nathan and the others watched them cross Peach Road and to go safely into Mrs. Woods' driveway. As they started up the drive they began holding hands. Nathan said, "I'm wondrous. Is there yet vigor in twilight?"

With Edith and Harold barely out of sight, Sergeant Fanny Gillespie and her girls pulled in. Stepping from the cruiser, she addressed Del, "Sheriff Puller wants you and Nathan to be deputized for the trip. He thought, to be more official, deputies would be better. He also has written orders for you and he said you'd better have the cruiser officially checked out to you. I think that's for our insurance coverage." She glanced around before saying, "Deputy Trip checked Harold and Edith out on the big Mack camper, we know, but the sheriff wanted to be sure they're both trained enough." She glanced again around but didn't see Aunt Edith and Uncle Harold. "Er, well, Del, he suggested that you also check them out on the Mack."

"Now just wait here a minute," Del joked, "you expect me to check out Fireball Edith?" His eyes looked to the sky then settled back onto Deputy Gillespie. "I'll ask but I'm sure they'll only smile. When Louie Watkins and I were kids, and so young that we were hardly all that competent on bicycles, Aunt Edith taught us to drive Doodlebug. It was a homemade tractor, made of Model A truck and car parts. She gave us minimal instruction and then turned us loose to ram around the farm. Louie and I are both good drivers and I'll credit that grand Fireball Edith for achieving our confidence. I'll ask on behalf of Sheriff Puller, ma'am, but I'm sure they're ready."

"Well, alright, but you guys drive on over to the office now, will you? Sheriff Puller is expecting you." Suddenly she held her palms toward them. "Wait. Please wait for the boys to finish a project in the shop. They'll be done soon, and can go with you."

Turning from the jubilant cruiser riders, Deputy Fanny at once became fully a mom. She took a step forward as if deciding to intervene but slid her gleaming brogans. She motioned and the others followed her into the shop. At a bench at the side of the garage/workshop Candy was holding two sides of the picture frame together while Miah tapped in a metal fastener that would secure the joint. Their hands were very close together and their heads were so close their hair intermingled.

Fanny's heart thumped anew when at a different bench, Hi gently held Sandy's hand in guiding the glass cutter along a straight edge. Their hair also intermingled.

Fanny stood a moment in wonder. She wondered, tried to remember; was her own childhood this short. Her thoughts glided back to a time when at a neighborhood skating rink she'd ran right into a boy and he'd helped her up. No, her thoughts brought a gentle smile to her face. No, childhood can end quickly, and in the space of a heart beat. Her gentle smile greeted Luisa as she stood holding open the door to the house. "Fanny," Luisa said, "congratulations. Come in, there's tea and we're baking a cake."

Luisa's also scanned the workers in the shop. Her smile was smug. "Sweet, isn't it?"

At the hermit shack Harold and Edith sat on the edge of the giant bed. They were trying to think of what could've happened to Roy Marlin but their interest kept pulling their attention elsewhere.

Chapter Seventeen

BECAUSE HI AND MIAH WERE to accompany Del and Nathan on the trip to Kentucky, the men waited patiently for the boys to join them for the visit to Sheriff Puller's office. Seeing the boys emerging from the work shop, Nathan won the dash to the cruiser and popped in behind the wheel. Del hopped into the seat opposite and grinned at Sergeant Gillespie who stood beside her daughters, the mom and girls with wondrous eyes keened to the boys.

Nathan jerked their chins into the air as they started on the route to town.

In town Sheriff Wayne Puller and Deputy Jack Trip had time to reminisce events pertaining to the costumes they'd placed in a sack while waiting the Platt men and boys. Their memories had them grinning broadly as Del, Hi, Nathan, and Miah entered the sheriff's office.

Indeed, Jack and Wayne were smiling so broadly that the very next modicum of glee would send them both into paroxysms of gutsy guffaw. "You're not dressed for the job," Jack said – and that did it; the two burst into paroxysms too overpowering for them to stand upright. Jack gradually slid downward until he ended on his knees where he held to a chair. His accomplice gradually laid his weight sidewise across his desk. Both merry guardians of peace slapped and slapped a knee, the chair, a desk. The four guests stood in amused attention until the lawmen straightened into presentable poise. "Here," Jack said. He handed a large square-bottomed grocery sack to Nathan.

Nathan stood holding the large brown sack with its Kroger label. His cohorts peered alternately at him and the big sack. "Look in. Look in." The lawmen were stepping foot to foot in an obvious bid to contain their glee. "Look in. Look in." Nathan handed the sack to Del.

Del upended the sack.

Badges and vests and bow ties cascaded at their feet. "What the? What is this?"

"Your uniforms and badges of authority."

"Huh?"

"We'd hoped you'd go along. The duds we had for a party last Halloween, the tin badges too. We had such fun that memory fuels our glee to this day. Oh, the deputy sheriff badges are real, of course."

"These go with the rest," Sheriff Puller said. He passed each a white Stetson. "Now," he said, "I'll deputize you men and sort of deputize you younger men. We want you to officially be on a Big Foot hunt on the way down there to Kentucky and back. You are to try for any information that may lead to the whereabouts of Roy Marlin. Ask if any other strangers were seen. Get descriptions, you know. Also, you may question those down there, Digger, you know, to see if more can be learned about our missing Roy."

"It's kind of for fun," Jack said, "but for real, too. You'll find that a badge and uniform will get you into places a smile won't. But a smile to accompany a somewhat ludicrous attire may also net results; as some folks have a sense of humor, you see."

The adult new deputies thrust into their uniforms. The boys hopped into uniforms and pinned on the tin badges. They slapped on their Stetsons.

Deputy Sheriff badges shouted from the left chest of the men as they too slapped on their official Stetsons.

The sheriff swore them to duty after which they stood while Deputy Jack Trip snapped a dozen snapshots.

"Well, good hunting, men."

Later on that day the deputies were to leave for Kentucky with Russell's bones. Presently, however, Sergeant Fanny and her girls were near to the last stage of their visit at the Platt home on Peach Road, that to be a brief celebration of her promotion to sergeant. Needing to relax, she nearly dozed while watching the newly appointed deputies carefully load their belongings around the box with Junior's bones. The ample trunk of the gleaming black and white cruiser, she knew would be room enough. Sergeant Fanny struggled to stifle a yawn, deciding to postpone a visit to the hermit shack where she'd been told that Edith and Harold were engaged. Now that a set of croquet had been decided by Omi's smack of the end stake, Fanny could sit back in her lawn chair to let final tension dismount, but her shoulders never met the chair before she was on her feet. "Oh, my, I said I'd go to the shack to catch their newest ideas."

"They didn't say they needed you, Mom. She said for you to come along after a while if you wanted to."

"Well, I did enjoy the drama of croquet. You four sure kept me on the edge of my chair." She stood up from the gaily-colored chair and folded it. "I'll go in to visit a minute with the ladies. They seemed earlier to be rushing about in the kitchen. That's why I came on out to be with you champions."

Sergeant Fanny entered the house. She'd chatted with the ladies in the kitchen but a moment before movement outside turned her gaze to a window. Aunt Edith and Uncle Harold had just reached the foot of Mrs. Woods' driveway. "They look tired," Fanny said.

"Hot green tea and fresh-baked cake ought to recharge them." Luisa and Clydis were busy assembling the paraphernalia needed for the celebration of Fanny's gleaming promotion. "I'll give a call to them; hurry them along," Clydis said.

She called from the kitchen window: "Yahooo! You two! Hurry along. Cake and tea are a-waiting the celebration."

The pair squeezed hands and she murmured, "Dear, how could they know what to celebrate with us?"

"Well, we didn't get hurt, but of course poor Roy wasn't found either." They quickened their paces, meeting Sergeant Fanny at the house entry door.

Fanny asked: "Anything new?"

"Er, uh, oh no."

"Nothing to report," Harold said.

"Well, come on. We're all here but you two. Luisa and the others have arranged a celebration."

"Oh?" Edith bugged her eyes and Harold put on a wry smile.

Luisa said, "Hurry, you two, we're to celebrate Fanny's promotion to sergeant."

* * *

At the Platt home on Peach Road the four new deputies again endured a photo session, the session concluding when Luisa and Grandma handed sack lunches.

Sergeant Detective Deputy Sheriff Fanny Gillespie waved them on their way.

Del squawked rubber heading south on Peach.

In the cruising car Nathan began conversation by asking, "Who do you have working your business back home?"

"Uncle Helio's trucking freshly combined wheat and oats from northern Ohio into the Anderson grain terminal near Toledo. Aunt Anna Mae will be riding with him. I've loaned my Mack and our forty foot Lufkin semi trailer to Louie and Sid Watkins. They'll be hauling their own logs until we get back from Kentucky."

"And Grandma?"

"It's hard to realize that our cousin Sunshine Hulda became twenty-three years old this summer, and that she's landed a degree in Social Anthropology. She'll stay with Grandma Clydis the rest of this summer."

"She landed that position, did she; in the Sudan?"

"Yes, sure, but it's to begin this fall. At first she'll be schooled by someone from the State Department on what to do and say, or not to do or say, sort of to avoid any international misunderstandings. To show that she's legitimately a student, I guess. She'll work and live in Sudan then until she defends her thesis. That's a step toward her PhD."

"What religion is there to study?"

"I don't know for sure," Del said. "The Sudan religion has elements similar to Christianity even though the religion there is said to be Islam. Sudan was taken away from Egyptian and English rule back in the late eighteen hundreds by a Mahdi and his religion was imposed upon religion that was already established. In their originally established religion they have the birth of humans occurring when God had a man and a woman come out from under a tree root out in the desert. Hulda wants to see how much of the original religion is still practiced today despite their being Islamic. It's a situation sort of like the Ghost Dance religion the Souix Indians were practicing at the time of the Wounded

Knee massacre. The Sudan case is also a mimic of religious elements found in the Inca people of Peru."

"I don't get their connection to the Souix."

"Inca also, you said."

"Regarding the Souix and the Inca, there's not so much a connection as there is a parallel. The Indians massacred at Wounded Knee had had Christianity clapped upon their already established religion. They believed they were Christians seeing as how they believed they understood about the messiah and the flood, but they grouped together and painted themselves and danced; acted like Indians, so the troops gunned them down at day break."

From the rear seat of the cruiser, Miah asked, "Why?"

"Outwardly they still were practicing too much of their traditional ways, so much so that the troops didn't see them as Christians but as savages."

"In what ways, the chanting and dancing around all painted up?"

"Yes, that's all that the troops saw. Actually later it was learned from survivors that this band of Souix had information about the messiah and of the flood all wrong according to Christian understanding of those topics. The Indians thought the messiah was to come at the end of the earth and to cause a great flood but would save the Indians and the buffalo by placing them on higher ground. That situation would be heaven for the Indians."

"That sounds a little like Islam, the messiah at the end, that is" Nathan said. "The messiah, al-Mahdi, would come and change all religions of the world into Islam and would then reign over his heaven on earth."

"Yup, that's it."

"It's confusing to have a messiah named Mahdi and also men named Mahdi."

"To us, sure," Nathan said, "but in Mexico many men are named Jesus. You may have heard a Mexican name pronounced like 'hay – soose'. That's what Jesus sounds like in Spanish."

"Really, well how about a father, son, and holy ghost?"

"I'm not sure how that goes in Islam. We'll need to ask Sunshine Hulda about that one day. She'd know where Mohamed fits in; and the ghost, too. That is, if they do fit in."

"I wonder where does Moslem fit in; Islamic, is it?"

"A Moslem is a believer in or adherent of Islam. I took a course in religions of the world about twenty years ago so I'm not really up on it any more," Nathan said. "I can't recall a trinity in Islam, but I recall one in Hindu."

"Is cousin Hulda going to study that too?"

"No doubt, so then we can ask her and maybe figure out more of Hinduism. The Hindu Bible, their main one, is called the Gita. Brahma, Vishnu, and Shiva are the trinity; that is Father, Son, and Holy Spirit. Note that the top rung of their social or caste system is called Brahman, very like their name for God – Brahma. Their trinity'd likely be their religion's front line, but also they have millions of other gods to pray to."

"Like Catholics? Don't Catholics have all kinds of saints; sort of like gods?"

"Certainly not millions."

"How about Buddhists? Like in China, does anybody have a choice as to being Buddhist or not?"

"Another query for Sunshine Hulda. Buddha, though, isn't a god. 'Buddha' means 'awakened.' A Buddha is a religious teacher, a person enlightened so a follower may be directed to appropriate courses of action."

"How about those Inca?'

"Yes, well, the Sun is the God of the Inca. Sun, the god, sent a son and a daughter and they were the first humans and began with peopling the earth. There is a ruin, an ancient city called Machu Picchu, dating to about five hundred years ago. The people there worshipped Sun, their god. Those Inca were defeated and the Catholic religion was forced onto them, but they still clung to their former religion. Finally the Catholics made saints of the principles of the former Inca religion, thus making that old Inca religion a Christian one."

"Well, golly! Uncle Nathan, does Sunshine Hulda know that story?"

"Sure, she told it to me."

"It sounds a bit like heresy," Del put in.

"Hulda caught those vibes, as well, but it did smooth things out."

"I wonder if she'll find that tool used elsewhere."

"I'd bet she will, as it seemed to help there," Miah said, "but, Uncle

Del, with only one god, I don't see why there're so many different religions; even one, Buddhism, that's headed by a non-god."

Uncle Del rubbed his head.

In changing the subject to one more answerable, Miah asked Uncle Del, "Which religion has the most people?"

"Last I read," Uncle Nathan answered for Del, "the largest religion is Christian with 600,000,000 Catholics and 325,000,000 Protestants. Islam has 475,000,000 members but is said to be the fastest growing religion. Additionally, I can guess there're thousands of other religions.

"Why so many religions; and how come the Catholic church divided to allow Protestants?"

"You have me there, Miah. Just be glad protestant Christianity is simple; and simplicity may have been a factor in that split which occurred in the 1500s. It's not at all confusing to a Protestant as to how one can be saved. And, also, I like Protestantism because even though you're born a gentile, you still have a choice, to be one or to change. You are free to choose the religious route you wish to follow. In Islam and in many religions or religious sects you'd be bound for Hades if you tried to change to a different route. Catholics, for example, have no choice but to be Catholic."

"If only one God for the entire universe," Hi said, "then why in the Star Trek adventures in space don't they meet beings who worship the same God as we do, or, presumably they'd have the same religion as practiced by those on the U. S. Enterprise?"

"Now you've discovered why I don't watch trash such as those outer space programs. They leave the omnipotent ever-present God out altogether. The Lost in Space program treats religion the same way as does Star Trek. Those two programs and any others of their ilk deny the fact of a one, and the only, God, and so they miss an obvious medium for communicating with creatures they encounter elsewhere in the universe."

"Likely, too, there'll be reruns forever, but Uncle Nathan I really like the special effects."

"That's not realistic, Cuzz. It's just run wild imagination. It's about as meaningful as squawking tires on dirt. I guess we're stuck with that special effect for ever."

"Say, guys, this is all getting heavy. My head's starting to hurt," Del said. "Let's talk about railroads and begin looking before I cruise right on past the site of the Wabash Cannonball. That'd be coming up soon."

Hi unfolded the map. With a finger he followed the route that Deputy Jack Trip had marked out. His finger tapped a circle where Jack had indicated a high point. "Hey, Dad, that Cannonball shop has ice cream too."

"And at that ice cream Cannonball stop," Nathan gloated, "I take over the driving of this lusty cruiser. In my turn fellows, watch me squawk 'um on dirt."

* * *

On the following afternoon, but one hundred fifty miles northwest of Manitou Prairie, at Leadford, Michigan, the big white camper slowed for its turn from Cross Road onto Jericho. In bucket seats Harold from behind the wheel strained to see ahead, and from her bucket Edith's neck cricked with her eyes pulling her head nearly to the massive windshield. Grandma Clydis also craned from the middle bucket seat. "There! There!" They all called at once as the arborvitae came to view. Long ago, when Edith was but a babe they'd planted the tree. 'It is Edith's tree. It is the tree she'll look for when coming home.' Edith had tears in her eyes. Grandma Clydis wept openly. "Home. Oh, home. Home. I do so miss my Clarence."

Sunshine Hulda pulled the camper door open even before its complete stop. "Hi, welcome home." They watched her lips move but heard only the roar of a Simplicity riding mower as Joe James was completing a pass. The Simplicity din dimmed into distance and suddenly lessened considerably as Joe disengaged the mower deck. "Delbert's here too," Hulda said, "hoeing the garden. Grandma, we expected you here a bit later so we did the folk's place first."

Her last words were muffled as Edith had taken her into a bear hug. Harold elbowed in to also hug his daughter. "Momma, Papa, we've missed you so; and Grandma, too."

"Hey, vagabonds," Delbert was jubilant as he walked up with a hoe in one hand and with a sack held in the other, "we were beginning to think we'd need to consume the garden stuff ourselves. I've picked snap beans, Swiss chard, and the end of the peas. Sweet corn will be ready in a day or so along with the tomatoes. How was the trip?"

"Great, we even threw in an unexpected adventure or two," his father said, but wasn't heard as Grandma grabbed the hoe and tossed it and grabbed the guy's head to pull toward hers, all while Momma bear hugged her eldest son sack and all and both ladies showered their grinning kin with murmurs and kisses.

"Papa," Sunshine moved back into his arms and pecked his cheek. "There's Canada Dry Ginger Ale in your frig and in grandma's. It has no caffeine. The ice tea has caffeine but the iced coffee is Sanka.

"No tea till the morning's light, then. Thanks, Sunshine. We sure missed you. All set for Sudan, are you?"

"All set for October. I'm to take some more classes. One on diplomacy, and then on what ever they say then I'm going by ship." In the near distance the Simplicity revved and pulled their attention to Joe who leaned forward over the dusty orange hood of the willing beast to urge the rider up a pair of planks and into his trailer.

Papa and daughter started toward Joe. "Howdy, Howdy, welcome you all!" He performed a western style dismount that missed the trailer's side to land him lightly upon the hard dirt of the driveway. He bee lined into a firm handshake from Papa Harold. "Welcome home. Your lawn's done too and your garden. One ripe tomato already; so congratulations."

The kids each grabbed a couple of suitcases and the group flowed into the massive kitchen. Grandma flicked a switch and the many bobbled crystal chandelier began to cast its cheer upon the green oilcloth table spread that covered the massive oak table. Soon the group had assembled under the chandelier and each held a mug of cool Canada Dry or of iced Sanka. Gab was from every direction, immersing them all in family affection. Finally, Harold announced the time as close to sundown. Edith and Harold piled into Delbert's car and they followed Joe out past the arborvitae and onto Jericho Road, beginning a three mile jaunt to the James' home. Edith and Harold were on the edge of their seats. "No place like home," Harold breathed.

"And our own bed wrapped around us," Edith cooed.

* * *

Before dawn at the old Groner home on Jericho, Grandma Clydis woke to the chirp of a robin. Her light summer covers went flying and she was on her feet quicker than her mind could assign a mission. In the kitchen she placed the percolator over the blue gas flame and stood beside the Westinghouse range still with no idea as to what was to be her task that day. At the first phulmp! her mind saw the beautiful coffee tumble about inside the perk dome, and she knew. Her hands came to her face and tears flooded over her fingers and cascaded down the back of her hands. She knelt crashing to her knees and her forearms came to rest on her thighs. Her face buried into her hands. Her entire body shook and her mind, her soul, her being cried out, "God in Heaven, please! Oh my precious, Lord. I love him. I miss him so!"

The flame too high, the coffee's enthusiasm exceeded the percolator confine and boiled over, meeting the insistent blue flame in a loud sizzle of steam.

Sunshine Hulda awoke and came running, entering the kitchen in a confrontation of Hell on Earth what with the steam, the glow of red and blue flame in the dim morning light, and with her beautiful Grandma prostrate on the floor, and with Grandma screaming for God to please let her see Clarence.

"Grandma! Grandma!" Hulda reached to still the flame and steam and that steam burned her hand even as she quelled the flame. "Oh, Grandma, Grandma." She knelt with her gram and held her, both lambs crying. "Oh Grandma, Grandpa Clarence heard your plea. He loves you still and forever and he wants you to be with him when it is your time." She pulled Grandma Clydis into her lap. "Grandma, he loves you and waits patiently for you. My dear precious Grandma Clydis, you must complete your work on earth and then go to join him."

"I know, I know, but Hulda, it is so hard; the hardest it has been in my life." Her sobs had quieted yet still jerked at her speech. "It's the robin. I woke to the robin. His favorite bird. Our favorite bird. The bird called to me to put the coffee over and its perk and aroma would bring my love to me. I'm sorry, dear, that a babbling old hag has alarmed you."

"No, Grandma, no trouble. Your love drew me. Come, your back is wet. Let me pull the gown off you. Come back into your room, into the brighter light."

In the better light she knew at once. "Grandma, you're burned! Scalded by the coffee. Wait here. I'll call the Nealy Clinic."

"Bring her in right away. Do you need an ambulance?"

"Yes, she should be lying on her tummy for transport."

During that night Anna Mae and Helio had arrived home with Del's faithful old Mack tractor, having finished with grain hauls in Ohio. Seeing that the big white camper was home ahead of them, they were thrilled to hop into it where slumber promptly claimed their tired bodies. Now they awoke to the shrill of an ambulance! Quickly they untangled from each other, their eyes snapping to the flash of lights outside the camper door. Pulling robes about them, their feet met the soft grass of the lawn even before the robes were tied. "Helio, hurry!"

Tying the robes on the run, they followed the gurney inside. They heard Hulda call, "In here. Her back is scalded."

"Hulda, what . . .?"

"Oh, Aunt Anna Mae, I'm so glad you two are here. I found her kneeled on the floor beside the range. The coffee had boiled over and scalded her."

"Your hand, too, is scalded. It's blistering. Go in with Grandma. We'll follow."

At the ambulance door, Hulda stood quietly as Grandma was pushed inside. In the quiet, no one spoke but the robin. Its chirp drew Sunshine Hulda's attention. "You darned old robin," she said.

Later, back at home on Jericho, Grandma Clydis said, "Hulda, bring Noxzema from the med cabinet in the bathroom. Put some, a lot of it, on your hand and on my back."

"But, Grandma?"

"Do it."

Sunshine Hulda looked to Aunt Anna Mae and Uncle Helio. "Yes," Anna Mae said. "It has always been our remedy for burns. It was invented first as a burn remedy rather than as a cleansing cream. We've used it all these years."

"But they've applied sterile gauze."

"Good. They did right, but now Grandma knows best."

The Noxzema was soothing and with aunt and uncle close at hand, Sunshine Hulda decided on a quick visit to her folks.

Behind cups of creamy sweetened Postum, she told her parents what had transpired. "Praise God you were there," Momma Edith said, "we must not leave her alone any more. Oh, praise God, you were there. And, Sunshine, keep on with Grandma's remedy. She's been our doctor all these years. In a day or so she'll have you mainly by soaking, gently wash away the Noxzema. By then the burn will have stopped its hurting for ever and you and she will be alright. By fall, not a trace of your burn will remain and, dear, I suggest you take a jar of Noxzema along to the Sudan."

"I hate now to think of leaving for the Sudan."

"Sweety, Papa Harold said, "you must stop with saying such nonsense. Anna Mae will be with her. She and Helio will leave soon on their trip to Alaska. Grandma looks forward to visiting with you while they're gone and with your aunt and uncle when they return. While you are away Grandma said she'd take a trip or two with Helio and Anna Mae when they are pulling their loads with the camper's white tractor."

Sunshine felt better. Suddenly a finger came to her chin and she said, "Is Uncle Helio joking? He said they were going to see whether Alaska has a town called Seven Mile."

"Joking, yes. We stopped with the big white camper once in Ohio, an hour short of our destination of Greenville. Hearing the town was called Seven Mile, your dad joked that Deputy Jack had sure taken us off course, and landed us in Alaska. Later, Grandma told Helio about the fun Jack and Harold had had over Seven Mile. Helio said there wasn't any town in Alaska that he knew about called Seven Mile, but he'd check and see for sure on his next trip home."

Sunshine Hulda rubbed her head, thinking: Old folks have the strangest humor. Her gentle smile remained as she said, "What of the hermits? Is that all solved?"

"No, unfortunately. Three men were involved. We found the graves of two of them but have no clue as to the fate of the other. Sadly, if there must be a single good guy in this tragedy, that guy could be Roy Marlin. Roy tried so hard to help his brother then Roy disappeared as into thin air. Babe Toberton of the Toberton dairy, you know her. Well, her daughter Fanny is a detective sergeant for the Manitou County Sheriff's Department. We were so thrilled to team up with her on the hermit case. The case is in her hands now and we're all rooting for her while at the same time we're wracking our brains to discover the clue that would lead to finding Roy."

"Should Grandma be still on the case?"

"Oh, sure. The deeper the better. Try to encourage her; to keep her mind away from Grandpa Clarence."

"I'll try, but the scalding occurred in the night, just before daybreak. She said a robin awakened her. Momma, I'm going to set an alarm and try to be up in time to shut up that old robin."

Momma chuckled. "You're a trooper, dear; a great companion for your grandma."

"Your mother's right," Papa said.

"Papa, I want to ask you about the Nation of Roughwater."

"Actually, your cousin Del and your Uncle Helio likely know the most about the Roughwater Indians."

"Yes, but Papa, you've mentioned before that a people can't die as long as their culture and religion survives. That's an anthropological idea and it relates, I think, to my work in Sudan. The people are as they are at least in part because they want to keep their past alive; at least their culture and their religion alive. That's why crucial parts of their past are held to with such rigor despite their having a new religion placed upon them. I want to see how much they've retained of their former religion and to get an assessment of how meaningful that is to them individually. I also want to determine the number of generations an idea may persist and why. That is, what keeps the idea alive?"

"At wounded Knee and for years after," Papa said, "the American Indians could be Indians only in secret. Whites were afraid the Indians would remain Indians, dangerous Indians, unless they were forced to live as whites. The Nation of Roughwater was formed in an effort to encourage all Native Americans, the Indians so called, to practice being Indian as much as possible but to show a white face to the whites. Their hope was that someday the whites would see that Indians were human beings and with the right of dignity like all other humans. That has gradually come about until at present we increasingly find folks striving to get others to believe they have Indian heritage."

"I wonder how much of a parallel I'll find over there," Hulda said.

"I've a hunch you'll find parallels all over," Momma said. "The Greeks had a god, an invented god according to a former pastor of ours, a god named Zeus. Using water and earth, Zeus formed the first woman and her name was Pandora. Also, there is at least one group of Native Americans who believe that where humans came from is that humans first emerged from the floor of the Grand Canyon. Despite the pull of Christianity, they still believe that, much as your Sudan people may believe the story of the first humans emerging from under a tree root in the desert."

"Another group," Papa said, "one closer to home; the Ojibwa or Chippewa, the largest group of Native Americans in Michigan, as you know. Well, they say their name means 'first people'. I learned about that belief at a powwow of theirs at St Ignace, but they didn't seem to know just where they, the 'first people', came from."

"There're so many beliefs, and, Momma and Papa, I can't believe they are doomed to Hades if their Bible or their traditional belief spells things out differently from ours. People all over the world believe in God. In Africa there is a region called the Serengeti. We, unknowingly, may see it as a vast pasture or zoo for us to safari into. But to the people there 'Serengeti' means 'Creator provided.' Creator provided; haven't I heard that expression voiced in our own Family Gospel Church?"

Chapter Eighteen

At various stops in Indiana and Ohio, the four deputies asked older community members about events some twenty years past. The deputies were trying to gain a clue as to whether or nor Roy as well as Digger had been on the trail of Larry. Their stops were quite brief because they had a time deadline for arriving at Raccoon Mountain, Kentucky with Junior's bones. Feeling that they really should devote more time to the Roy issue, they decided it could be efficient to begin a meander along the north bank of the Ohio River near North Bend, Ohio. The meander would lead into Cincinnati and the bridge across to Covington, Kentucky. Their route, they hoped, would be a logical one for a person or persons walking to Kentucky.

To their good luck, an old timer at North Bend recalled an incident nearby that occurred while he was a fledgling Hamilton County Deputy Sheriff.

"Yes, there was others seeking a look at Big Foot," he said, "northerners, they were; at least two of them. One was dressed like a hunter, with a bird pouch in his jacket, you know, and he wore L. L. Bean boots. I talked with him a while. He said that he'd heard Big Foot stories all down through Indiana and now Ohio. I heard his name, but I don't recall it. The other fellow was wearing moccasins and they actually looked homemade but before I got to him he'd disappeared. I asked Mr. L. L. Bean if he saw that other fellow, not Big Foot, and did he know this other fellow's name, but he said he didn't even see that fellow with the moccasins."

The four deputies were expecting a report of Big Foot and one other, who they knew to be Digger Marl but until that chat with the old deputy they hadn't gained a clue pointing to a possible presence of Roy. The four had talked of the incident that night in a Cincinnati hotel lobby and decided to call Grandma Clydis in the morning. Aunt Anna Mae answered the telephone and they learned of Grandma and Sunshine Hulda's scalding. They decided then to call Aunt Edith and Uncle Harold. Sunshine Hulda answered the telephone.

"Hello you deputy officers, where are you?"

"In Cincinnati. How is Grandma? How are you?"

"Fine. We went to the hospital and now Grandma has us plastered with Noxzema. What's up with you?"

"Tell Aunt Edith and Uncle Harold to both pick up. We may have a clue that Roy Marlin was seen down here."

"Nathan, what have you learned," Uncle Harold said.

Nathan could hear that Aunt Edith had also picked up. "A Big Foot was seen at North Bend, Ohio and an old retired deputy sheriff said he also saw a hunter wearing L. L. Bean boots and that he saw another stranger wearing what appeared to be homemade moccasins. The two men showed up a day or so after the Big Foot was seen. Those two men were the only strangers around but the moccasined man disappeared before the deputy got to talk with him. Can you tell us what sort of man we're looking for in Roy?"

"I'll read the description we've assimilated," Aunt Edith said. "Five foot seven, medium build at around one-sixty pounds. His molars were gone also. Full head of reddish brown hair. Come to think of it, Nathan, we haven't tried to see where Larry or Roy would've obtained their shoes. Self constructed moccasins may be the answer. Why are you looking for Roy down there?"

"Sheriff Puller asked us to inquire. That old deputy here didn't mention reddish brown or ample hair. Deputy Jack said that Deputy Clydis and Sergeant Fanny had notions about Roy. We called Grandma but talked with Aunt Anna Mae. She said about the scalding and that Grandma was finally sound asleep."

"I'll call Detective Sergeant Fanny and will fill you in when next you call in. Tonight, will that be?"

"Yes, we're running behind schedule and need to bee line now and pick up on the Roy and Digger clues on the way home. It'll likely be nine or so when we call you back."

"Good, you call Grandma tonight around nine then. We'll be there with Grandma and we can all talk together on the telephone."

"Grandma okay, is she?"

"Yes, their burns hurt but Dr. Nealy says they're going to be okay. We'll hear from you tonight."

Del kept the lights flashing and used the siren from time to time on the one hundred forty-five miles to London, arriving at the turn onto Raccoon Mountain in just a tad over two hours. From the house Margie, Hal, Jill, and Digger led out for the parlor in town. Business was quickly concluded at the parlor including the official legal transfer of the remains. Then their badges flashing, Del collared Digger and Nathan collared Jill. They occupied separate rooms in the funeral parlor. Margie and Hal had some loose ends to tie with the funeral director then they sat down with Hi and Miah. "Are you really deputies? You seem so young."

"Sheriff Puller swore us in as unofficial deputies but in uniforms like our dads. We are authorized to gather information."

"About what, or who?"

"Roy Marlin. Ma'am can you tell us the color of his hair?"

"Dark brown with just a tinge of red, not rusty red like Larry's. Larry always went bare headed and we think the sun lightened his hair and brought the red out. Roy and Russell Junior preferred to wear baseball caps which kept their hair from the sun's influence."

"How about shoes? Where did Roy and Larry get their shoes?"

"Roy could wear Senior's or Junior's, or Digger's shoes, all the same size. They made Larry's shoes from deer hide, Digger has a shoe repair stand, and they sewed car tire tread on them for soles, but Larry was barefoot that last time we saw him."

"Any particular about Roy's clothing; a favorite hat, perhaps, or a preferred style of pants, shirt, or jacket?"

"Just overalls, not Levis, not bib overalls either, and a solid-color shirt. His hat didn't have a team name on it like today's nor an adjustable band at the back. He preferred the tan hat although khaki was available at the hardware."

"Thank you both. Can you think of other info that would help to identify him?"

"Clean shaved, he didn't like a beard. Digger kept him supplied with Burma Shave so he didn't need hot water or shaving mug and such, but

Larry plain refused to shave or be shaved. Larry could get very mean if he was pushed. Roy got on the best with Larry."

The funeral director came into the room, interrupting their interviewing of Margie and Hal Sweeney. "Gentlemen and ma'am, there's someone here to see you."

An old man who was bent about double at the waist came into the room. Margie rushed to his side and placed an arm across his shoulders. "This is very good of you, Preacher Jacob. You would've truly liked my Russell Junior."

Preacher Jacob rocked his head backward and shifted his weight to the rear until it seemed that Margie was his entire support. She eased him into a chair. "I'll talk some at Junior's service. I came today to say that I would and to say about Big Foot. My cousin never preached no more after Big Foot nigh killed him when it yanked down the revival tent."

"Oh, my dear; when?"

"Sir, was it recent?"

He focused his tiny round eyes upon Hi. "Twenty years ago. Me and Cousin Curly Ben Forge went on a tent revival tour. We took turns preaching or running the roads to tell of the revival and it was his turn to preach. The tent was all lit up with Coleman mantel lanterns and he was praying to have them for sure know the world was about to end, praying real loud, he was, then there was screaming and a beast tore out the tent post and swung it around and the whole shebang went up in smoke; folks never did come back. We took it as a clear sign that we shouldn't be in the tent revival ministry.

"He didn't preach no more at all but I did I took hold of the little Raccoon Mountain Church until my son Jimmy Seth took that church over. I heard from my cousin Sheriff Dewy John that you were hunting that Big Foot to this very day."

"Sure. Thank you. My dad and I and my uncle Nathan and my cousin Miah, here, are deputized to collect information about Big Foot. Margie and Hal looked at Hi in disbelief that Preacher Jacob couldn't detect that he was reciting to a mere boy, one who struggled to keep his voice pitched like a man.

"Yes," Miah said, himself pitched as low of voice as he could hold, "we also want to know if strangers were in your midst at that same time as Big Foot was. Did you see any strangers?"

"Uh, all was, as this was a revival and folks came from afar; mostly from the mountains north and west of Victory. Me and Cousin Curly Ben Forge were strangers, too. We'd traveled a fair piece all summer with our tent, traveled with a cart and mule. The mule ran off; scared, too, of that Big Foot and the fire."

"Sir, can you recall the time of year that was?"

"Er, yup, we was meeting the first week of June."

Hi turned to Margie and Hal. "In June of 1951. You folks were around at that time?"

"Hadn't before heard of it," Hal said, but that'd be near about when Larry was here all right."

"And Digger Marl too?"

Hal rubbed his head. "Ah, now I don't think he was; huh Margie?"

"No, just Larry."

"And Senior left out to find Larry."

"And Senior never was all right since then, we understand. He didn't talk about seeing Larry?"

"Said he didn't see Larry."

"Well, you've all been very helpful. We thank you very much."

"Preacher Jacob," Margie took his hand, "where was your revival when Big Foot did that sinful deed to you brothers and to the people? Was it here at the mountain?"

"No, up at Victory nearby to East Bernstadt. We called us the Victory Revival."

"We'll stop in there to talk with folks," Miah said. "Thank you, kind sir, for your report. God is truly by your side."

* * *

"Hello." The hello sounded like a chorus. "Who is . . ."

"Edith, let me speak. We must take turns. Nathan, we all talked at once is what you heard."

"Yes, Grandma, I thought I'd gotten the Gospel Chorus."

"Well, I'm gonna talk mainly. What have you found out?"

"The boys found out. Del and I struck out talking with Digger and Jill but Hi and Miah talked with Margie and Hal and an old pastor named Preacher Jacob. He and a cousin were holding a revival at Victory. We're housed in Bernstadt tonight right near the small town of Victory.

Folks here at Bernstadt recall when you folks were here in the big white camper. At supper we met folks who recall youins but none recalled the revival that was attacked by Big Foot. Tomorrow we're going to work to the northeast of here. That's where folks assembled from to come to the Victory Revival. What have you on that moccasined stranger seen at North Bend, Ohio?"

"Not Fanny nor us could make him. Digger, yes, we agree that one of the strangers was Digger even though Digger hasn't admitted to've followed Larry south, but the man with moccasins isn't enough like Roy Marlin."

"We did get a description for Senior from Jill. That's for when Larry was here back in June of 1951. Senior always wore a broad-brimmed hat as protection while mining. He wore red or blue plaid shirts and black pants with a wide black belt. He wore heavy engineer's boots; altogether a typical miner's get up."

"That's not the description Fanny gathered on him while he lived here, but Fanny's description would rather match Russell Junior as Roy, so Senior changed a lot. That moccasined man seen at North Bend doesn't sound like either Senior or Roy, but the other man there fits Digger."

"How are the Sweeneys?"

"Good, Aunt Edith. "They seem happy. They put up some tents and rented cots and chairs and tables and when we were leaving already most of the Manitou Prairie folks had arrived and moved in. Talk was so generous that it'd sure chase out any Big Foot. The relatives melded so grandly it was a pleasure to see. I'm sure no one missed us as we pulled away."

"Good, now what about that revival?"

"Hi and Miah will describe it to you. They've written it all down."

The boys told all they could of the Victory Revival. Aunt Edith came on to talk with Nathan: "My, that sure was a frightening affair. It should help you guys a lot when you go around that area tomorrow. Using their descriptions, I suggest that you ask if anyone saw either Digger or Senior. That failing, ask if any had seen Roy. Fanny says it looks more and more unlikely that Roy went south with Larry that last time; that is in June of 1951. None of us has found evidence that Roy went south."

"Grandma, what caused you to think Roy may have been here at that time?"

"He'd know Larry better than anyone. It's awful to think it, but Fanny and I thought just maybe it'd be a case like 'Of Mice and Men.' Get it?"

"Yes, gosh that would be terrible if Roy turned out to be George and Larry turned out to be George's simple-minded friend."

"Yes, you see the parallel. You recall that Lenny killed a bunny and he killed a woman. Locking Lenny up would've been a terrible tragedy for Lenny and perhaps, but almost certainly, for many others. George killed poor simple-minded Lenny. A man said to George, 'That's all you could do, George.' We'd thought that it may be that one, or all, of Digger, Roy, and Senior killed Larry. Larry, we know, is buried in an old mine shaft of Senior's. It looks now like Roy is not implicated in Larry's demise."

"Well, we'll search by using their descriptions tomorrow. We'll check in again tomorrow night. Nine at night, OK?"

"Yes, we'll all be here at nine."

* * *

Hi and Miah keep their badges partly hidden under their vests, thinking they'd pass more readily as 'official' deputies. All four of the party stayed in uniform, wearing their vests, bow ties, and their white Stetsons. Expecting to command the most respect along the way, Del and Nathan displayed deputy sheriff badges on the outside of their vests. The foursome drove the narrow winding curvy roads northeast of the town of Victory, stopping to interview anyone they saw.

Typically an encountered person would stand foot to foot and would know 'nothing about no revival, fire, or Big Foot', but around noon they encountered an old woman picking dewberries along a roadside. She didn't hear them stop the sheriff's cruiser.

"Ma'am."

She jumped a foot then held her pail of dewberries behind her. She stood stock still and ran her eyes over the strangers. "Ma'am, those are fine looking dewberries and we can see you're pickin' um right what with long sleeves and with gloves with the finger tips removed. We can go along and pick our own dewberries and won't bother you none but we need to know if you heard of or have seen a Big Foot. Big Foot, say, at the revival over at Victory or of a revival tent afire anyplace like over at Victory. Oh, a long time ago, that would be."

She glowered at them. "You law? Dewberries ain't nobody's. I ain't agoing to make no wine out of them." She traveled the foursome with her squinted eyes, finally settling them on Hi. "Junior, you ain't but a boy, are you?"

"Yes Ma'am. Me and cousin Miah are unofficial deputies from Michigan. We're here to learn about Big Foot that was here when you were a younger like Miah and me. I'm Hi. What is your name?"

"Beulah. These dewberries ain't nobody's." She moved the pail to her front and bent to pick more of the large black dewberries, each berry surrounded by very briary vines. "Ain't nobody's."

"Yes, Ma'am, you are right to pick um. When you were half your age a Big Foot struck a revival tent over at Victory."

"Were a man, no Big Foot. Some mad Yankee from north. Burned the tent and nigh killed us folks."

"That's correct, Miss Beulah," Del said. "Did you -" His eyes met hers, and she glared at him, stopping his speech in mid sentence.."

"Who you?"

"Del, I'm Hi's daddy."

"Talkin' to the boy."

"Yes, Ma'am."

"These boys is half lawmen. Their badge is half hidden. I'm talkin' with these half lawmen. Two other Yankees came nosing that day and the next. Said they was after that other that burnin' Yankee."

Nathan ventured to say, "Boys, the descriptions."

"A man about five foot seven," Miah said, "who wore a tan cap with a bill like a baseball cap, Ma'am?"

"No, never."

"A man wearing engineer's boots and a big brimmed black hat -- "

"Saw him."

"Thanks, Ma'am."

"And a man wearing rubber boots with leather tops. He was -- "

"Him, too. They chased that other Yankee and shot at him over along the Rockcastle. We saw him in a black coal truck."

"You saw a black coal truck?"

"Yep, an old Mack truck from down around London, we saw. Raccoon

Mountain was writing on the door. Said that was coal in it covered up with a tarp but we hadn't never before seen coal toted that way."

"You have been very helpful. Thank you, Miss Beulah."

They were soon on their way toward Manitou Prairie. Del was driving the powerful Plymouth cruiser. Nathan turned to the rear seat to converse with Miah and Hi. "We were sure lucky we had you half deputies along. We must have tried to interview a dozen others before we ran into Beulah. Good going, guys."

"Dad, can a horse see very well?"

"One near Beulah, was there?"

"Didn't see one but on the way down, I watched horses and now that we're out of those Kentucky Mountains, we're passing some again. They always point their ears at us."

"A horse whether Kentucky or not," Del spoke up, "but I've noticed it more out west where they still work cattle, sheep, even hogs, and other horses and such with horses. A horse points its ears to the direction of its interest. It may turn to that direction next, as in driving cattle, sheep, etcetera, or when danger or excitement is sensed."

"But yet they do seem to have good eye sight," Nathan said. "My guess is that they can zero in on direction best by using their ears; sort of supplemental to the eyes. People use their ears to do a similar trick in aiming our eyes toward a sound."

"Blind people always face the sound as well. Ears do more than just hear, then?"

"Yep."

"I wonder if UFO people have ears like us and horses. Those UFO folks that were reported to've been seen in New Mexico had big, big eyes but no obvious ears. I'd think they'd need ears like ours or the horses."

"Yes, seems like it."

"I wonder then if UFO people were actually seen that time in New Mexico"

"I'd say, likely, seeing as UFOs have been seen for years, even centuries. But if God is all over the whole universe, he would've made beings like us, I'd think, so you've made a good point with concern for those ears."

"How did we get here from you guys' success with Beulah?"

"She acted strange," Hi joked. "Maybe she was a UFO person."

"I wonder if in heaven we'd see all of the other aliens that passed the Pearly Gate. That seems likely to me. I'll bet they'll have ears, big ones."

"Too deep for me," Nathan said. "I've been confused about what to expect in heaven for all of my life, I think. At first I thought the folks were talking about our brother Jimmy being there."

"Jimmy?"

"Who?"

"It's seldom talked about but we had a brother born before I was born. That'd be after your Uncle Ward, but Jimmy died before I was born. He has a grave marker, though, at Cannonsburg cemetery."

"Gosh, Dad, we didn't know that."

"Seldom talked about, but when I was real young, say around three or four, every Saturday night the family listened to a country music program on the radio; no TV back then. I knew by that age that our brother Jimmy was in heaven and the folks would quiet us and say 'Little Jimmy was coming on'. So I figured Little Jimmy was in heaven and that's why we listened faithfully to that radio show. You've noticed that Grandma Clydis uses the term 'dickens' a lot, though not so much lately. Well, the folks must have used 'dickens' a lot also so when Little Jimmy added Dickens to his name, that when he joined the Grand Old Opry, I figured our brother, Little Jimmy Dickens was in heaven."

"Would our Little Jimmy be there along with those aliens?"

"How could he get saved? He wouldn't know about Jesus."

"I don't know, but I'd think aliens must be in heaven somewhere and so would our brother Jimmy be. I think when you're too young or for whatever reason you had no way of knowing about Jesus, God makes an exception for beings like that."

"What do you now think heaven is like?"

"I don't know, boys, but I decided when very young that I wanted to go to heaven because it would be the place that had all of the correct answers. I'd figured that out by about the second grade. Already by the second grade it seemed to me that about everything I learned in school was a pack of lies according to the church. I knew that that couldn't be, but I didn't dare to say about it. I waited until the preacher had an invitation service and I raised my hand."

"Gee, not in Bible School?"

"Nope, right during church."

"How come where we go to church now they just sprinkle water on you but in Uncle Naveapse's church, they dip you under?"

"Just the type of church it is," Del put in, and it's a strange thing about that. You don't need to be baptized to get into heaven but you need to have been baptized to join a church. It's a case where people's law seems to be over-riding God's law. I don't know if that's why Uncle Nathan's not joined a church."

"Well, I didn't know of that requirement," Nathan said, "but I know why I've never submitted to being baptized. But now, and are you sure of this, Miah? You just get sprinkled at our church?"

"Yup. I asked about it."

"I may do it then. The scriptures say to be baptized and then to go on and practice being Christian. Not that Jesus said baptism is a requirement to be met before one attempts heaven. Rather, he said to get baptized and go out and teach or preach. Being baptized with all of us, the whole family, would be great.

"In our family we each knew when to be baptized. Each one older was baptized, by dunking, you see. Well when Melanie got baptized, I asked her, 'How was it?' She said, 'it was cold, Nathan.' Then after Ward was baptized I asked him. 'How was it, Ward?' He said, 'it hurts your nose, Nathan' so I never was baptized because I never did like cold water and I didn't want to get my nose hurt."

"Let's do it, Dad; by sprinkling."

"We'll look into it when we get home."

"I've already done it," Del said. "I thought baptizing was necessary to get into heaven. Brother-in-law Charles Naveapse did it. It was right after the truck accident and, believe me, I knew then what I wanted to do. No Hell for me. I got saved all over again to be sure and I got baptized."

"After you hurt your eye?"

"Eye socket, mainly. Yes, I got baptized right after that whack and after the semi trailer tires burned right off the Lufkin. Your Aunt Dosia went through the truck terror alone as I was unconscious, but it sure scared me when I learned what we'd been through. The tubeless truck tires like we have now are less likely to catch on fire. They're not as dangerous as the old non-belted tires containing tubes back in the 1950s."

"Anybody hungry?" Miah rubbed his tummy.

"We'll catch the next truck stop."

In the truck stop just north of Lexington their necks craned to see the pictures of trucks and truckers on the walls as they passed through to a window-view table. Del was the last of the foursome to be seated. "Those truckers from around here?" he asked the waitress.

"Yes, some. Guys, what will you have to drink?"

"Milk."

"All milk?"

"Yep."

"The special today is meatloaf, potatoes, gravy, and string beans."

"That's for me," Del said and he rose from his chair. The others stated identical food preference. She turned toward the order window and nearly collided with Del.

"She from around here?" Del pointed to a woman depicted with one foot resting upon the front bumper of a large olive drab army truck.

"I'll ask." Del went on along the pictures and had just completed his scrutiny of them when again he nearly bowled the waitress over. Struggling to steady her tray of milk glasses and a milk pitcher, she said, "The boss is a trucker; drives a Kenworth. She said that's a friend of hers."

"No name, huh?"

"She'll be out with the dinners."

The boss set the food and said, "That's an army rig, a five ton used to haul a bulldozer. And that lady, that's Annie Redden; well, Annie Barker now, and she's in Utah now, but she also was in the army. Drove every size truck they had, but she started here in Kentucky. Annie was the first female in the United States of America to hold a commercial driver's license. That's the CDL, you may know, that truckers have to have."

"Sure know it," Del said. "First lady to hold one, huh? My wife drove an eighteen-wheeler once."

"Can she back a triple? Can you?"

"I'd bet she'd try it if a situation warranted. Me, I've only backed singles."

"Annie won a truck backing up contest in Australia. She won it backing a triple. Are you surprised?"

He rubbed his hair. "I guess not. I've found out a woman can do most anything. A friend, he reads a lot, well, he told me about Amy Clarke, the lady who fought beside her Confederate husband at Shiloh. I see a lady trucking once in a while. I'm not surprised. A triple, by gum. I somehow caught that she was a special trucker when we first came in here."

"Where are you sheriffs from?"

"Michigan. We're deputy sheriffs investigating a Big Foot sighting that occurred around here about twenty years ago."

"Not hot news, I guess."

"No, but your Annie, the trucker, is. My mother-in-law is writing a book about trucking. You wouldn't happen to have Annie's address."

"Sure. I'll get it."

That afternoon they stopped for refreshments in the town of Seven Mile, Ohio and were surprised in finding Seven Mile was also the name of the river that flowed nearby. They found tourist cabins to rent along that river and Del called his in-laws. Helio C. Outhe raised the receiver. "How do, Outhe's and Groner's."

"Dad, it's Del. We've found some cabins in sight of Seven Mile River so we're staying the night here. We've news for ma for her book."

"Seven Mile River, huh? Amazing. Through Seven Mile town then? Anna Mae's out at the camper. We're heading out for Northway Village, Alaska early tomorrow. It's good that Sunshine Hulda can stay with Grandma. We're taking a long way home, not leaving Alaska until we hear that Sniffer and Snifferette have arrived out in Maine. She wants to visit Prince Edward Island, Canada. That's the area where Lucy Maud Montgomery based the Anne of Green Gables books, her books starting in 1908. Then we'll wander on down to pick up the dogs. Here's your ma-in-law."

"Del, honey, where are you? Did I hear Seven Mile?"

"Yup, river and town both. You ever hear of Annie Grace Cook, or Redden? She's the very first female CDL holder in the USA. She was nee Cook, but Annie Grace Redden in 1943 when she was granted the license in Kentucky. Now she might be Annie Grace Barker, her friend here said, as Annie may have married anew. Amazing lady. Should I send my info to you at Leadford?"

"No, send it to Helio's family in Alaska. Son-in-law, you've done super good sleuthing there. Thank you." She recited the Alaskan address. With a book about finished, I've begun scouting for a new book topic. I'd like serendipity somewhere in the title. It's like your finding Annie

Grace. We were way out East, a while back, and met serendipity when a hotdog sign grabbed our attention. In gab with a fellow customer, he said 'Oh home of the famous hotdog sauce, huh?' That took us by surprise, but he was correct, such a sauce does exist. In Leadford in the thirties at the close of prohibition, a tavern owner named Hyde and two brothers, Harold and Howard Bailey, teamed with a retired Army cook named George Myer to concoct a hotdog sauce. The recipe is still a secret; even kept in a bank vault. The sauce is exclusive to that tavern at the stoplight in Leadford. Such stories as that really grab me. Keep on the hunt, you treasure, you. We heard of you four deputies and your travels. On your way home, er, that is to Manitou Prairie now, huh? How did the boy deputies do?"

"Hi and Miah proved to be the best at getting information. Folks pretty much clammed up for me and Nathan. The boys just looked so darn cute in their outfits. We'll be in Manitou Prairie by noon tomorrow."

"Great, we look forward to hearing the wind-up of that hermit business. Edith said they still don't know what happened to Roy Marlin except Digger said that Roy went away; I guess; also that hermit Larry said, 'Roy's gone.' A real pack of mysteries that hermit shack turned out to be, but it's been a godsend for Grandma; kept her mind occupied."

Chapter Nineteen

The four Michigan deputies called Sheriff Deputy Sergeant Detective Fanny Gillespie around four in the afternoon, wanting to catch her before the end of her shift. "You've gathered enough facts to confirm that Roy wasn't there so he can't be implicated in Larry's demise. Meanwhile there's no proof that Digger and Senior took care of Larry even as the info on the use of the coal truck is interesting. Larry's end, by whatever means, put an end to any further Big Foot encounters; no further Big Foot threat. Gentlemen, you've done a good job. Come on straight to Manitou Prairie."

"We'll telephone Grandma Clydis tonight, but we think we've done what we can down here. Likely we'll drive straight through tomorrow, as you said, arriving at Manitou Prairie around noon. Our family is there at the home of Nathan and Luisa Platt. Then you can retrieve your cruiser at any time. Sure was fun to travel in it yet we don't envy your using it on duty; duty that, we're sure, isn't all fun."

Del, Dosia, Hi, and little Virginia Louise left for their home at Ellington after breakfast that following day, Del needing to return to trucking. "Paychecks need to kick up a pace if we're to keep our heads above famine," Del'd joked.

In the wake of their departure, Luisa sat with Nathan around an ort vested breakfast table. They scanned the mess, each in regret that they said they'd do the dishes. Had they said, "Your chores first before you go visiting," the kids would've pitched in.

"Where'd they all get to?"

"Miah left for work at the cemetery, Omi and Cia are visiting Sandy and Candy, and Nic went fishing with Alvin and his dad. Luisa scraped the plates all onto one plate and Nathan began gathering silverware – but then stopped. "What's the hurry, anyway?"

She pushed the stake of soiled plates aside and turned to the sideboard, reaching for the large fragment of grave marker, wanting to look it over a last time. "Mr. Istir wants to finish repairing the grave markers tomorrow. He has waited for Miah to return from Kentucky. I want a last look at this thing."

"Sure. I'll start dishes." He pushed up from the table. He scrubbed away until finally the dish drying rack was filled. His hand reached to comfort the small of his back. His thought was that she'd decided on a nap. His mind's eye focused his easy chair where soon he plopped to switch on the Detroit Tigers.

Meantime in the garage workshop, Luisa'd smoothed a sheet of paper over the grave marker and taped it securely to the bench on either side of the marker. Next she rubbed with a carpenter's pencil. A few holes showed up clearly as white unmarked spaces in the smear of pencil lead. Keeping the holes clearly in mind, she paid no attention to the large letters known to be on the marker. She scanned keenly for any other letters. Two faint arcs were visible. She installed a paper ninety degrees to its predecessor and again wielded the thick-leaded pencil. She applied more sheets of paper and with different directions on each for employing the pencil. She tried over and over again until her aching hands could take no further abuse. She sat on a chair near the bench. Her hands ached so badly she felt only pain when she rubbed those tortured hands across her cheeks.

The Tigers fell apart in the third inning and Nathan switched them off, instead deciding to catch them in the ninth. He yawned and stretched and knew he needed exercise; and that the lawn could use mowing. In the garage he encountered Luisa with her hands held against her abdomen with the beautiful hurting hands holding one another. "Gosh, dear, let's push to get past your doctor to a specialist someplace."

"The stone, I think there's something else written."

Using the known letters and the three distinct holes of the marker as a guide, they stacked the pages she had rendered one at a time on top. On each paper she'd rubbed the pencil lead in a different direction. Nathan poked with a pin along the arc-shaped lines and many short straight lines and slanted lines. He repeated the process for all of the other sheets she'd prepared. Then lining up the clear spots of the pages, she held the pin-poked pages to the window light and tediously studied along the rows of pin pricked holes. "R-O-Y." A gasp escaped her.

"Nathan, hurry; go and call Detective Fanny Gillespie!"

In the woods near the hermit shack Nathan and Luisa approached the giant hermit's humper. They could see where Old Sniffer had insistently dug. Old Sniffer had left with the others to go back to Leadford and Nathan said, "Sure wish we had Old Sniffer here now." They could see at the edge of Old Sniffer's excavation where Luisa had found the large fragment of grave marker.

As a joke Nathan decided to make like Old Sniffer. He began to toss duff and dirt back from between his legs. "Wait!"

"Huh? Sure, I'll gladly wait. This dog mimic vastly hurts my neck and back, anyway."

"What bone is this?"

"What?" He reached for the bone. "Praise God! Luisa, you've a metacarpal bone there. It's a human hand bone!"

She dropped the bone as though it were a hot rock. In the distance they could hear the cruiser siren wailing and knew it'd be Sergeant Detective Fanny Gillespie on her way.

They ran from the hermit shack venue on a bee line for Mrs. Woods' yard. Fanny skidded to a stop as they approached. "F . . . F . ." They were puffing too hard to speak clearly.

"Fanny, please c ..... come."

"Yes, please come," Luisa puffed. "We've found Roy."

The End

About The Author

T. F. Platt enjoyed his first writing success in grade school, discovering that he could entertain an audience by reading aloud a story that he'd written. He wrote for fun through grade school and into high school. There he found that writing and giving a speech was as rewarding as had been his earlier triumphs. He went on to serve thirty-one years as a college professor of biology. While a professor he published articles in the scientific press and also served many years as the National Editor of an annual science honorary magazine. Along the way Mr. Platt became a pilot and logged many hours flying a Piper Cherokee Archer.